Nicholas Blincoe was born in Rochdale and now lives in London. He is a journalist and broadcaster, working for *The Modern Review* and BBC Radio 4. His previous novels, *Acid Casuals* and *Jello Salad*, both received outstanding reviews. He has also written screenplays and short stories, including 'Ardwick Green', which was published in the bestselling anthology *Disco Biscuits*. Previously, he was a founder member of Britain's first white rap group, signed to Factory Records and completed a Ph.D. in contemporary philosophy.

Also by Nicholas Blincoe

ACID CASUALS
JELLO SALAD

NICHOLAS BLINCOE

MANCHESTER*SLINGBACK*

PICADOR

First published 1998 by Picador

an imprint of Macmillan Publishers Ltd
25 Eccleston Place, London SW1W 9NF
and Basingstoke

Associated companies throughout the world

ISBN 0 330 36920 2

1 3 5 7 9 8 6 4 2

A CIP catalogue record for this book is available from
the British Library.

Typeset by SetSystems Ltd, Saffron Walden, Essex
Printed and bound in Great Britain by
Mackays of Chatham plc, Chatham, Kent

Thanks to Robert Blincoe, Leila Sansour, Martin Delamere, Chris Sharratt, Richard Thomas, Lisanne Radice, Jane Gregory and Peter Lavery for their help and advice.

Thank you to Raissa Sansour for her hospitality.

MANCHESTER *SLINGBACK*

CHAPTER *ONE*

Davey Green stood at the bar, loosely penned, drinking an Old Fashioned and resenting the low balustrade surrounding the bar area. A sign read: *No drinks at the gaming tables.*

Earlier that evening, he'd been worrying about the state of his suit. Looking at himself in the mirror of his low-star Marylebone hotel room, he got as far as making up a rule: Never buy a thing from a place with Mister in its title. He'd been robbed by *Mister Sox, Mister Fire-Surround* and *Mr Hi-Fidelity*. Now he could add *Mister Bollocks Suits* to the list. But once through the casino doors, he started to relax. Very few of the punters had made anything but the most sluggish attempts to satisfy the suit spec. Most wore some kind of sports-jacket-and-matching-trouser affair. Hardly anyone of them suited with style. Quite a few were wearing towels on their heads, Ariel-white under the dimmed-down lights.

Davey arrived in London forty-eight hours ago. What he always said, getting to the smoke was nothing but a drag. The journey was a wretch, both the ride and the come-down ... riding out of of Piccadilly Manchester and touching down at Euston. Eu-stoned? You bet. The weird tinny taste of McEwan's coloured his breath as he stepped off the train and he hadn't sobered completely since. Forty-eight hours . . .

That first night he was wearing an anorak with a cagoule hood. Eskimoed up because it was pissing down. The first thing he had to do was bag a membership card. He took a short bus-hop from the station to Baker Street, followed by a long trek down the wet streets until he found the casino doors. The law demands that all punters join a casino two full-clocked days before they place their first bet; and Davey was the law. So he paid his dues and stood in the gilded and tufted lobby while he filled out one of the casino's stat forms. Then he found himself a local hotel and spent the next forty-eight hours in hotel limbo, limbo-dancing, porn-channelling.

Davey leant back on the bar, keeping half an eye on the bartender. Everyone working the casino had their specific uniforms. Bartenders in dark-blue waistcoats, croupiers in a lighter shade. The pit bosses were allowed to wear jackets. The more clothes they got to wear, the higher they'd got on the casino scale. Right at the dizzying peak was Jake Powell, the manager. He got to wear an evening suit . . . and a good one.

Davey called the bartender over, nodding his head slightly so the bartender would follow his look.

Over on the far side of the room, Jake Powell was moving between the tables, like a prince caught under alcove lighting.

'You know that guy Jake?'

The bartender was unsure, not knowing whether

Davey was asking a question or beginning a sentence. 'You mean Mr Powell?'

Davey just winked. 'Me and him, kiddo, we go way back.'

The bartender looked doubtful, but who could blame him? Compare one with the other: Davey Green and Jacob Powell, one looking like shite and the other definitely not. Davey hadn't seen Powell in almost sixteen years. If he wanted to mark the changes he could say the lad had put on some weight but, then again, he would have had to. Anyone over six foot couldn't stay ten stone for ever. Powell was still slim, around thirty-four years old. And he had the advantage of the only well-thought-out suit in the place.

Davey told the barman to line up another: 'I'm just off for a slash.'

The lavvies were something else. Black marble with gold trimmings, every surface a reflecting pool angled to catch Davey's bad points. You want them enumerated? Davey took a long hard look and decided he was being too hard on himself. What he looked like was just a little worse for forty-six years' hard street wear but it was nothing to skrike about. All it meant, he was sometimes underestimated, sometimes overestimated. It was what you'd call situation-sensitive, and either way he could exploit it.

There was a young Arab kid standing at the wash-basins, splashing water into a loser's face, his hands shaking so much the water was squitting everywhere. By the time Davey joined him at the basins, the marble was dripping but the kid was semi-dry and ready to go on his lonesome way . . . although he wasn't yet out of trouble. A step from the exit, he ran up against the lavvy attendent who was armed with a canister of eau-de-cologne. Davey heard the hiss as the poor kid was hit by a quick-burst spray, followed by the clink of coins ringing off the attendant's plate: the lavvy man's tip. Judging by the sound, it was nothing more than busfare but the kid looked wrung out. Worse off than before, and now he didn't even smell so nice either. When Davey came to make his exit, he was already lavvy-savvy. He hammed up a sign of the cross to keep the perfume vampire away. But he tipped the man all the same.

His latest Old Fashioned was sitting on a casino own-brand circle of tissue paper. Smiling up at him. He took a sip and called the bartender over. 'Tell Mr Powell to step over, will you. I want a word.'

He got an 'Okay', followed by a mumbled 'Sir'. Seconds later, he saw a waistcoated messenger float across the floor and approach Powell with a backward nod towards Davey's spot at the bar. Powell took a look but registered nothing. Perhaps he was too far away to recognize him – good old Detective Inspector Green. It was sixteen years after all . . . and Davey wasn't an inspector back then.

Powell took his time, keeping to a slow stroll, and even pausing to talk to a member of his staff en route. When he eventually squared up to Davey, he said: 'Can I help you, sir?'

Green smugged him out. 'It's been a while, Jake, lad. But, yeah, I reckon you can help me out again.'

Powell showed nothing, just calm, as he said: 'I don't think so.'

He delivered the line with a casino smile and a wave to the bartender. 'We like to make the first drink complimentary for new members. Though it'll have to be the third in your case. Good luck at the tables.'

Powell turned and walked away. Davey hadn't reckoned on that, the lad coming over so suave. In the time it took him to walk over, he'd found out Davey was a new member and was finishing his second drink. Even worse, he'd also guessed this couldn't be an official visit, not if Davey had gone to the trouble of putting his name to the membership list.

Normally, Davey Green relied on presence and sleek wit. Above all, the ability to scare the shit out of people like Jake Powell. But there was his first mistake ... assuming Powell was still the same kind of person, still not quite a grown-up. Haring down to London half-cock, Davey just hadn't thought it through. For the kid to run a busy casino, he must have had some kind of temperament transplant.

Davey started after him, catching up by the second roulette table. 'You don't think you'd better take me to a private room, find out what's on my mind?'

'No.'

'What if I cause a scene?'

'That's why we have security.'

'Maybe if I started by saying you offered me your arse over in the lavvies.'

'I've had worse said about me. This is a casino.'

There – a fragment of his Northern accent showing

through. But it didn't give Davey anything to work with.

He decided to regroup.

Jake watched as Davey Green swivelled and rolled and headed back for the bar. Looking at the back of the man's head, Jake felt his own pose slip a little.

A girl, one of the waitresses, caught his look. 'Are you all right, Mr Powell?'

'Mm.'

'You look like hell.'

'This is hell and I'm in it.'

Over the next hour, Jake took another turn around the tables, always careful to keep his back to the bar. This should have been an all-sorts night, a mix of weekend punters, social gamblers, fun-lovers and all-out addicts. The bigger the mix, the more the different styles worked to dilute the overall ambience. But tonight it seemed that not only was everyone losing, everyone cared about it, too. You could feel the fretting in the air. A single note, close to the head, bouncing off the tables like a scream.

A woman with bruised luck held a chip over the number twenty-three, then veered off for twenty-eight. The bet made, her fingers fluttered away, casting uncertain shadows on the last of her last chips. Next to her a fat man was cropping his pile with pudding fingers, craning the top half over the baize to cover the junctions of three separate four-number bets; the remainder pushed with his free hand to cover the deuxieme twelve.

The croupier dinned out the order, 'No more bets,' and swung the wheel like he was doing it in his sleep. As he released the ball, a punter in a white suit dropped five blue chips onto the table, calling a bet on the quarter of the wheel around the zero.

Jake shot a look over to the pit boss, not so much because the bet was late but because the croupier had managed to hypnotize himself. One of Jake's jobs was to keep the somnambulists circulating, make sure they never settled into everlasting repetition. Into anything predictable. The pit boss caught the look and clicked his tongue at the croupier. The boy jolted awake, called the number twelve, and settled the bets before withdrawing from the table.

White-suit had guessed what was happening even before the number came up. Now he was shouting that he wasn't going to be fucked about, he wanted his lucky croupier to stay. The pit boss gave the standard apology: it was time for the boy's break. But it didn't go down; white-suit had a stack of imagined slights and a Bible's worth of rights. Wanting to know what they thought they were pulling on him? Acting like he expected them to chain the boy to the table. The guy should have known he'd blown it; shouting only fractured the peace. And, once that happened, there was no chance of any rhythm reasserting itself. White-suit had hexed himself. Just another proven loser trying to bid up his luck against the weight of the casino.

Jake gave him a moment, hoping the truth would dawn on him before it was a matter for security. It worked. The guy stopped, glared round and shut up.

Finally stomped off for the bathrooms. Whatever was going through his head, he was beaten. Maybe later he would see another fragile spiral of predictability and hope to ride it out.

Jake kept an eye on him as he marched across the casino floor, only losing him as his trajectory crossed with Davey Green's. The policeman had left the bar and was wandering among the tables.

The rest of the night, Jake was trailed by bursts of Davey Green. The man pumping out a stream of bullyboy northern comic patter as he chose the best locale for his lonely chips. No one had ever gone to such trouble just throwing twenty quid away. A small man, nicotine-yellow face and watery eyes, but he kept up the club-comic act to the end. Over at the cheap-shot roulette tables, Jake heard him talking to the girl croupier, saying: 'I tell you what, it looks like I've had me fucking chips, what do you reckon?' Even singing: snatches of early Kylie and, one time, starting on Dead Or Alive's 'You Spin Me Right Round'.

There was a woman in a sequinned jumper, padded shoulders and juggernaut earrings standing next to him. Green looked her over, winked and said: 'You feel lucky, missis? 'Cos I tell you, I feel like a lucky little punk.'

Jake carried on doing his job but was not so engaged that he didn't notice Green leave. It was about three in the morning and the man was telling the world that solitaire was the only game in town, the words slurred into a drunk chug-along as he made for the exit. He wasn't the last to leave, but it was close. The casino was emptying down to the last few freaks all chasing despair like maniacs. Jake hated that he was so good at his job. Keyed to the main chance, making it sit up and work out. If he yawned at the other side of the room, he could send the balls or dice into a spin. Maybe it was a disease. Wherever he went, he shrugged through the chaos that ripped other peoples lives apart, just like it was nothing. Leaving him in his own little black hole: nothing but pure depression. Jake was sunk deep into it by the night he left Manchester. He kept with it over the years until it had outlasted the drugs, the alcohol and all of the cigarettes he'd given up smoking. Recently he'd begun to think about Prozac, but could never make it to the doctor's for a prescription because he worked nights and slept most of the day. All he knew – the great joke – was that everyone he met wanted to be more like *him*.

The bartender came rushing over. 'Quick, the toilets.'

Jake started running, without knowing the problem. It had to be bad. He saw the brush first, lying on the carpet feet from the gents' door. Another two paces and he saw the attendent, stretched out on the marble floor with blood washing out of his face.

'What happened?'

'That guy – the nutter in the white suit.'

Jake knelt down, finding the bump of a pulse in the man's soft neck. The move left a tacky residue of blood on his fingertips, musky and sweet from aftershave. The bottle was shattered, leaving only the pump-cap: its silver snout and plastic-tube tail making it look like an alien bug crawling on the tiles. Jake looked back to the old man and saw the splinter of porcelain embedded in the gash below his eye, a fragment of the china saucer the guy used to collect his tips.

'Anyone called an ambulance?' Jake was up and already moving for the door. 'An ambulance – do it *now*.'

Baker Street was empty, nothing but the full-length reflection of the streetlamps and soft young trees in the rainwater road. Jake looked up and down, and ran for Portman Square; it opened up ahead of him, empty. Sidetracking, he crossed the road, trying to listen for the sound of an engine or the squeal of a taxi brake, anything to pinpoint. To chance. When he caught it, it came from the mews behind the burnt-out kosher restaurant: the beep of a car alarm and the flash of a white suit. Jake came running, keeping to his toes. The guy heard him at the last second, and turned to get a punch full to the face.

Jake dummied the first kick, putting it high into the guy's chest because the balls seemed too quick. Better to leave him with the taste, pause for his sight and breath to return, then just begin over, working him over. The guy reeled as he caught a back heel to the side of his head, an elbow driven into his chin. Then an almighty hoof square to his gut that lifted him off the ground. As his body flopped to the cobbles, Jake was thinking: *break his fucking spine*. One time with a boot heel, just fucking stomp it. But he stopped himself in time.

The man had left his car keys jutting out the door lock. Jake opened it up and took a look around the leather-upholstered lux interior. There was nothing he wanted, nothing in mind but finding his bearings and running through the odds. Maybe he could fake a car crash. *The guy ran himself over, m'lud.* There was a briefcase under the passenger seat. Jake flung it out, making sure the steel-tipped edge bounced off its owner's head. He flipped open the glove compartment, a *London A–Z*, a bottle of Admiral eau-de-cologne and a cheap electronic calculator, freebied and discarded, blazened with the name of an offshore banking outfit. Jake took the cologne and walked back to the body.

He put a few boots into the man's ribs, waiting for him to curl into a ball before kicking him over. Kneeling on the cobbles, Jake grabbed a handful of hair and started working with the atomizer, pinching the man's nose tight-closed as he sprayed the syrupy gunk over the back of his throat. The man thrashed; Jake just shifted his knee to the guy's chest and kept pumping. The guy's eyes started goggling. Jake sprayed them too, as much to give him time to swallow as to blind him.

The perfume smelt sulphurously volatile behind its saccharine sweetness. Jake could set either the man or his car on fire, though it might attract attention. The fire-station was two blocks away. Anyway, he was beginning to bore himself now and he couldn't think of an easy way to end it. All he could do was walk away; leave the man gagging and thrashing on the road. A slo-mo thrashing after the beating.

Ahead of him, someone said: 'Nice one, son.'

Jake looked up to the narrow entrance of the mews, between the shadows of the buildings.

A Manchester voice saying, 'Why didn't you just fuck him?'

Davey Green stepped out of the shadow. He was wearing a quilted schoolkid's anorak with the collar turned up. The crowning touch was the thin nylon hood, close to his scalp like a swimmer's cap and pulled tight with a draw-string. He looked like a novelty condom, but he seemed happy in himself. Saying: 'Come on, Powell. You know we've got to talk.'

CHAPTER *TWO*

1981 oh yeah . . .

. . . Jake was heading for the boys' room when the drag act started in the main bar. Sean and Fairy stayed behind, hutched into a corner booth with two other geezers: one elderly, one not so. As Jake stood, the older guy twisted in his seat and pinned his gaze on Fairy, saying: 'Now your friend's going to miss all the *fun*.'

Fairy threw Jake an arch look and said, 'He'll be back.'

'Oh, don't let him rush on my account.'

The guy's voice had that fruit-rich bub-bub-bub of public schools and old dead queers. Jake couldn't tell if the accent was genuine or affected. Maybe something the man borrowed one time on shore-leave and never returned? There was a merchant-navy tattoo on the back of his hand, a slurred dash among the liver spots. The same hand he used when he lit Fairy's Sobranie Cocktail, Fairy reaching out with two flirtatious fingers, the cigarette twitching between them as he blew a smoky *thank-you* across the table.

'My pleasure.'

The man was a fixture in Good-Day's. He had his own seat, his regular glass of gin, and his trademark wheeze that mixed emphysema and alcoholism into a

kind of chuckle. Fairy laughed alongside in his hiccup-
ping giggle. Sean just sat silently.

'And where's your other friend tonight?'

Fairy said, 'You mean Johnny? He's in Berlin.'

'Ah, Berlin.'

Fairy was seventeen, short and disabled by problem
hair and acne, but at least he was cheerful. Pretty-boy
Sean always wore a spoilt, bored expression. Tonight
he was using it to keep a distance between himself and
the second guy, the one they called Corduroy Man; his
voice the same rustled whisper corduroy makes between
shrugging thighs.

Jake was glad to go. Anyway, he needed to adjust
his mascara ready for the night ahead.

He was applying the final touches just as the drag
act moved into her encore routine. Jake heard the
opening chords, revved his eyelashes in time to the beat,
and pulled a last stare. His face in the mirror was so
white, the eyeliner came across like pure insolence. As
he came swinging through the lavvy doors, he could
believe the applause was for him. Not that it was . . .
just it was a plausible scenario.

He looked over to the bar and saw a long-necked
queen, dressed in Carmen Miranda hat and platforms,
standing on the bartop and working her stuff. Her
patterned skirt was rucked at the front to show her legs
and, as she sang, she swished it one-handed back and
forth. It was her entire stage routine. There wasn't
enough room on the bartop for any elaborate choreography but this was *ba-sic*: just two steps to the left . . .
hustle . . . two to the right . . . and shake times two. The

song – Jake was guessing – was called *Rui Ruiz*: it had the exact same tune as *Louie Louie*. He had no idea where she found a salsa instrumental of the song but he knew *Louie Louie* had been covered more than a hundred times, the most covered track in the history of rock-and-roll. He had one by Iggy and the Stooges: tape not vinyl.

Up on top of the bar, Queen Carmen looked like she was stomping the heads of the crowd, but she had a great voice: digging deep with a bass growl for the *Oo-Ooh Bab-ee Now* and turning the standard Yeah-Yeah-Yeah-Yeahs into apache whoops of *Ay-Yay-Yay-Yay*. Another thing in her favour, she kept the Hispanic lisp going the entire song.

While Carmen was working, the bar staff at Good-Day's got to take a pace back and relax. The only contractual stipulation, they had to smile and jig and generally provide backdrop camp until the act was over. This was a Thursday and, according to the schedule devised by Lady Good-Day, Thursday was guest-act night. The rest of the week the staff were the entertainment and had to pull lip-synchs and disco line-ups twice a night, every night. About a month back, Lady Good-Day asked Jake if he wanted a job.

Jake laughed him out. 'The rings you put your boys through, I think I'll stick to hustling.'

What Lady Good-Day said was, 'How do you know what rings I put them through?'

Carmen's song ended with a Latinate flourish, something percussive which she underlined with everything she had: winks, twitches, hand flutters, crotch rotations.

15

Jake turned away, glancing back to the gents. The blacked-out porthole in the door doubled as a mirror. It worked for Jake. He was eighteen, skinny and tall. Tonight, his hair was slicked back Berlin-style. He was wearing a dark suit to underline the look. In the bar-room light, the suit looked nowhere near as worn as it had done in the charity shop.

Good-Day's was rammed and, once Queen Carmen got off the stage, there was an almighty rush for drinks. It was so bad even Good-Day herself was working, repeating every order in a voice like a klaxon, tagging obscenities to every line. Lady Good-Day was maybe forty-five, a truly fat guy with two fully-grown double chins and a baby on the go. Another reason Jake turned down his offer of work, Good-Day was a notorious grope. Gay or straight, everyone got the same offer: *Blow Job or No Job.* If it wasn't an absolute condition of employment, Jake bet there were more who'd done it than admitted it. Lady Good-Day routinely claimed to have schlepped it up everyone in Manchester so no one could depend on him for the authentic figure.

The PA popped as someone switched it back over to the juke-box. The first song out was Edwin Starr's 'Eye-To-Eye Contact', coming up on the chorus. There was some singing along, bursts of the short staccato title-phrase from pockets around the bar, followed up with hand movements . . . *I'm looking at you* with a snapped salute that segued into a sly pointing gesture. Jake cast his eyes to the floor, anxious in case he was singled out by some old guy who had once spent a night buying his drinks and was now looking for a return on the outlay.

Out in front of him, a couple of dancing men took a turn and spin, their shoulders moving up and down and their elbows sticking out like clipped wings.

Jake swung around to their side and pushed into the crowd without melting, swaying at the waist as he walked because it felt like the only way to move in his suit. His navigation was set to the sound of Fairy's hiccup laugh, so high and sharp it was wired to dental pain.

Sean and Fairy were still in the corner booth, entertaining the same two men. When Jake was close enough to make out the gold band on the filter of Fairy's Sobranie, he stopped and watched as the old emphysema guy made another great play of lighting it. It was an easy route through to Fairy: put him in the spotlight, even if it was nothing but the flame from a cheap Ronson, and the boy would follow you like a dog. The effort the old man put into it, he knew the score. So long as he stayed in character, Fairy would keep on dreaming this was something more than routine sleaze: it was jazz-age decadence and he was Sally Bowles. Fairy lived for every moment he got to see himself another way, even a second or so was pure pleasure. Missing the point that Sally Bowles was just another loser. Though maybe Jake was being unnecessary; maybe Fairy knew that much. Maybe that was the attraction.

The Corduroy guy was maybe forty-five. Sean was still sat beside him, but was tilting away each time the man moved in. Two paces away now, Jake watched as the man leant forward and asked if Sean had ever been to the Lake District. 'I was up Scafell Pike last weekend. Just incredible. You ever go walking?'

Jake clamped his lips tight on a smirk. He could imagine pale, skinny Sean struggling against nature, but only as some kind of cooked-up play scene, never for real. If the guy really wanted a *Boy's Own* romance, he should have advertised. A seedy drag bar down the Village just wasn't the place.

Sean said, 'No, and I don't climb rocks or sail fucking boats either.'

It finally shut the man up.

Jake laughed. Not too loud, but he hit a lull and everyone heard him. Fairy, who was nothing but predictable, screamed first.

'Get *her*, covered in slap and gagging for it.'

Jake hated that high-pitched queen humour, and Fairy knew it. But the boy was already too drunk to scare with a look, so Jake forced a smile and said, 'Okay, Fairy . . . Which one of these two is paying for it?'

He nodded down to the ring of glasses on the table, every one of them three-quarters empty.

The old guy said, 'Allow me,' holding a twenty out in a raw, eczema-eaten hand. 'Would you mind?'

Jake wavered, letting his lip curl into the same bored expression Sean was wearing. As he shrugged and leant over to take the note, he left the traces of a mild sulk hovering like a cigarette kiss.

'So who's having what?'

Sean and Fairy asked for Grolsch, the outdoor queer wanted a pint and the old guy was a gin. Straight – definitely no tonic: he couldn't use the stuff. There was a full Schweppes bottle standing on the table by his JPS packet. Jake nodded okay, and turned into the crowd.

Some arsehole had called 'YMCA' up on the juke-box . . . so how down are you feeling, young man? Jake slithered for the gaps as the crowd closed around him.

At the bar, Lady Good-Day popped a couple of dimpled mitts on the bar top and threw Jake a wink.

'Jakey, y'alri-ight, ducks? What's your pleasure?'

Good-Day always spoke in a mincing nasal drone, more marked when he was in his drag-wear, but it was just a matter of degree.

Jake shook his head. 'Nothing. I'm off.'

He pushed at a side door and leapt out into the damp swirl of Manchester. No one at his table even saw him go.

For twenty quid, Jake would drop his friends – count on it. He hit the Village, looking for possibilities, floating twenty pounds above the gutter. The attraction of Good-Day's, it stood halfway between Chorlton Street Bus Station and the canal, at the heart of the Village. From where he stood, he could see most of it: a terrace of stooped-roofed buildings like a row of old farmhouses somehow dumped in the city and left to decay; the wide gutter of the canal and the semi-derelict mills that crouched above its banks; the overhang of the multi-storey car-park and, beneath it, the coaches pull-ing into the station in a tight bend, their headlights bleeding into the wet night. Tonight the Village was doused in drizzle that could have been chilling but wasn't. This was mid-December, but the rain was nothing but a late autumn flush. All Jake needed was a blast of speed, just enough to readjust the aperture and turn the coaches' dull beams into sharpened pinpricks. When he set out walking, he knew, whatever direction he took, he was never more than two minutes from the nearest gramme.

Turning to face the multi-storey, he picked out a figure sheltering in the doorway to the pay-lobby. As he got closer, a car passed by and the figure snuck towards the light. Like a soft dissolve, a child's face flickered by the door-jamb, and then faded. It was a rentboy's move, showing out for the passing trade. If the car had slowed, the kid would have stepped out onto the pavement. By the time the driver circled the block, he would be waiting, ready to talk terms. Not that the boy played it right. There was too much diffidence in his manoeuvre, leaving too much guesswork for the punter. Jake recognized him but didn't know his name. When Fairy first pointed him out, almost a month ago, he christened him Slappy. It fitted. He had the kind of looks that tempted rough handling. Jake got a helpless feeling whenever he saw him but mostly he just looked away. Tonight, while it was still early and the wet was an added disincentive, there was no one else around. Even the chip shop was empty, inside and out.

Jake crossed the road to see what Slappy knew.

The kid met him in the doorway, his bony face catching whatever light was around, his hair cut in a skinhead that made him seem even younger, like a refugee snapped during a louse scare. Though he was maybe sixteen, maybe seventeen. Any younger and he would have still been in care and Jake had seen him often enough to know he was no part-timer moonlighting from a home.

'Anyone been around selling whizz?'

The boy nodded. 'I don't know his name: the one who wears the white wig.'

Jake knew. 'Yeah? Paulo. Which way did he go?'

Slappy pointed across the road towards the Rembrandt. 'In there.'

Jake nodded thanks. He was stepping out onto the road when the boy called him back.

'Do you like Bowie?'

Standing there, Jake felt that old helplessness settle on him. The question was so naked and needy, the kid must have been in solitary the day they were teaching social skills. And the worse thing, Jake did have opinions on Bowie, all of them bad. He was the original misfit: the only Bowie Boy with no time for Bowie the man. But he wasn't going to stand in the street and pull his demolition routine. It was certain the boy didn't want to hear it. He wasn't looking to get shot down, he just wanted to belong.

Jake just nodded and turned. Saying, 'Later, mate,' as he headed for the Rembrandt's door.

There was no sign of Paulo, not even his peroxide wig above the crowd. The Rembrandt was reaching its mid-evening plateau, already medium rammed. Jake brushed a hand under his stray fringe and took another look, craning upwards for extra height. A voice to his left called him over.

'Jake, hiya. You not going to let on?'

Two girls were sat at a table, frisking the ice in their soft drinks with a couple of straws. Jake knew them both in a vague way but had only slept with one of them.

'You going down Devilles later?'

She was called Rebecca, lived in Bury or Prestwich and had a car. He thought she might be an art student, or doing her A-levels at sixth-form college.

Jake nodded, 'Yeah, I was thinking.' He had the money now, at least. Though he could probably get Rebecca to pay his way, if he met up with her later.

Her friend was called Debs. Both girls were twinned as Siouxie Sioux, with a mass of black back-combed hair above eyes Cleopatratized with a kohl stick.

'What about the weekend? Are you going to Pips?'

It was certain, although Jake pretended there was some doubt. He said, 'I'm letting Johnny have the final say.'

He remembered now, Debs had her black-made eyes on Johnny. It was around November, she and Johnny had brushed shoulders in Pips, and towards the end of the night she had found him again and asked if he knew any parties. There were always parties but the problem was getting to any of them, which was how Johnny found out Rebecca had a car. He made her give a lift to all of them, Sean and Fairy as well. The four of them cramped in the back of a mini on the ride out to Flixton and the house of someone whose parents were away.

Later, Jake had taken Rebecca upstairs to a polyester-draped room with a double bed, and assumed Johnny would do the same with her friend. A couple of hours later, Johnny came bursting into the room, saying they'd gotta run. He'd spent the night burgling the houses on the lower side of the street and wanted to get away before the neighbourhood woke up.

Debs asked where Johnny had been hiding; she hadn't seen him in a month.

'Still in Berlin. He's back tomorrow.'

'You got to make him come to Pips.' She held out a packet of cigarettes. Jake took one.

'I'll tell him.' Before he walked away, he said, 'Maybe see you later in Devilles.'

The clientele in the Rembrandt was pretty much a pick-and-mix of the Good-Day's crowd. If there was a difference, it was that the Rembrandt gave powder-room to a few-plus trannies – Jake didn't know why. If he had to guess, he would say Good-Day operated a subtle queen-dissuasion policy because, with his looks, the guy couldn't be desperate for competition. Good-Day was one end of the beauty scale. And right at the other end there was Paulo . . .

Jake felt a pull on his shoulder and turned. Paulo caught him with a wink, a sure blush-maker.

'Jake, hiya.'

The way Paulo was dressed, he was a self-made wonder-slut; tight black pedal-pushers and an off-the-shoulder top that showed off his half-caste cocoa skin. And, set above it all, the shock of white hair. Paulo was pure Manchester but claimed to be Latin-American:

like the white wig, the '-o' was nothing but an affectation.

'Paulo, I was looking for you.'

'You were looking for me?' Paulo sucked on his teeth, making a *tut* sound like the negative-image of a kiss. His eyes cast towards Rebecca and Debs. 'I thought you were too busy scouting out those horrors.'

Jake gave him the wide-on innocent look, like Paulo was making an honest observation. 'Is it my fault everyone's gagging for me?'

'Like you don't encourage it. Your problem, you want to decide which side you're playing for.'

Jake shrugged. 'As long as I'm in demand.'

'Well a word of advice, honey. You gonna walk around giving everyone puppy-dog eyes, you want to think about waterproof mascara.'

'I tried. It gets under my contacts.' Jake angled for a reflection off the pub's window. 'You saying I got panda eyes?'

'You look like a tart that's been pissed on.'

'Please, Paulo. I'm a fucking customer. Show some respect.'

Paulo grinned. 'Oh, business?'

Wherever it came from, Paulo always had the best speed: crazy white crystals of amphetamine sulphate. There was a rumour it was manufactured locally: Jake didn't know or care, so long as he had money to pay for it. He followed Paulo's patented butt-swing over to the telephone, giving it just a shade less hip movement, himself. While Paulo picked the receiver off the wall, Jake dumped some change on the top of the box: the twenty he'd stolen from Fairy's elderly friend tucked underneath. Paulo turned, giving another kissy *tut*, and made like he was picking a thread off Jake's shoulder. No one saw the real move, the way the wrap flicked out of his fingers and disappeared into the hankie pocket of Jake's suit. A moment later, Paulo took the note and slipped a tenner – the change – alongside the coins. The last thing he did was hang up the receiver.

Jake was laughing. 'No reply?'

'Don't take the piss. I don't want to get barred from this place as well.'

'Is it right you got barred from Good-Day's?'

'I tell you, I barred myself. That fat cow gives me the fucking creeps. I get through the door, I can smell her salivating.'

Jake was wondering whether to go to the bar, or at least make the offer. Turning it over: how long could he make the tenner last?

Paulo saved him by asking first. 'Just so it doesn't look too obvious you only stopped by for the pharmaceuticals.'

Jake was going for a Bacardi and Coke.

Paulo said, 'Me too. Thanks, honey.'

Jake took another look at the note. Then shrugged and turned for the bar. It was the moment the sirens started.

By the time Jake joined the crush at the pavement, the whole side of Good-Day's was lit up with blue strobes. Outside the pub doors, a line of police formed a cordon, stopping anyone who hadn't already run from getting out onto the street. Jake knew Sean and Fairy

25

were both under-age. He hoped they made a getaway. From where he stood, he couldn't see a thing. He started worming for the front of the crowd. Only as he broke through at the front, he realized they weren't raiding Good-Day's at all. He watched as a pair of cops came trotting round a corner carrying a two-man battering ram and saw they were heading for the Zipper Store.

The back of an unmarked Transit swung open. These cops were in full riot gear: helmets, shields and batons. They clattered out of the van and started jogging down the street, moving into closed ranks. It was genuine choreography, no doubt something they practised at cop-school. When they were maybe twenty paces from the Zipper Store, a second team came pounding from Canal Street in parallel formation. Both teams were dragged up in scary black body armour, ready to put a pincer lock on the store-front. It was not like there was any opposition. As they formed a corridor, either side of the door, the police came with the battering ram. No opposition there, either. The wood cracked and split, fracturing at the first assault, and caving with the second. As it fell, the two cops with the battering ram fell back and a third stream of cops, these in regular dress, made for the doorway and disappeared inside.

Outside Good-Day's, the Rembrandt and all the other smaller bars, packs of men stood in the rain and watched. Carve the Village open and you got to check out the full cross-section: Bowie boys, clones, queens, straight-looking, old geezers, also a sprinkling of fag hags and a few fewer dykes. All out to watch a bad night turn sour. The whole show had been running almost weekly since the Chief Constable had declared he was God's Cop and he was ready for a genuine crusade.

Jake felt someone panting at his shoulder. It wasn't Paulo; he'd disappeared the moment the sirens started, and they hadn't stopped yet. Turning to look back into the crowd, Jake saw Slappy standing there. The kid was breathing hard but it wasn't excitement. It was more like this was bonfire night and he was one of the dogs they forgot to lock away before the fireworks started. The police lights parasolled across his face, painting it with white and blue stripes.

Jake said, 'I tell you who's a Bowie fan . . .'

He pointed out Fairy, over on the far side of the road. The recognizable head of problem hair popping up between the crowd as the boy hustled for a clear view. There was no sign of Sean.

Slappy said, 'What's that?'

It wasn't worth repeating. Jake shook his head and turned to watch the first of the police come out of the Zipper Store. Still in single file, all holding cardboard boxes in front of themselves. Inside: magazines, pin-up calendars. Even greeting cards.

From this moment on, it was plain routine. Jake didn't know why they even bothered with the riot cops. Did they think, one of these nights, the Village was going to erupt? That it was going to go up in flames like Moss Side had that summer. Maybe one man seriously believed it was going to burn, though not in a riot. Chief Constable James Anderton, spokesman for God in Greater Manchester. Maybe one other, Inspector

John Pascal. There was no sign of Anderton himself but you wouldn't expect to see him until the photo op at the press conference in the morning. Inspector Pascal was there, though. Now the streets were guaranteed peaceful, he had appeared out of one of the cars and begun directing the loading of boxes into a Transit van.

Jake watched Inspector Pascal at work. The man had a semi-military style: the kind of act he could have carried off without props, although he was holding a truncheon. All told, he was a different type to his boss, Anderton, who was queer for the Old Prophet look, the thick beard and swept-back hair. Pascal preferred to stay clean-shaven and neat. Still, it was Pascal who looked more like Charlton Heston.

Jake had seen enough. He pushed away towards Piccadilly Gardens. He was just passing the bus station when he heard the dull slap of tennis shoes off the wet pavement, and looked over his shoulder. It was Slappy again, nervously following him. When Jake turned, the boy stopped. It was maybe something in Jake's expression: something of the grim touch Pascal had been wearing. Jake reset his face before he waved the kid over.

'You got a cig?'

Slappy nodded hard and started fumbling at his pockets. The left-hand side of his Harrington, he felt something and reached through the zip to pull a crumpled pack of B&H out of the shoplifter's pocket. The way he ran up and offered it over, it was a tear-jerker.

Jake took one and said, 'Let's get out of the rain. You got any money?'

Slappy nodded again. Jake jerked his head: *Okay then, this way.*

He took him round a corner where the narrow street and the high buildings took some of the sting out of the rain. As they turned into Silver Street, Jake ducked into a service door and waited for Slappy to pull out his matches. The kid was an outdoor smoker. When he lit the match, he held the box upright and slipped the flame into the recess of the box drawer. Jake hunkered over the light, sucked hard and waited for the cig to fizz and settle, before he asked the kid his name.

'Kevin Donnelly.'

'Jake Powell. Come on.'

He moved off sharply. The kid had to jog to catch up, holding his hands like a bantamweight, his cig cupped inside a rabbit punch. They were maybe ten yards from Portland Street now, cresting round the side of the Britannia Hotel. And, only now, Jake finally caught sight of the white Cavalier. Already it was idling up to the kerb in a shower of gutter spray. It was a police car: unmarked but always recognizable.

Jake would have crossed the street, making like he'd seen nothing, but the Cavalier's back door was swinging open.

Out of the front seat, a voice saying, 'Get in.'

'You what?' Then, 'What for?'

Detective Constable Green poked his head round the door. 'What do you mean what for? For fucking *sus*, you little puff.' Giving a sigh as he turned back to his driver. 'You believe this? Some people haven't the fucking sense to get out of the rain.'

Slappy – Kevin Donnelly – was backing away. If he walked any further he'd be jammed against the wall of the hotel. Jake looked right and left, letting his breath out. He wondered how long it would take for DC Green to find the gramme of speed. He thought of running out into traffic along Portland Street and across the reservation towards Piccadilly Gardens, but his suit was beginning to feel heavy with rainwater, and there were so many cops in the area. How far would he get?

As he climbed in the back of the Cavalier, DC Green shouted over to Donnelly. 'You too, son. Don't be shy.'

CHAPTER *THREE*

Detective Inspector Green was impressed, so he said. The man was sucking on a cig, strutting around the flat like he had a warrant. All the time keeping up his one-sided conversation. Saying, 'We're talking London prices, right. So you got to be doing all right at the casino. A super-duper croupier – management even. Give it me straight, what's a gaff like this set you back?'

Jake was stood at the kitchen sink, waiting for the kettle to boil, and washing the blood off his knuckles. Basically closing his ears and staring into space. The view out of the kitchen window was his favourite, looking out across the ornamental rooves of the other mansion blocks. Coming up to four in the morning, and there was nothing moving between the pavement and the night sky but black cabs on the shortcut from Edgware Road through to Baker Street.

The man he was trying to ignore, DI Davey Green, was just five yards away: walking, talking, smoking one of his old Rothmans . . . spying. Heaving himself from room to room, and then padding back to fill the kitchen doorway. This exact second, Jake couldn't actually see him, but he hadn't managed to shut out the sound of his voice.

'Oh, look at that. There's a message on your answer machine.'

'That's okay.'

'I'm just saying. Like, you feel you need one of these gadgets, you probably got some kind of dizzy social whirl going. I don't want you missing anything important. Your life falling apart just because of me.'

'It'll keep.'

Jake turned from the sink and dabbed at the graze on his hand with a clean tea-towel. Somehow he had scraped the skin off his second kuckle when he was fighting that guy. He wasn't sure when exactly. Call it a mystery: it wasn't like the man put up much of a fight. He just rolled over and took his beating. Staring at the dry wound, Jake thought he might have caught the man's tooth.

Davey Green was still obsessing on the answer machine. Now asking: 'You want me to play it back, or what?'

'No, leave it. It's okay.'

He had already seen the flashing light of the message indicator. He could guess what it was: a short word from his partner to say Milan was okay, there were no insane hijackers on the aircraft, no devices in the hold . . . everything funky and hunky, just adorable. If there ever was a real emergency, he could be paged at the casino . . . He was there every solitary night. The message could keep because, so long as Green was in apartment-colonizing mode, Jake wasn't going to give him the least edge. He didn't want the man to know what kind of shape his life was in. You gave him the smallest fucking window, he would come whooping through, riding a pack of sniffer dogs.

Green didn't give a shit about the guy Jake half killed: whether he was ambulance-ready or able to walk. Green had his own approach to police work: the victim could bleed to death and all he cared about was could he grab a hold of it, make it work for him. As he walked Jake away from the crime scene, he started spinning a whole string of jokes, speculating on the relation between being queer for violence and queer in general. And he fed Jake a proposition: they could discuss it with the local bobbies, get their informed views, or they could find somewhere quiet to talk. Jake weighed it up: the police station maybe five minutes' walk away or one of the all-night cafés on Edgware Road. What'll it be? Green said, 'How about your place?'

Since they'd reached the flat, Green had shut up for maybe five–ten seconds at a stretch. Jake couldn't swear to it being even that long. He could hear the squish of the man's DM soles, the rubber on the wood floor as he scoped the shelves of books, videos, the CD collection. And every couple of steps that voice again.

'You like to do a bit of reading, then?'

Jake said, 'Some.'

Green had finally taken off his anorak with the ridiculous hood. The suit was no improvement, but at least it wasn't physically hurtful on the eyes. It was more of a psychic jab. He was running down the shelves now, ticking off the titles with his cigarette fingers:

'Oxford Companion to Renaissance Literature, Auto-biography of Malcolm X, Chinese Horoscopes by Dr Nick Land, Christopher Marlowe by Dr Faustus . . .'

Jake walked through with the tea-tray, just in time to see Green lip his cigarette and reach up with his free hand to pull a slim purple book off the shelf.

'Kant's Critic of Judgement. Looks like a fucking laugh. Jesus, you seen this, just about every word underlined.' Flapping the book open, his finger flattened to the margin notes. 'Someone's written "groovy" here. What's that: is it a philosophical term or what?'

Jake shook his head, it wasn't his book. He set the tray down on the table. The full rig: a teapot, two china mugs printed with Van Gogh's sunflowers, a sugar bowl and only one spoon. The milk jug he left in the kitchen, selecting the Tetrapak instead. He didn't want to give Green too many joke locuses. How would that end – watching the man short out because he couldn't decide what to take the piss out of first? It was bad enough the tea was Earl Grey. Jake intended to let it brew awhile, but Earl Grey never coloured up too dark. It was certain Green was a strong-and-milky man. You could tell by looking at him.

Green said, 'You shacked up with a student, right?'

'About ten years ago. She works for a record company now.'

'She?' Coming over all surprised, like he was aud-itioning for the police pantomime and the director really wanted to see those double-takes. 'You shacked up with a chick?'

If you saw her, it's how you'd want to describe her.

Until she set you right. She was out of the country, now, trying to persuade a new-age Italian composer that his CD of ambient electro was finished. Before she left, Jake had asked, 'How can you tell?' The music dribbled on for one-hour-fifteen, minor chords over a synthesized rattle like the sound of a plug chain caught in the leak of a warm tap. He could have told Davey Green any of this . . . if it had been any of his business.

'Little Jakie, all grown-up and hetero. Who'd have thought it? You taken the AIDS test, then?'

'Fuck off.'

'No, I'm serious. What with you having a past history, you got to think about it.' The man paused, his mouth open, either dumb or enquiring. He looked like an uncooked American doughnut, but Jake wasn't sure what impression he was actually trying to create. 'The reason I'm asking, it's got to be something that preys on you. Yeah? Every time you shoot your load, you wonder what's wiggling up between the spermatazoa?'

Jake said, 'I was just thinking you look like shit.'

Looked it, talked it, acted like it. Everything but rise to it. Green was still pondering the great issue. 'You know, Jake lad, something I was wondering: you see a paisley pattern, like a dressing gown or, say, the lining to an anorak . . . does it make you wonder whether you got iffy spunk or what?'

'No.'

'But it will do now, eh?'

'Yeah,' Jake said. 'But I'll think about how you thought of it first.'

Was that a point? Green didn't look bruised. He

had slotted the philosophy book back onto the shelf, stubbed out his last cigarette, and was looking round for somewhere to park himself. Jake was sat on the settee, making like mother and pouring an inch of milk into his flowery mugs.

Davey Green squirmed into the chair opposite, saying: 'I like a higher back, me. Get to my age, you always gonna look for lumbar support, know what I mean? On top of which, I did my fucking back in – must be five years now – pulling some cunt out of the Rochdale Canal.'

'I wouldn't take you for the heroic type.'

'What?' A two-second pause before Davey realized there was a misunderstanding. 'Oh. No, the guy had been dead two days. I was just trying to haul him to the side with this boat-hook. I think I overstretched myself, pulled some kind of muscle and never popped it back.'

He groaned a bit, his hand in the small of his back at the exact problem point. Then he took another look at the mugs. 'Ooh, tasteful. You get them out a catalogue? Best give me three spoons, son. Keep my blood levels bubbling. This looks like it could be a long night.'

The thing with Jake Powell, boy and now man, he never said anything in custody. Or nothing apart from simple answers to direct questions. It wasn't something he had learned. He didn't have the benefit of a family background in crime: maybe an uncle who fancied himself as a cell-block barrister. What he had was arrogance and a kind of inner sufficiency. Davey glanced over to the clock: four-fifteen. At this rate they'd be up all night.

'Maybe I should have asked you for a coffee – what you reckon?'

Jake said, 'Whatever . . . Espresso?'

'Fuck no. I'm a Birds Mild man. Give it me grey as dishwater and I'm laughing. It's my tea I like to have a bit of colour.'

He pulled a face at the mug, staring down at the off-white mess and wishing that he hadn't started on that sperm rap. He closed his eyes, downed it in one and dumped it back on the tray. Saying: 'You left some washing-up liquid in the bottom of that.'

'The tea's perfumed. You've had Earl Grey before.'

Give the lad that one. 'You're right. I interviewed this stripper once, she was suspected of over-stepping the lap-dancers' code. The two of us sat there in her dressing-room sipping Earl Grey because she reckoned it gave her class.'

Jake said, 'What I think, you're still watching those Columbo reruns. You still reckon you can hassle out a confession if you come across as a big enough arsehole.'

'You think I'm putting this on? I really *am* an arsehole . . . ask my wife.'

The night Davey Green first met Jake, he remembered hauling him off Portland Street with little Kevin Donnelly. It was a memorable night, what with Inspector Pascal and the vice squad pulling one of their major numbers down in the Village. Now, that was pure hassle: sending the riot cops to raid what was basically a gift-shop. Davey liked to think, the way he did things, there was a little more finesse to it. Not on the surface, perhaps. But something in the overall style. Maybe, later on that same night, he had made a mistake mentioning Columbo to Jake: once you give away a part of the trick, you find the whole magic's gone.

DC Davey Green, sitting at his interview desk, twisting open the carefully folded wrap and saying: 'The fuck's this. I'm a Sweet 'n' Low man, myself.' It was a good line. It was even true. Back in those days, he was still married and his wife had put him on the saccharine substitute.

He got the initial details, name and age, etcetera, and he found the speed easy enough, tucked into the top pocket of Jake Powell's suit. But he was still feeling his way round the lad's psyche: the specific shape of his personality.

What he was getting was pretty much nothing: a whole mix of signals.

Maybe, three-quarters of an hour into it, he said: 'You like Peter Falk? Columbo, right. He's the kind of guy you can underestimate, basically because he looks like a no-mark. But the thing is, when he gets on the sniff, he's a fucking hound. Does he have a dog, too? A bloodhound or something, just to underline the point? I've a feeling he has, but I might be wrong. Anyway, what Columbo's got, is tenacity. That's the central thing. You also know that he's super-intelligent, but that's more of a secondary motif. It's really his tenaciousness that gives him the edge. And that's like me. That is my basic style, I'm tenacious as fuck. It's the one factor you really got to grasp if you want to get under my skin. Then the other thing, my secondary quality if you like, I'm not so super-intelligent. What I am is a twat. And I reckon the last thing you want, now you're living in Manchester and acting like cock of the fucking walk with all your little bum chums, is Manchester's biggest twat dogging your every step.'

Davey was leaning over the table by now, his head only another head's length from Jake's. And he was taking it unbelievably fucking loud, almost shouting without shouting. Not so much to convey anger or emotion or anything. Just to convey sheer fucking noisiness.

Because, what Davey had figured, over the course of their first meeting, was that the junior Jake Powell was a smug little git but he was also intelligent. Sitting in that puce and cream room in Manchester's Bootle Street police station, he was easily intelligent enough to feel the noise and swallow the Davey Green deal. Becoming a grass wasn't so bad. There were plenty worse things he could think of, given the time, given a few more hours in that over-heated little room with its crappy colour scheme and the decibels ratching up to Concorde levels. It helped, too, having the gramme of amphetamine sitting unwrapped between them on the interview table.

It was a shame there was no amphetamine this time around. Because the truth was, Green was having trouble finding any leverage. Pushing his way into Jake's life hadn't been a problem, but now he'd reached a wall. He lit another Rothmans and took a Columbo squint through the smoke haze. Look at this apartment: the hardwood floors, the designer cons, even the flower-power teacups. Maybe it was his warped prole soul but Green felt like there was some kind of impregnability deal going on here. He couldn't see any loose flaps, and he had no way to get under the lad's skin. Maybe he'd blown it, and Jake's snitching days were long gone.

A four-minute stretch while Green sipped at a second mug of tea and worked through another cig and a half. As far as Jake knew, the room had never been this full of smoke, but Green was clearly getting off on the fug.

Finally, Green said: 'You follow the news back home?'

'Manchester?' Jake shrugged. What should he be looking for? The football scores, maybe? Manchester City ripping through a string of managers and tripping down to the bottom of the league. A few less predictable bombshells, like the IRA tagging Marks and Spencer's. Jake had a phone-call off his Manchester aunty a few weeks after that happened: she wanted to know why the bastards couldn't have bombed Debenhams; no one goes there.

Green said, 'The reason I'm asking, I been making the papers quite a bit. Ever since I brought down that paedophile ring, I been getting heavy press action.'

A pause.

'You haven't seen me?'

Jake shook his head.

'Yeah, well, I'm no beauty but, you know, the face of Manchester crime prevention. They could do worse. You sure you haven't seen it?'

'I'd have remembered.'

'I bet you would. The second I saw you tonight, I knew you recognized me. Your old Smiley – your boss. I got to say, you were about the worse fucking snitch I ever ran.'

'Why are you here? You think I know anything about a paedophile ring?'

'Let me get the story out. That's always been your problem, wanting everything arse-first . . . does your girlfriend complain about that?' Green put up his hands: a play at conciliation. 'Sorry, just a joke. What I was saying, we found out these juve homes round Cheshire, Warrington, also Liverpool but that's out of my jurisdiction, all of them were run by benders. The last seventeen or so years, they'd been buggering the boys, organizing swap meets, all kinds of unpleasantness. Anyway, I cracked it.'

'Seventeen years too late.'

'I got to act on information received. It's not as if you told me anything about it. You being my shit-hot bum-boy sneak and all.'

'The police knew.'

'Well, this is the peculiar thing. That's the conclusion I been coming round to, in the course of investigations, as I been rehashing the old files.'

'Is that why you're here? The police are so corrupt, you got to blackmail old snitches into lending a hand?

Because, if it is, you can forget it. I haven't lived in Manchester in fifteen years.'

'You're getting warm.'

Jake looked at him, 'Or you're here to shut me up and maintain the spotless image of the Greater Manchester Police Force.'

'Good guess. But it's more of a collateral thing. A friend of yours has turned up, bludgeoned to death out on Saddleworth Moor. To tell you the truth, I'm amazed we found him, you know our record finding any bodies up there. Anyway, little Kevin Donnelly, when did you last see him?'

'Donnelly's dead?'

'If he's not, he's going to have to walk round the rest of his life with his dick in his mouth.' Green paused. 'I should have said there was some mutilation involved. It wasn't pretty.'

CHAPTER*FOUR*

It was after midnight when Jake stepped out of Bootle Street police station. This was the old Victorian lock-up smuggled into a narrow back street in the centre of Manchester. Maybe there was a logic to hiding the police out of the way in a street so narrow and overhung: the idea that whatever happens between police and thieves, it shouldn't take place in public. DC Green was steeped in those kind of subterranean deals and had his own reasons for taking Jake there.

Outside, the night was steeped in streetlight amber and soaked in a mist of water, rain held in near suspension. From Jake's angle, the night was creeping by while he was moving at double speed . . . like Billy Whizz, running around the raindrops and only getting wet if one melted against his speeding cheek. Billy Whizz, for certain. It had to be a first, snorting speed off the top of the cistern in a police-station toilet. When DC Green returned his little packet of amphetamine, Jake had headed straight for the lavvies. He was new recruit to the police's informal network, so why not get a little informal around police officers?

Jake started running up the street towards Albert Square, keeping his face turned to the slit of night sky above him. He wanted to see the stars through speeding eyes. When he heard someone call his name, he spun and almost fell.

'Donnelly?'

The boy was standing in the back door of what looked like a bank or shop, only a short step out of the rain, his eyes like a cartoon squirrel pictured in its hole.

'How long you been there?'

Donnelly shrugged. 'An hour?'

At least.

The boy was shivering. 'They didn't do me for nothing.'

Jake never thought they would. What could they do him for; he'd been walking down the street when DC Green picked him up. Arresting rentboys was always a problem, anyway. The Chief Constable's official line was there are no puffs in Manchester. If they caught Donnelly bent over a car hood with a mechanic buried in his back passage, they'd hope the guy was carrying a wrench so they could charge Donnelly with going equipped.

Donnelly was holding out his pack of cigarettes. Jake took one and moved closer for a light from the shared match. Huddled together in the doorway, his face was inches from Donnelly's. The boy's cheeks so pinched and sharp they reminded him of sides of wind-dried duck, the kind he saw hanging in the Chinatown shop windows.

Jake said, 'You okay?'

It was a stupid question; the boy was risking pneumonia. He must have thought it was worth it: wanting to stick by his new compadre. But the way it was with Jake, any show of affection made him tighten inside. Now, standing so close he could almost taste the cigarette burr inside the kid's thin smile, Jake watched as Donnelly's face flickered out of focus, losing its hopefulness and clicking into something else: a look that read equal parts horror and resignation. It was a long second before Jake realized it was his fault. What had happened, he knew, he had sneered down at the boy with something like distaste – or worse. The way Donnelly recoiled, it was nothing but a response.

Jake tried to fix his expression, flashing a smile he hoped looked warm rather then crooked. He tried an apology.

'Sorry. I'm pretty fucked up.'

'It's okay.'

'Yeah, well.' Jake couldn't just leave the kid. 'Come on, let's get a drink.'

Bernard's Bar lay a couple of streets over, on King Street South, a chintzy cellar venue: part log cabin, part swinging discotheque. Jake walked ahead of Donnelly, past the spotlit fish tanks on the stairs and down to the underlit bar. Bernard's was one of the few gay bars outside the Village: standing up for itself outside the ghetto and catching a shade different clientele. These men tended to be wealthier, professional, aged thirty to fifty. That was the plus. The minus: they were mostly clones. Anyone who came walking off the street, they thought they'd hit an ugly moustache party. Even late

Thursday, the place seemed full. Catch it on the week-end and it bristled.

The wooden-topped counter started at the door. Jake leant against it and sent a psychic thought-beam into the back of the barman's head. The guy turned on cue.

'Two Pils.' And turning to Donnelly, 'That all right?'

'Uh-huh. Ace.'

Jake wondered, the way the bar guy bent over into the fridge, was that choreographed. Knowing he had to pull the same move a thousand times a night, he tried to get it perfect. Tilt and down, one-two, and lift and squeeze, one-two. The guy surfaced with the two bottles, smiled and said, 'I took them out the back, they should be a bit cooler.'

Jake just nodded and passed over a couple of quid. After what he'd been through, he wasn't going to worry about the temperature. The beer was good, though. Combined with the speed, it was Holy Communion. Jake reached inside his suit, pulled out a half-full pack of Rothmans and flip-topped it towards Donnelly.

'Here. Sorry, I don't have a light.'

It was only as the kid sparked up, Jake remembered that he hadn't had any cigarettes earlier. Donnelly knew it, too, if he thought back. Why else would Jake have bummed one off him all those hours ago on Chorlton Street? And even though Donnelly didn't seem to have guessed the cigs were police-issue, it still gave Jake a shock of guilt. A shock and an aftershock: this was going to become an everyday anxiety, something he would have to get used to now he was a police informer.

Jake covered, coughed, rationalized: Donnelly probably assumed Jake was holding a pack all along and had only asked for one earlier as a kind of Borstal Boy reflex, making the new kid pay in tobacco. Though Jake had never been in Borstal; he'd only read the book. In his Harrington jacket, Donnelly looked like he'd only been released a month.

'Your mate's waving you.'

Jake looked up to see Donnelly pointing across the heads of the clones, towards the back of the club.

'What?'

'Over by the chimney, that's your mate, isn't it?'

Jake stared, seeing Johnny sat on the raised Swiss-style hearth, his back to the unlit pile of logs that was Bernard's unique decoration statement. He had a beer in his hand and his hand held above his head, yelling: 'Jake!'

Jake couldn't believe it. Johnny was supposed to be in Berlin until tomorrow evening.

'Johnny?'

Jake pushed by a couple of beefy blokes wearing flight jackets and locking handlebars. As he manoeuvred round them, he shouted, 'What you doing here?'

Johnny was grinning through his long blond fringe, 'Had a bit of business, mate.'

There were two men with him, both with short-cropped hair, tennis shirts and blue jeans. As they stood, Jake noticed the jeans were belted too tight and too high. Men's waists should run from hipbone to hipbone, not straight across the navel, but a lot of the clones wore their jeans high. Jake didn't know why. Maybe

47

the attraction of super-tight pants. If they moved their waist up, they could fit a smaller size. Perhaps they liked to brag they'd had the same waist since they were eighteen. These two men were in their mid-thirties and would have looked identical except that one was six-two and the other was five-seven. Whatever business Johnny had been doing with them, it was over now. He was just shaking their hands and telling them he'd see them tomorrow, around nine.

The smaller one said, 'We're having a dinner party, so come a bit later. Say, nine-thirty . . . about that time we'll kick back the rug and put some records on.' He had a campish lisp that became even stronger when he said, 'Bring your friend.'

He left with a coquettish look over at Jake.

Jake gave Johnny a grimace, 'The fuck's with her?' Using the same tone the guy had used.

'I'm selling them some videos.' Johnny said. 'And I told them I delivered. What's the matter, you don't fancy a party?'

Jake made the correction. 'A dinner party, and we're not invited. It sounds more like we're the after-dinner entertainment.'

'You think they'll want to play hide the After Eights?'

Johnny was laughing. But Jake was a little more worried. Anyway, Friday nights they usually went to the Poly Disco on Aytoun Street. In fact, the place they first met – though they'd seen each other around before then. Counting back, it was probably less than a year ago but it seemed a lifetime. So, if Johnny asked him one more time, Jake would go and help him deliver videos to the guys' party. He'd missed Johnny the last few weeks he was in Berlin.

Johnny was the blond bombshell and Jake was the brunette, and although one was bleached and the other dyed, that only underlined their different complexions. Johnny looked rosier, Jake just looked pale and intense.

'So what's been happening? I miss anything?' Johnny asked.

He definitely missed something tonight. Jake said he'd tell him later, but already knew he would never say anything about his conversation with DC Green. 'What about you? Why didn't you let on you were coming back early?'

'I didn't know. It was luck, I got a lift straight through to Amsterdam and then another to Watford Gap. I did it in about twelve hours.' Johnny always hitched. 'Anyway, I tried to find you at Good-Day's. Sean said you'd skipped out with this old guy's money.'

The way he said it meaning: *Smart Work, Mate.*

'Yeah, twenty quid. I bought a gramme with it. You want what's left?'

'Top one. I tell you, I'm wrung out. I haven't slept since . . .' He had to stop and think that one through. 'What's today, Thursday? I woke up Tuesday, about six in the afternoon. What's that?'

Jake palmed the wrap over. The sum he could do in his head. 'Fifty-four hours.'

'Jesus Christ, as long as that. No wonder I'm fucked.

I've got to get some of this down.' Johnny rubbed his hands together, keeping that amphetamine warm.

He was about to head for the powder-room but paused, a crease forming between his eyes. 'Who's that?'

Jake had forgotten about Kevin Donnelly. He swung to the side, waving Donnelly over as he shouted an introduction.

Johnny already had his hand stuck out for a formal shake-meet. Donnelly only had to thread his way through the crowd, he'd find a new friend waiting. A second ago, he looked like a boy in a bubble of loneliness. All it took was Johnny to flick a switch and he was floating inside a warm 40-watt bulb.

Johnny clamped the kid's hand and patted his arm. 'Good to meet you, mate. Back in a second.'

Jake and Donnelly stood there and watched Johnny bounce into the crowd. The way his hair moved, the shimmy could have been created for a shampoo ad. Johnny's hair always looked like that . . . when it hadn't been washed. Usually, he wore it lacquered-up and back-combed into a quiff mountain.

Donnelly said, 'I seen you around together loads. Not recently, though.'

Jake told him, 'No. He's been staying in Berlin – cornering the European pornography market.'

Donnelly looked puzzled, but didn't bother with a question, 'Right. Do you want another Pils?'

Jake had nearly finished his drink. Speed gave him such a thirst he wouldn't even notice he was ripped until the sixth or seventh bottle.

'Yeah, same again. And get one for Johnny.'

Donnelly disappeared. Jake could either stand there, alone, or he could follow Johnny round the dance-floor and into the gents. The toilets were impossibly small. Or was that cosy? Just one cubicle, a two-man tin urinal and a basin so small you could wash one finger at a time, maximum. When Jake got there, he had to wait for a guy to zip up and leave. He spent it usefully, putting in some time at the washbasin mirror. As the guy left, he tapped on the cubicle door.

'Open up, it's me.'

The bolt slid back. Jake watched the disc swivel from red to white and pushed on the open door. Johnny was straddling the toilet, a Pips membership card in his hand and the speed laid out on the porcelain cistern top. Jake rebolted the door and asked if there was much left.

'Yeah, I couldn't believe it. I thought you'd leave nothing but the glucose; snort all the speed from around it.'

There was a joke that Jake was tight-fisted. Or, rather, it wasn't a joke but Johnny had enough charm to make a joke of it.

Jake watched as Johnny rolled a something-denomination Deutschmark note into a tube, took a breath, and whooshed the speed down: it took him just two smooth goes. He finished by wiping the side of his Pips card down his tongue, grinning while he did it. It was true, there had been plenty left. Paulo always gave good deals.

Jake said, 'It taste better with foreign money?'

Johnny opened out the note and licked across its

surface in two fat tongue swipes. He pulled a face and considered the question. 'Actually, no. I got to say, it just doesn't do it for me.'

Jake laughed.

'I'm serious, mate. They're smaller, they're printed on crappier paper and they don't have the Queen's head. It's just not the same.' As he was talking he passed over the empty wrap. Jake screwed it up and popped it in his mouth, chewing the dregs out of it.

As they left the cubicle, a guy looked over from the urinal and threw an arch look, backed up with a grin. Jake ignored him but Johnny grinned back, telling him to put it away – this was a no-small-dick zone.

'Like you'd know.'

Johnny left with a dirty cackle, following behind Jake as they headed back to the bar. The DJ had just put on a Hazell Dean track and there was a rush for the pocket-sized dance-floor.

As they stood back to let the stampede pass, Jake said, 'You didn't say, were Sean and Fairy mad at me?'

'What do you think? They reckon that money had their names written on it. They'd been humouring the old bastard all night.'

'Fairy wasn't humouring; he'd fallen in love. You know what he's like for those old school Quents.'

Johnny shuddered. 'Jesus, I saw the guy. I'm no expert but he was on his last legs. If Fairy went down on him, the guy would have pegged out. I'm not kidding.'

'So I saved him.'

'You saved them both. Saint Jake, that's you.'

Half of the men in the bar were up on the dance-floor, now. Even spilling out to the sides to dance on the carpet. Over on the raised hearth where Johnny had been sitting, a couple were up on their feet and jogging to the music. Standing for the anthem, their hands in the air. And, just to their side, there was Kevin Donnelly. He wasn't moving, just looking confused with a hard-bitten, no-tears look on his face, a bottle of beer in his right hand and two others in his left.

Johnny pointed over at him, 'Your boy's missing you.'

Jake said, 'What do you make of him?'

'Sad fucking case. He works the Bus Station, doesn't he?'

Jake nodded, 'Pure psycho-bait, you can tell just looking at him.'

The relief on Donnelly's face when he saw them walk over – Jake thought it could melt a heart: even his, if anyone wanted to try and find it. What millions of prehistoric years did to fossils, amphetamine did to his heart in seconds ... pure ventricle calcification. He should sell his body to science, let everyone else sell theirs to trade.

Donnelly passed over the spare bottles. Johnny apologized for keeping him waiting. Saying, 'Cheers,' as he held up his Pils bottle for a unification clink. 'This is a Welcome Home Me party.'

Jake said, 'Mr Manchester. Cheers.'

Over the next hour, Johnny told them about Berlin. One story: an old German queen he'd seen walking down the Kurfürstendam in pink leather hotpants and matching biker's jacket and cap.

'The geezer had to be sixty.'

Jake said, 'Did you go over the Berlin Wall?'

'Nah, I didn't understand that bit at all.' Laughing. But he told them he'd visited a back room in a bar and seen stuff that would make your eyes pop . . . or water. 'You imagine what the cops would do, they find that stuff happening in Manchester? They'd call in the fucking army. Probably the Salvation Army, too, knowing Anderton.'

Johnny had already heard about the raid on the Zipper Store from Fairy and Sean. He asked if Jake had seen it.

Jake told him, 'Some. I walked away.'

'Fairy said it was that same Inspector again, on the spot to personally supervise the operation.' Johnny couldn't remember his name. 'Pascoe?'

'John Pascal. What did Fairy say about him?'

'He claimed he was wearing a sandwich board: he'd got *Repent You Bum-Boys, The End Is Nigh* written on it.'

It was almost plausible. It could even be a quote from the speech he'd give at the press conference in the morning. Opinion was divided on Pascal, whether his preacher-man style was an act to win promotion or whether he was serious when he spouted warnings of hellfire and damnation in his *Manchester Evening News* interviews. Whatever, the city was being pushed to extremes: a council hooked on Marxist-Leninism, and a police chief convinced he was overseeing Sodom and

Gomorrah. There was a rumour that said Anderton wanted to be the next chief of the Royal Ulster Constabulary where there was a better class of god-fearing Protestants.

Johnny said, 'I heard Anderton wants new body armour for his men: steel-lined keks to protect their backs.'

Jake had enough speed inside him to top that line. He could have gone all night, spraying out God's Cop rumours, high on amphetamine-fuelled wit. But the DJ was spinning out a new song that demanded a change of mood, 'Zoom' by Fat Larry's Band, and he wanted to get up there and start dancing.

'You up for it?'

Johnny didn't need asking. He was already across the floor; shugging, frugging, negotiating elbow space between the high-stepping clones doing their cowboy-style dance.

Times like these, they really needed Sean, a genuine soul devotee but with a sense of humour. It was Sean who taught them the Zoom dance, a dumb-show illustration of the lyrics beginning with a swoop of the hand zooming down like an airplane, and back up to the eye for the love-at-first-sight lyric. Johnny wasn't doing badly, though. He was catching every move on the beat and keeping a straight faraway face, the way Sean did it. The trick was to get the mock-seductive look of a black American soul singer: eyes hooded, lips just slightly apart in a pouting smirk.

Jake was cracking up, as he always did, doing the Zoom. It put him a beat out of step and he had to hurry to the rhyme – boom! – miming his heart exploding out of this chest with love. He and Johnny fell into synch. Kevin Donnelly danced alongside but didn't try to follow the moves; he just kept to the beat in a quiet, unshowy way. You needed to look down at his feet to know he could really dance: a series of natural soul-boy steps, perfectly done.

This was the end of the night, at least as far as Bernard's Bar. Johnny had zero money and though they could have hustled a few drinks, Bernard's was basically a couples place and even the few men cruising the area were really looking for soul mates. They weren't stupid enough to believe they could put a down-payment on a romance for the price of a beer. Jake bought one more round and let Kevin Donnelly buy another and that was it.

Somehow – maybe the frayed ends of his nerves after his night in the police station – Jake was feeling wired by the time he hit the street. Wired and frayed, like an electric cable whipping through the Manchester drizzle. You could practically see the sparks as he charged Albert Square. Johnny ran beside him. Kevin Donnelly dribbled along, fifteen yards behind.

CHAPTER *FIVE*

Fifteen days after the death of Kevin Donnelly, but only four hours since he heard the news, Jake Powell was sober and suited; wearing a dark tie, a dark overcoat. Nothing strictly funereal but it felt sombre enough. He had an overnight bag at his feet, a polystyrene cup of Euston cappuccino large in his hand. The coffee was whack.

The arrangement they made before DI Green left for his hotel was they would meet by the papershop at 9:15. Jake was there early, Green was running late. If Jake wanted confirmation, he could take a look at the electronic flip-board above his head: the Manchester train was leaving at 9:30 whatever happened. Maybe Green needed his sleep, maybe he'd miscalculated how long a five-minute taxi along the Marylebone Road could take in rush hour ... but he'd arrived now. For the past few minutes he'd been padding across the mouth of the double shopfront, twisting the strap of his wristwatch and pulling at a Rothmans. Jake was wondering how much longer it would be before the man recognized him. He was cutting it fine.

Finally, it happened. Beginning from a dead start, fifteen yards away, Green came pounding across the station floor, shouting: 'Powell? That you?'

Jake nodded hello.

The guy looked like a seizure case. 'How long you been wearing specs? I didn't fucking recognize you.'

Jake shrugged. 'I wear glasses during the day, contacts at night.'

'Well get another fucking pair. I been walking round the last fifteen minutes. Didn't you see me?'

Jake said, 'The train's about to leave.'

The platform at Euston stank. It was years since Jake last headed north and he had forgotten the smell. It was something specific: flat and dull but strong. He didn't know why the other stations should smell different. And, as usual, once he caught it, he remembered two other smells, both of them breweries: the McEwan's plant opposite his old flat in Hulme and the Boddington brewery next to Strangeways prison. There was a link there: the Manchester-bound train, the Manchester smells. You didn't have to be a Proust to dig it, though it would be lost on Green. Running for the train, the man had enough problems breathing. There was no way he could smell anything.

Jake kept pace with him, thudding down the ramp and running along the side of the carriages. The first four coaches were all First Class. Green didn't even look at them. He certainly didn't notice Jake drop back a pace and side-step into the No Smoking carriage. As Jake passed through the swish inner doors and bobbed down the aisle, he watched Green struggle along the platform outside. It was a kind of dumb show, the man passing breathlessly in and out of the frames of the sealed glazed windows. But, as Jake found his seat, it took a slapstick turn.

Green's mouth was already open, grabbing the oxygen he needed to power himself along, but now his mouth began to remould, getting ready to speak. And as it moved into conversational gear, Green began to turn his head, casting a look to his side. And because he couldn't see Jake, the look arced further and further until his head was facing backwards and his feet were pegging for the front. It couldn't last. Green went into a jelly-roll spin, dropping his old blue sports bag to the platform as he stopped and took a good hard look around.

Jake's seat was on the platform side of the train. By the time Green spotted him, Jake had emptied his coat pockets onto the table and was stretching to stow his bag on the luggage rack. Green stared up, no more than three feet away but separated by the double thickness of the window. The glass muffled all sound, but Green had easy-to-read lips.

'The fuck you playing at?'

Jake's ticket was in his inside pocket, tucked into an embossed envelope. The idea behind the envelope, he guessed, was to give First Class passengers a sense of added value. He slipped the ticket out and flashed it at the window: let Green have a good look before he folded it away again.

At a guess, Green was saying: 'You infantile little twat.'

Jake smiled and mouthed: 'See you in Manchester.'

Green stood on the platform with his crummy sports bag at his feet and a copy of the *Mirror* in his hand, and said: 'You know you're impressing no one, you git.'

Emphasizing the words by beating on the window with the rolled-up newspaper.

A whistle started blowing somewhere up the platform. Green wavered, the paper caught mid-whack as a uniformed guard came jogging by with one arm raised in the air. Watching from inside his coach, Jake believed he could see the cogs turning as Green tried to gauge the time, looking up the platform and turning back to Jake. Then he grabbed his bag and hauled off, really gunning for it. Jake watched, thinking: *You thought I'd spend another three hours listening to you?* Still, it was a childish trick.

Then, as Green disappeared around the curve of the platform, Jake noticed for the first time: with his anorak and his old sports bag, the man was dressed exactly like a schoolkid. How could that happen, a man goes through his whole adult life without ever putting any more thought into his clothes than his mother did on his first day at school.

As the train moved off, Jake made a pile of his things, all of it reading matter: a newspaper, a magazine and a paperback. By the time the steward came round with his trolley, he had finished *The Times*, which he neither liked nor disliked and bought because he had a theory: every empty decision he made, in some way it kept him saner; closer to having an open mind, becoming a floating voter. Although *The Times* was cheaper than the other broadsheets, so perhaps it just made him a price-sensitive consumer.

There were two other passengers in this short stretch of First Class: a bearded man who was working on a laptop and a woman Jake recognized from a soap – *Coronation Street* in fact. Jake was third along the steward's route. When the man arrived, he asked for a coffee and got a cup poured from a stainless-steel pot: presumably ground and percolated because there had to be some kind of First Class dividend. The stuff tasted like real coffee.

'Anything else, sir?'

Jake nodded. 'Yeah. If a fat guy comes asking where I'm sat . . . tell him I'm in a no-smoking compartment. I want that stressed.'

'Yes, sir. No smoking.'

Jake nodded. That was it. He was paying for the room: room to breathe, room to stretch.

He dumped the paper and opened his magazine, flicking through to the fashion pages. If he ever lost his job at the casino, maybe he should try modelling. How would that be? One of Green's first plays, last night, was to talk about Jake's job security. Asking, for instance, how it looked: '*A casino manager kicking shit out of his customers. I was just wondering?*' The man had a point; it could be time for a vocational shift. Looking at the featured models, Jake guessed he was older than most of them, but not all . . . these weren't the kind of stripped kids used in the women's mags. And it was a fact: Jake looked like a model. He had people, strangers even, come up and tell him. He believed them.

Years back, in a kind of post-crisis blind, Jake started wondering if his whole appearance was an illusion. That what he thought were his good looks were nothing but a self-delusion. Maybe he'd spent so long staring so hard at himself in mirrors, he'd put a gloss on his worst features. Now, even after he'd taken to wearing thick-lensed, black plastic specs, it didn't matter. He still got mistaken for the alpha-model male . . . *Mr Fuck-Up* disguised as *Mr Fuck-You*.

Another time, he wondered why he never let himself go. If he didn't, it was because the idea of leeching into a slob was just another route to self-obsession; not only disgusting but somehow arrogant . . . and a definite kick in the teeth for anyone who wanted him around their bed or their life. All round, he was happier if he looked clean, neat, together. His game-plan, so far as it went, was just to walk and act as close to normal as he could. If he felt no real connection with the guy trailing him across the mirrors of men's rooms or appearing like a ghost in the train window as an InterCity flew by on the opposite track, it wasn't like he could wish him away. Any more than he could help noticing the man looked all right and dressed better. Maybe he shouldn't become a model. If he could pick the suits and set up the shoots for these magazines, then that seemed like a job with a little more dignity. He could do it, he was sure.

Jake was staring at a spread: specifically the cuff on the trouser leg of a woollen suit. The material was so thick and soft, the hem had become bulky and eye-catching. At least it caught Jake's eye, used to staring at minutiae and trying to postpone the moment when he had to face the full picture. The only reason he never thought he was a thirty-four-year-old burn-out was because he'd been posing as a burn victim since he was sixteen. He once read somewhere that a sure sign of clinical psychosis is when a patient starts repeating the words *'black, dull, empty'* over and over. Jake tried it for five minutes. It sounded okay but it would, wouldn't it? He didn't know if he was feeling it for real.

The train paused in Stoke, less than forty-five minutes from Manchester Piccadilly. When DI Green tapped on the window, he caught Jake off-guard, deep into InterCity auto-analysis. As Jake snapped to, the first thing he saw was Green's grin. The man looking cheerful, holding two tins of McEwan's Export and a Scotch egg. Half a minute later, he reappeared in the aisle, rolling between the seats. So unsteady on his feet and so loud as he sat. Jake was only surprised it took him so long, thinking he would have just flashed his shield or whatever it was called, and promoted himself to First Class.

'How you doing? Comfy?'

Jake nodded, Fine. He didn't know how the other two passengers felt. Both of them, the laptop man and the soap actress, had looked up. Green stared back at the woman, a brief look of panic on his face until he recognized her.

'Fuck me.' The words coming in a rushed hiss, sotto voice. 'You're not going to believe this: I thought it was a friend of my ex-wife's.'

Jake believed. He had thought the woman was a friend of one of his aunts. That was the trouble with soap stars: they were only recognizable obliquely, through a chain of association.

Green popped the top of a McEwan's and took another look round as he settled down. He found the No Smoking logo, top centre of the window. 'Nice touch, Jake. You think, because I can't have a cig, you've got a psychological advantage?'

'I'm feeling okay.'

'Yeah, well it's the impression you're working on. You did all right last night, didn't you? Holding onto your decorectum while I'm doing my best to monster you.'

It was true. Green charged the flat like a stud bull, sure he was packing a savage wad.

'The way you clobbered that guy, you could be looking at GBH easy.'

Jake shrugged. Maybe.

'Oh, easy. But say you got a good lawyer and managed to pull a provocation deal. Even line up a few character witnesses and play the previous-of-unblemished line . . .' Green paused, like it was worth a thought. Though the only thing he was chewing over was his Scotch egg. 'You never know, it might have worked. It would have been a good laugh at my expense, anyway. Seeing it's my fault you don't have a record already, me being such a self-sacrificing twat when it comes to my snitches. The embarrassment of incidents from your past – I could have written a classic charge sheet. What do you reckon?'

Jake shrugged again.

'And how would that go down on a gaming-licence application?'

'Bad,' said Jake. 'But when it comes to casinos, any kind of criminal record is a bar, no matter what the charge. If I got one now, I'd be through.'

'What, back counting cards or spinning that roulette job? Busting your gut in one of those stupid waistcoats, the oldest kid croupier in the West End?'

'Something like that.'

'It's what I thought. I got to say, I liked the idea: the symmetry. You know, the innocence Davey Green bestows, yea he even takes away. Of course, the later I left it, last night, the less sense it made me going to the local cops. I mean, what if that guy had died ... how would I look, then? Standing like a knob, saying, Yeah, I was an eye-witness but I thought I'd let him croak.'

Green twisted his Rothmans packet around, then slapped it to the table, his great grey hand covering it entirely.

'And so there I was, enjoying your hospitality and drinking your delightful tea and letting time tick away. All the while, thinking: fuck, but little Jakie's grown into one smooth git. Then, this morning, I got another idea. Suppose this wasn't the first incident of its kind...'

Green was looking up at Jake now. A smile in his eyes like he was asking: *How does that compute?*

Jake said, 'Is that why you were late this morning?'

'Mm-mm. I had to find a friendly copper who didn't mind me having a diddle through his incident sheets. I got to say, that area's like the *X-Files*, it gets so many unexplained attacks. And all of them within fifty yards of the casino doors. So far, no one's volunteered a description, but going off the modus operandi, it could be the ghost of Bruce Lee.'

'Bruce Lee? Why not Bruce Wayne?'

'Who?'

'Batman.'

'What, the guy in the tights, makes the boys wonder?'

Jake nodded. He had to say, even at the comic-book level, what he'd been doing was hard to justify. But if he tried to claim he was protecting his staff, it sounded worse. They weren't the reason. What it was, at the hard core of the matter, he liked kicking the shit out of bad men ... he couldn't get enough of it. And, like Bruce Wayne, you had to suspect the reason was buried in his past.

Jake said, 'You thought that was why I agreed to come back with you? I was worried you might dig a little deeper, find a shed full of new stuff to hold over me?'

'I was just fact-checking, getting background.'

'That I'm a dangerous psycho?'

'Well, you certainly got a temper.'

Green settled back, smug in his seat. Jake didn't care. The truth was, there was no way Green could have blackmailed him into taking this trip. Losing the casino gig bothered him less than Green could imagine. It wasn't simply that Jake wasn't a gambler; that was one of the things that had recommended him to the casino's owners in the first place.

Jake's real problem was he disliked gamblers. Their nervousness, their beliefs, the things that turned them on . . . night after night, he felt he was surrounded by people who made his flesh crawl. Picture a Krishna-ite toting his bells and lathered in Vaseline, whining for a fix. That's how he saw gamblers: pervert junkie zombies. And it was time he quit flitting between a martyr and a third-rate vigilante. This trip back to Manchester, it was either a final attempt to push the self-flagellation act or a route to recovery. See some bad men . . . atone for some dead boys . . . all that stuff.

Jake said, 'I was thinking, how did you identify Kevin Donnelly? He didn't have any family.'

'Fingerprints.' Said matter-of-fact. Donnelly, of course, had no police sponsor. Just a yard-long criminal record. 'Anyway, the lad had plenty of family. A mother, two or three fathers, and God knows how many sisters and brothers.'

Jake was startled for a second. All the orphans together, sharing a flat in Hulme, he always assumed Kevin Donnelly was the genuine thing: a bona-fide orphan. Not just a slim Jim Morrison-style fake like the rest of them.

CHAPTER *SIX*

Jake's flat was 283 Robert Adam Crescent, though there was no number on the door. One way to recognize it: someone had spray-painted *Hommoes* in vertical letters from top to bottom. Jake might have taken it personally but it also said *Niggers* in fresher paint, left to right. The door, like the window, was covered in plywood inside and out. This was primarily a security measure, though the window did open onto the kitchen and Jake was glad no passer-by could see the state of his sink. Hulme housed a mix of people, but even the worst of the scum kept a cleaner house than these four queer boys.

Jake put the key to the lock, saying, 'Homme Sweet Homme.' Johnny stood behind him, stamping his feet. Kevin Donnelly was a pace further back, hovering like he was still unsure how far Johnny's invitation stretched – just to the walkway, or all the way through the flat's front door.

It was actually Jake's flat . . . at least, it was in his name so he claimed the rent benefit cheque although it had never yet been used for rent. There was a bundle of eviction notices skewered to a nail on the inside of the door. All of them unread because no one was ever evicted from the Crescents. If it ever became council policy, they could always fill out a fresh application at the housing office and move to one of the empty flats further along the block. The next time, they would have to rent it in Sean or Fairy's name – Johnny had already used up his turn. Maybe they should think about moving, just to solve the kitchen-sink scenario. Although Jake would miss his monthly cheque, and couldn't imagine how the sink could become a bigger problem.

Pushing the door open, he caught a snatch of Fairy singing along to the record-player: '*Boys keep swinging . . . Boys always work it out.*' Bowie's bass theatrics made it an easy song to parody. Effortlessly easy, because Fairy would never knowingly parody the divine David.

Jake let Johnny pass him in the doorway, and stopped Kevin Donnelly, saying: 'Listen to that and tell me you still like Bowie?'

Donnelly just grinned and nodded – so what could he say? Anyway, Jake found himself inexplicably moved by the song tonight. Almost to tears, despite Fairy's tinny campiness . . . it was the unbelievable truth. Maybe the speed was hazing his judgement but one line was really doing it for him: '*Heaven loves you . . . the crowd shouts for you.*' Imagine if that were true, that just being a boy got you a solid blast of adulation, stretching from heaven to earth . . . *and nothing stands in your way.*

The living-room was filled with cigarette smoke and lit by strings of Christmas lights. Inside, Fairy and Sean and four others were improvising a party. Fairy was working the hardest. With the combined noise, Fairy's singing and the noise from the record-player, no one heard the front door but they couldn't miss Johnny's grand entrance. He charged the room, yelling 'Alright'. In a second, everyone was shouting, 'Johnny! Jake! Alright!'

Jake nodded around the room, playing it wary as he probed for residual anger. If Fairy was still steamed about him skipping with that old guy's money, he wasn't showing it. Maybe he'd forgiven and forgotten, maybe the surprise appearance of Kevin Donnelly was acting as a distraction. Johnny was dragging Donnelly into the room, and anything new Fairy could not resist.

Johnny was pointing round the room, providing a full roll-call of introductions so Donnelly wouldn't feel shelved. 'This is Rebecca. This fox here, this is Debs. Alright, Debs . . .'

Rebecca was on the settee. Debs had been dancing with Fairy but was still now. She had a shy smile for Johnny.

'. . . the one asleep there is Domino and . . .' Johnny broke off, looking at a small kid crouched by the armchair where Sean's boyfriend, Domino, was sleeping, '. . . you got to forgive me but who the fuck are you?'

The kid said, 'Sorry. David.'

Jake didn't know who the fuck he was either.

'David. You alright, yeah?' The kid nodded. Johnny gave him a full grin. 'Okay. Then we got Sean here and, last up, Fairy. Everyone: Kevin.'

Johnny had invited Donnelly back as they were

crossing the roundabout below the Mancunian Way. They were running across the carriageway, avoiding the underpass and dodging the minicabs, when Johnny looked back and saw Donnelly tagging behind them.

Johnny was saying: 'I told him he had to come back. No argument. You know he's living in a DHSS-approved B&B. I said, no way. I've been through that and those places are suicide pits. Isn't that right, Fairy?'

Fairy nodded. 'Death by Bed and Breakfast.'

'Listen to him, Kevin. He knows. I swear, the council's got a meat truck moving round constantly, just picking up the bodies. Like, what are they called: those twenty-four-hour gun cars the cops have on call, just waiting for an armed response. Or one of those nuclear convoy things where the missile trucks are always moving so the spy satellites can't track them . . .'

Johnny was running out of moving things, his mouth was willing but his general knowledge was giving out.

Jake said: 'A shark.'

'Yeah.'

There was a bottle of Pernod on the floor, trapped between Domino's ankles. The bottle looked about three-quarters empty, so that might be why the boy was coma'ed. Sean's boyfriends might have trouble holding their liquor but they could pass as novelty drinks cabinets.

Jake was reaching down to free the bottle when Rebecca said, 'I thought I'd see you down Devilles, Jake.'

He looked up, said, 'No', shaking his head to let her know that it was too long a story. So far, he hadn't said a thing about DC Green and Bootle Street police station, and neither had Donnelly. When it came out, it could look strange: Jake keeping quiet on something like that.

'How was Devilles? Is that where you linked up with Sean and Fairy?'

She said it was. Jake was wondering now why she was out at all: wasn't it a schoolday tomorrow. He said, 'Have you broken up for Christmas already?'

'Last week.'

He brought the bottle over as he sat down next to her. He could see now, through the dark green glass, that the Pernod had been diluted with blackcurrant. It was one of Fairy's recipes. Jake passed the bottle to Rebecca, and when she shook her head he remembered she had a car and was probably driving. He took a swig, realized Fairy had used Vimto not blackcurrrant and started giggling, with his mouth already full.

'What's the matter?' Rebecca was smiling, glad to have a hook as she tried to connect. Jake shook his head, meaning that he couldn't speak, not that he didn't want to. Thinking: this had to be the national drink of Manchester: Pernod and Vimto. Was that a Vimtod or was it a Permo? Which made Domino permo-glazed.

Up above him, Debs's dancing had subsided to a basic shuffle. She swayed in front of Johnny as she asked him about Berlin. Her first question: had he been out clubbing? Johnny began telling her about The Jungle or *Der Shungle* or something; a name that Jake hadn't quite caught the first time and still couldn't make out.

Apparently, the inside of the club was fitted with scaffolding and steel walkways which made Jake think of a building site. To their left, Fairy was fussing around Kevin Donnelly, asking if he needed a drink. When Fairy began looking around, Jake guessed he was searching for the Pernod bottle. He took another swig and held it out. Fairy passed it on to Donnelly who rubbed the neck with the sleeve of his Harrington, playground style. When he realized what he'd done, he blushed through: the colour of the drink he was pouring inside himself.

Sean was sat over by the record player, thumbing through the box that had SEAN painted on its leatherette skin in Tippex. When his head flicked up for a moment, Jake caught him casting a sulking glance over at Domino. Or maybe it was concern. Jake remembered, now, that he'd heard something about Domino and diabetes. It came back to him: the boy once passed out in a stairwell in Pips. He'd been trying to drag his way to the snackbar to find a sugar sachet when the diabetes overtook him. Jake had heard the story secondhand. It might have been Sean who got the sugar. Jake could only picture someone crawling up a sheer staircase, groaning 'Sugar . . . Sugar . . . Sugar.' *Yes, Honey?*

Jake started giggling again. Rebecca put her arm around him, cosying up as he smiled back at her.

'What is it?'

He shook his head again; it wasn't worth saying out loud. He breathed in, recognizing the smell of her hairspray. Elnett Extra-Hold – the same brand he used. Her fringe was fixed in a row of spikes, pointing down in front of her face like a security fence. It wasn't designed to be impregnable.

'Who's he?' Jake pointed at the other kid whose face had begun to seem familiar, but whose name had been re-erased.

'David? He's at sixth-form college with us.' She meant her and Debs. The boy was in a huddle next to Sean, crouched over the records but searching through the wrong box. He had something by the Human League in his hand and a connoisseur's look across his face. It was wasted on Sean, who'd pulled out a disco twelve-inch. As it started up, Jake recognized 'Imagination' by Imagination. David leant the Human League record against the front of the hi-fi cab, as though they operated a queueing system.

The flat was a third-floor maisonette right at the top of Robert Adams Crescent. The front looked down into the broken circle of the four Crescents and over to Moss Side. The back windows looked onto the Aaben Cinema and across to the Ship Canal. The idea of a maisonette, Jake assumed, was to recapture the glamour of a council house but set it in the bright modern utopia of a tower-block. There were three bedrooms upstairs: his, Johnny's and Sean's. Fairy had been the last to move in, so slept downstairs in a makeshift lean-to at the back of the living-room. Any guests, if they weren't asked to share a bed, crashed on the settee. He guessed that's where Kevin Donnelly would be sleeping, unless Fairy turned out to have an interest.

Jake took another circular peek around the room

and realized both Fairy and Donnelly had disappeared. If they were using his bed, they were both dead.

Jake was almost on his feet when Johnny came dancing over, holding a bottle of poppers in his hand. 'You want some?'

Absolutely no moment of indecision. Jake took the bottle, removed the loosely screwed cap and covered the neck with his thumb. He took a snort up his right nostril, a quick gulp of room air, and another snort up his left nostril before he passed the bottle sideways to Rebecca. What was it with poppers? Primed up, he was nothing but a ticking time-bomb. Johnny stood in front of him, watching intently as he counted down the seconds. When it came, Jake felt the muscles at the base of his neck vibrate and begin to spread, like g-forces were flattening his face. Spreading wider, the muscles opened around his mouth until his lips were stretching into a rictus grin. The sound coming out of his mouth, this inhuman cackle, set up new spasms. His cheeks were pleating like curtains and opening out to his ears, his eyes were staring upwards, flickering and boggling. Everyone else's eyes were on him.

He had one hand gripping Rebecca's knee, the other holding onto the settee cushion. He knew what he looked like: His Holiness the Pope courtesy of Francis Bacon. And he was pushing into the purple until it crested, receded and he was coming back to earth. He could hear his laugh now, human again, the manic but recognizable giggle. Then the echo. He turned to his right, it was Rebecca, giggling with him and wanting to share the moment. He puppet-nodded his head in front of her to keep her giggles coming. She had a hand in front of her mouth to cover her quaking smile. Above it her eyes were watering in their violet Cleopatra frames. As she began to subside, he was asking, You alright?

Her soft giggling, 'Yes.'

'You sure? Y'alright?'

Watching her head nod as he nodded up and down in front of her, moving closer until their lips met and they began kissing. She began a little too hard. The sharp point of her tongue probing like a little snout, but he kept his lips soft and she began to respond. Soon they were slipping together, moist without being wet, in and around each other's lips in shallow dives. He bared his teeth for a moment and felt her bottom lip glide across their serrated surface, then she nibbled his lips for a passing second.

They were beginning to work together, he could feel her relaxing as he moved a little deeper. Every shared slip of their tongues diluting the taste of spearmint that hovered on her breath ... and probably the taste of aniseed and cigarettes on his.

It was Rebecca who broke away. He didn't know why until he heard Fairy's voice above them, saying, 'Jake. Jake.'

He shook his head, 'Yeah?'

Something was upsetting Fairy. 'Can you come over?'

'What is it?'

Fairy pursed his lips, 'Can you come.'

Jake got up, stroking Rebecca's shoulder rather than strain for an apology, and followed Fairy out of the room. Fairy opened the front door and they stepped onto the walkway.

Johnny was leant on the pebbled concrete rail, ten yards from the open door, as though he was searching for privacy.

When Jake asked him what was going on, he shrugged and said, 'That kid, Slappy,' using the name Fairy had given Kevin Donnelly on the night they first noticed him. The boy had been hovering at the kerb by the Bus Station, looking uncertain before he climbed into a beaten-up Transit van. As the van pulled away, they saw the driver's face, unshaven and grey as an emery-board. The man scanned the street for live witnesses, then nodded his head backwards. Kevin pushed between the two front seats and disappeared into the rear of the van. They'd all seen it, but Jake was the first to speak, barely laughing as he said, 'He's going to get fucked over.' Fairy had said, 'A slappy – give him six months and you'll hear his sphincter flapping as he walks.' It was the kind of obscene image Fairy hoped to carry off with a camp twist. It turned Jake's stomach but, when he shot Fairy a look, Fairy hadn't looked too happy either.

Jake said, 'Donnelly? What's up with him?'

'He's up in my room skriking.' Johnny's face was drawn. He hadn't slept in how-many hours now and even the amphetamine wake-up call couldn't override his tiredness.

'Sling him out. You want to get to bed, mate.'

'He's in my fucking bed. You brought him here. You talk to him.'

Jake could have said, It wasn't my idea. You invited him. But he got the feeling he was supposed to be constructive. 'What's his problem?'

Fairy said, 'He can't take rejection.'

'You go up, then. Give him the benefit of your experience.'

Fairy didn't laugh. 'I've been up. He's really upset.' The stress on *really*. 'It's not Johnny's fault.'

Jake looked down the bleak corridor, curving away to their left with the granite sweep of the Crescent. The wind had blown the rain across the deck of the walkway, leaving only a ragged line, closest to the wall, still dry. Where Johnny was stood, leaning out over the parapet, the wind sprayed round his head.

Jake motioned back to the open door of the flat. 'Come on. We going to stand in the rain? I'll go up and talk to him.'

He led the way. At the door to the living-room, he held up a finger for Rebecca – give me one minute – and walked up the stairs ahead of Fairy and Johnny. At the closed door to Johnny's room, he stopped and waited.

'So he's upset. You reckon someone should make some tea.'

Johnny's shoulders slumped. He said, 'I'll get it. Maybe I need a coffee.'

He was dreaming. What were the chances of finding milk in the flat? And anyway, Jake had never even seen Johnny brew up before. Jake waited outside the bedroom for a moment longer, listening to Johnny's feet drop on the stairs. At the foot of the stairs, he heard him say, 'Anyone want to put the kettle on?'

Fairy was shooting looks from Jake to the door. Jake sighed, said, 'Okay,' and pushed into the room.

Kevin Donnelly was the shape under the duvet, a shallow heap across Johnny's double mattress. The bottle of coloured Pernod stood at the foot, Jake moved it a few inches to the side and sat at the edge of the mattress. He nodded to Fairy, implying *You take the other side.*

Fairy hunched over the figure, delicately drew the duvet back and said, 'Y'alright?'

Kevin Donnelly's face came up – just as slapped and bitten as it always looked. There was a smudge under one of his eyes but no sign of fresh tears. The boy had pulled himself together, or pulled himself in. Something in the boy's eyes was both accusatory and bitter. 'I'm okay.'

Jake was ready to brush it off as nonsense. If that was the way the boy wanted to play it, who wanted to get personal?

Fairy said, 'He was at Colchester Hall.'

Jake knew the name: a care home close to Cheadle Hulme, Stockport.

'Yeah, when?'

Kevin was sitting up now, the duvet had fallen off his shoulders onto his lap. 'I left a year back.'

Fairy was saying that Donnelly had been on remand since then, but Jake wasn't listening. He was looking at the pin-scrawled tattoos across Kevin's arms and shoulders: spiders' webs, the wavering square letters *'MUFC'*, fragments like *'cut here'* followed by dotted lines, *'skins forever'*, *'Madness'* and *'kev kev kev'*. All in biro-blue, almost the shade of the veins that spun across his arms and chest below the too white skin.

Donnelly saw him looking, flinched and drew the duvet back onto his shoulders.

'Colchester Hall,' said Jake. He didn't know what else to say. They'd met a few other boys who'd passed through the place . . . rentboys on the streets around the Bus Station and others trying to blag a drink in Good-Day's. Counted besides the ones they knew, the ones who decided to make a career out of getting fucked over, how many others were spread around Manchester?

Fairy said, 'He was there three years. He should have been released earlier but his housemaster per-suaded the social workers he needed more time, saying he was beginning to get through to him.'

A line like that – a dry, dropped hint about the horror – always cropped up in a story about Colchester Hall. Every story so closely followed the same patter, Jake almost believed the place was fiction. If it was real, why had it never been busted? Then he'd meet someone else who'd been there and he'd get a new jag from the story, an edge that made him know it was real. Then he was left wondering, if a place like that existed, how could he be one of the few people who knew what happened there? It seemed impossible when he'd never even seen the place, couldn't even say exactly where it was.

Kevin Donnelly, chicken-wrapped in the duvet, said, 'You do like men?'

Fairy nodded, Yeah sure. Jake shrugged, noncommittal.

Donnelly said, 'This one master, he told me he could tell just by looking at me. That it was what I wanted, so in that way I was just like him. He told me I could stay in his room all the time, except when he needed it for another boy.'

'He kept you in his room?' Jake spat the words out. 'What? Chained down?'

'I wasn't chained.' Donnelly's voice was quiet . . . but there was nothing simple in what he was saying.

Fairy was trying to reason with him, saying that rape was rape. 'Or what about a teacher who forces himself on a girl, he can say she likes boys, so what? It still wouldn't make sense.'

'Most of the time, it was better in his room. Once he'd told everyone else I was a puff, I had them on my case. Kicking the shit out of me or fucking me . . .'

Johnny walked in, holding two mugs and slurping the top off one of them. 'You want a brew?'

He held it out for Donnelly, who took it.

Jake said, 'What's happening downstairs?'

Johnny shrugged. 'I'm wasted, man. I think they're all still here.' Turning to Donnelly, 'Look, there's no problem you being here. I wouldn't have asked you, if there was. But I got to crash. You can take the settee or whatever, any way you like. But I got to get my head down.'

Jake nodded vigorously, 'Find yourself somewhere

to kip. There's no problem.' He was on his feet now. 'I got to get downstairs, you know . . .' He gave another shrug. When he left, he was holding the bottle of Pernod.

Jake detoured by the bathroom. Looking in the cabinet mirror, he saw his slicked-back hair had loosened. A shock of black swung over his forehead. He had to say he liked the effect. Looking down, he saw someone had left the bottle of poppers on top of the sink. He took two quick shots of Pernod then unscrewed the poppers' cap and took a whiff of that. The amyl gave the last of the amphetamine a kick-start. He wasn't laughing this time but he felt juiced up. The idea of flailing round the settee with Rebecca some more, wondering what she wanted from him or, worse, feeling guilty because he either wasn't talking or wasn't listening to her, he wasn't up for that . . . a too-slow game for Billy the Whizz.

The bathroom door pushed opened and Domino walked in, fresh out of his suspected diabetes stupor but still looking dazy-eyed. Jake stood there with a bottle in either hand and his face pounding red. He said, 'Go ahead, mate.'

Domino unzipped over the toilet and started peeing. After a second, Jake said, 'Hutch up.'

They stood either side of the bowl, plaiting golden streams as Jake felt his penis thicken in his fingers and watching Domino's piece, jerking as it filled with blood. He stroked his own and popped his foreskin back over the bell-end. Domino did the same. As they shook together, Jake whispered, 'Straight across the hall, the black door.'

He let Domino go first, nodding directions from the shelter of the bathroom door. When he darted past the open door to Johnny's bedroom, he saw they were all still there, drinking out of the mugs. He thought no one saw him.

He and Domino were unbuckled, facing each other with their trousers around their ankles. Jake had hold of Domino's buttocks in both his hands and the boy's shirt open. He bent him backwards so his mouth could reach to suck on his nipples.

Fairy was stood in the doorway, looking in.

'You twat, Jake.'

'Get out, Fairy.'

'What about Sean? What about the girl down there?'

Jake unlocked Domino and took a step out of his trousers and a step towards Fairy at the doorway. 'I don't give a fuck. Get out.' He had his fist curled, only at waist level, but he was raising it higher.

Fairy backed out, shocked silent. Jake slammed the door behind him. When he turned, Domino had dropped to the bed and was beginning to unlace his Doc Marten's.

CHAPTER *SEVEN*

DI Green was already on the platform, smoking the cigarette he had been waiting for since Stafford. Jake gathered his bag, his coat, helped the soap actress heft her suitcase down the train steps and onto a trolley. Green never lifted a hand. He stood looking at the woman as though he was still suspicious of her . . . she might turn out to know his ex-wife after all.

As Jake joined him, Green stretched and straightened, pulling back from the sign he had been leaning against so Jake finally got to read it: MANCHESTER PICCADILLY. That was it, the moment the city chose to wake up and hit him between the eyes.

'So, now I'm here,' Jake said. 'What do you expect me to do?'

DI Green took another drag on his cigarette, letting the actress get a good head-start before he followed her towards the ticket gate. 'Do? I don't know. Just ask around, gather information and pass it on.'

'Ask who? I don't know anyone.'

'You just heard Donnelly died. You're curious, appalled . . . so you're digging up old acquaintances.' Green didn't seem to have either a plan or the patience to think of one. 'Use you're chuffing imagination. I mean, your whole life was play-acting, you should be able to make up some story.'

Jake could have said it wasn't his whole life; he was only a kid at the time. He didn't. Instead, he said, 'How am I supposed to find these old acquaintances? It's been fifteen-sixteen years.'

'Yeah, so? Sixteen years is nothing.'

'Not for you, but for the people I used to know . . .'

It was something so obvious, even Green could have thought of it. In fact, had already thought of and even made into a joke.

Jake said: 'It's the difference AIDS makes. Even if I could find anyone I used to know, how many of them do you think will be dead?'

Fairy, for instance.

Five years ago, Jake got a polite letter, redirected from the home of an aunty he didn't remember having mentioned to anyone, let alone Fairy. The letter asked if he would like to drop by and pay a visit, although Fairy hadn't actually written it – the letter explained that Fairy had already lost his sight. The tone was polite, distant, striving to be formal against what seemed to be a natural demotic strain, the signature bracketed with the words *Si's Friend*. Fairy's real name, Simon Hartley, was used three or four times in the letter, often enough to jar and eventually to strike a chord. Jake had never forgotten Fairy, only his real name. By the time he received the letter, Fairy was dead so Jake went to the funeral, instead. It wasn't far away: Golders Green Crematorium. He learnt that Fairy had moved to London a couple of years before to take up the job of head stylist at a department-store salon. While he was standing around at the wake, Jake took a look at the photographs Fairy's lover had dotted around their home. Remembering the frizz of thin reddish hair Fairy had at seventeen, Jake was surprised how normal the hair looked in the photos of the pushing-thirty Fairy. It was a romantic story in many ways, someone who had overcome personal handicaps to achieve excellence . . .

The second Jake thought up the 'personal handicap' line, he felt guilty. It was just something that had come to him, standing in the hallway of this strange, overly-coupley Golders Green flat. Even as it flitted through his mind, he tried to excuse it as the kind of flip campery Fairy liked to use, something that could be churned over until it almost resembled stoicism. Then he felt worse because he no longer knew anything about Fairy or how he'd changed. That feeling passed as well. Fairy's friends (*Si's friend's friends*) were a clutch of jolly, puddingy queens – though not particularly effeminate – and the flat was decked out with the kind of suburban reflex that might claim it was aiming for theatricality or irony, but really only wanted to settle into cosy homeliness. Though the flat was nice.

Jake was still standing in the hallway when he ran into Sean, stepping out of the bathroom with an eyebrow arched against the scented candles standing round the tub. There was a moment's awkwardness: should they hug or shake . . . what? Jake stuck out his hand.

Sean took it. 'You look good.'

Jake didn't need to say, You too. Wearing a good suit, a truly beautiful shave and with his natural jet-black hair, Sean was smart and smart-looking, a winning combination. At the time he was a TV producer. Jake had seen his name once or twice, wafting through the credits of different TV programmes, but he was already on the verge of abandoning producing to run his own company.

When he told Jake this, Jake said, 'Good one. Make a million.'

He said he would.

Jake never got around to checking it out, but Sean probably had his million by now. Set against Fairy's suburban queens, he came over as a very different life-style gay, rarer but still recognizable: someone who held on to his natural fastidiousness with such determination, it was now baked hard, dry and unbreakable. Jake knew Sean would apply it with a formal, ruthless cruelty to every aspect of his life. It was an English type, or an Anglo-type; any place where fastidiousness was treated with both suspicion and awe. It was a trait Jake had recognized in other succesful men, if not at first hand, at least in news photos or TV reports; some politicians had it, also some film producers. Maybe Jake had something of it, too. Maybe not. Whatever was hard-baked inside himself, it felt more like meanness than carefulness. Still, he and Sean made a pair that after-noon. Standing around Fairy's flat and avoiding drink-ing the sweet sherry.

Sean had got to hear of Fairy's illness by a similarly

circuitous route, via a friend of a workmate of an ex-lover. It was long-winded but, still, Sean lucked out, if that's the word: he managed to catch Fairy on his deathbed. The way Sean told it, Fairy was nothing but a bladderless mouse skeleton, shrunk into hospice bedware.

Jake said, 'Well, he was a good friend. It's my loss that I never saw anything of him.'

Sean nodded. 'Mine too.'

'You remember the night I got off with Domino? I still feel guilty about that, not because he was your boyfriend . . . I mean, it's not like I'm overjoyed by that aspect, but you do stuff like that when you're young.' Jake paused, feeling he'd made a bad start, but Sean just nodded him on; he understood. 'What I do feel bad about, even now, was the look on Fairy's face when he caught us in the bedroom and I threatened him. He couldn't believe I could just turn on him like that. That I would beat him up.'

'What can I say? You were a shit.' Sean smiled, like it was something they shared. 'But what were we – sixteen, seventeen?'

'I was eighteen.'

'Well, anyone with an ego, they're always going to be a shit at eighteen.'

'Anyone who's an arsehole is a shit at that age,' Jake said. 'Not that you were.'

Sean waved it off. 'But Johnny and Fairy definitely weren't.'

No, they weren't. And now Fairy was also dead. Like Johnny was dead, more than a decade ago.

There was a beat there. A pause while the air seeped out of the conversation bubble. Sean tried first to fill it.

'Did they ever catch the guy who killed Johnny?'

Jake shook his head.

'What was it? Someone he picked up at Chorlton Street Bus Station?'

Jake shrugged. He couldn't say.

'A psycho?'

Jake said, 'It would have to be, the state of Johnny's body when the police found it.'

Back on this side of the tracks, DI Green finished his cigarette with a croak and an ounce of phlegm, and began to panda down the platform.

Jake, walking beside him, tuned back to hear him spiel a justificatory line, saying: 'Yeah, it's been a while. A lot of the faces are dead . . . so why'd you think I need you? The police have changed, you know. We're not still chasing the puffs with cattle prods and bibles like we did in John Pascal's day. We got a gay liaison unit . . . even *I* have meetings with them, you believe that? I get to serve on a committee co-ordinating the Queer Up North party they run around the Village. I didn't go fannying about round London because I got problems with puffs or with AIDS cases. I did it because I got problems with a specific case. This murder and the first one. And because of your intimate ties to both of the deceased, I decided to go looking for you.'

Johnny. Someone who never waited around to find the rumours of a gay plague were true. His body was found hacked and dumped on Caldenstall moor. And now Kevin Donnelly had gone the same way, it seemed the police were willing to reinvestigate. Or, what made it worse, all but willing. A sleazy old copper was ready to take a couple days off to reactivate an old snitch, and that seemed to be all. The end.

Jake said, 'You believe it's linked, Johnny death with Kevin Donnelly's?'

Green shrugged. 'I don't know.'

'You're not willing to stick your fat fucking neck out.'

Blandly, 'Not particularly. Not at the moment.'

Jake stopped him at the barrier, hissing so no passer-by could hear, although he felt inclined to shout it out: 'You couldn't solve Johnny's murder back then, you fat cunt. How you going to do it now?'

DI Green was still nothing but bland, cop-like as he shrugged past Jake. 'Things change. We got a handle on that whole kiddy-fucking party ring: all the evidence we need to put everyone away. There's just the matter of loose ends.'

'Is that what you're calling it?' Jake was right on Green's tail. 'Two murders.'

Green rolled on towards the black-cab queue, holding up a hand as though, just this once, he might admit he'd edged over the acceptable border. 'Just a figure of speech, son. And, whatever you call them, they're still loose until they're tied up . . . which is what I'm working on. Trying to decide how to do it, whether to tie them together or not. And how exactly I should bundle them up with this Colchester Hall business.'

Here they were, edging towards a locale Jake couldn't begin to recall without feeling sick, no matter how long ago it all happened. He was a pace behind Green as they stepped out of Piccadilly Station into the pale grey sunlight of Manchester. The sweep of the ramp that led up to the station entrance carried a shock of the familiar without seeming any less distant, a part of the un-nostalgic past. Take him, inter-citying to the crock at the end of the rail track, and he still wasn't prepared. What he really wanted, he now realized, was for Green to spell it out. He'd been waiting all this time, steeling himself for something that had never come.

So he said, 'Why don't you just say it? You brought me back because you want me to find Gary Halliday?'

'Kevin Donnelly's old housemaster? Why would I want you to find him? I know exactly where he is.'

Jake's stomach was turning, his knuckles were burning white on the handle of his bag. 'But you want me to go see him, in that place?'

Green looked confused. 'What place? Colchester Hall?'

Jake nodded, Where else?

'He's not there. We closed that place down weeks ago. He's on remand, awaiting trial.' Then, like he was thinking of it for the first time. 'But since you mention it, you could go visit him . . . I've booked you in for the morning. How does that sound?'

CHAPTER *EIGHT*

Johnny was waiting for him on the landing. Jake edged round the door of his bedroom, his jeans in his hand.

'What time is it?'

'Eleven-thirty,' Johnny said. 'So get a move on, you slapper. You don't want to be around when Sean wakes.'

Jake knew it, working hard at unravelling his trousers for a quick getaway. Sean had an evil temper – the fact he kept it wrapped most of the time only made it more scary. Call it cowardice, call it betrayal, or call it like it is: Jake's best move was to skip out early and leave Domino to face the music. As of this moment, Domino was still sleeping. If the boy had any sense, he would run the moment he realized Jake had slipped the sheets and disappeared.

Johnny said, 'I tell you, you owe me the fucking moon for this.'

Jake nodded, peering over the stair-rail to check for life or movement downstairs. 'Who's here?'

'You don't need to worry,' Johnny said. 'Rebecca left last night, which is another thing you got to thank me for. The state I was in last night, you think I wanted to kick a crying girl out of the flat, then spend another hour listening to Sean and Fairy going on about what a git you are – all that plus the crazy kid you picked up last night and dumped on me.'

'So everyone hates me?'

'They always did, mate. I tell you, I wouldn't have anything to do with you if I didn't need your help. So get a fucking move on.'

Downstairs, Fairy was still sleeping inside his make-shift blanket tent. Kevin Donnelly was awake, though, sitting among the kitchen debris and drinking a cup of tea. There they were, the two of them working on a vanishing act, and Donnelly was asking if they wanted a brew.

Johnny put a finger to his lip, telling him to hush.

'Anyone asks, you haven't seen us.'

Then he grabbed his kitbag and nudged Jake ahead, out of the door and into the Manchester morning.

They were stepping out of the shadows of the undercroft beneath the Crescents when Johnny said, 'So, how was Domino? Was he worth the aggravation?'

All he was doing was trying to needle Jake. Johnny knew Jake never talked about sex. At least, not in detail. He preferred to stick to the abstract level. That way it was guaranteed to sail right by Johnny.

This time Jake just shook his head. Then tried for a diversion: 'So why did you wake me? What am I supposed to be helping you with?'

'The three Ps: piracy, pornography and peddling smut.' Johnny held the neck of his kitbag open and let Jake see inside. It was full of German porn videos. 'There's a guy I know, he's got the equipment to copy these . . . then, tonight, we go out and flog them.'

'What guy?'

'A loony, you'll see. He lives in Elmin Walk over there.' Johnny pointed to the low-rise blocks marking the end of the Hulme estate.

Then, a few paces later: 'You were saying, what position does Domino play? Catcher . . . hitter, or what?'

Jake said, 'You ever heard of the Marquis de Sade?'

Johnny's eyes swivelled, 'Yeah? You gave him a spanking? I didn't hear it.'

'What do you think?'

'I don't know. You're the one brought it up. Day Sade, the sadist geezer, right?'

'I asked if you'd heard of him. It was a general-knowledge question. Congratulations, you passed.'

The story Jake was thinking of was biographical, not something de Sade wrote, unless it came from one of his letters. Apparently de Sade paid his valet to bugger him first thing every morning. There was no mention of whether the valet enjoyed it or not, or even anything to suggest it was an unusual demand. De Sade believed it set him up for the day, so from that point of view it was nothing but a daily exercise routine. Neither de Sade or, as far as Jake knew, his valet were specifically homo. Maybe the old guy had a prostate problem and figured that was one way of dealing with it. The story set up so many spin-off suggestions, it was the kind of thing that once you knew, you never forgot. But the reason Jake thought of it now was he couldn't begin to understand how anyone could launch their day with a bout of buggery. When Johnny came creeping into the room to wake him, Jake took one look at the boy lying beside him and just wanted to get the fuck out of the duvet.

Johnny said, 'I was only asking, 'cause I thought old Dommo was all right, the time I gave him one.'

Jake burst out laughing, 'And you were calling me a twat.'

'The difference is, I was suave about it. Sean didn't know a thing about it. And Domino was up for it. What could I do?'

'What can we do? Everyone in Manchester wants to shag us.'

Johnny had to say: 'It's not easy.'

No, but *they* were. And most of the time, it felt incredible. Not the sex, admittedly. But the feeling that there was no one who didn't want to sleep with them.

They crossed the road by the Sir Henry Royce, past the wired-in five-a-side pitch, and headed for the entrance to Elmin Walk. For some reason, these flats had always been considered a shade more respectable than the Crescents. Walking up to the first floor, Jake said he'd always wondered how the other half lived. When Johnny stopped, it was outside a maisonette flat that looked more cheerful, all round, than Jake's place. The outside was faced with wood, a little like a Blackpool chalet.

Johnny re-reminded him that the guy was a nutter; tread carefully. 'He's called Junk.'

'Junk? The guy's a scag-head?' Jake didn't like the

sound of that. Somewhere, perhaps, there was a sphere for glamorous heroin addicts, an exclusive club where William Burroughs swapped junk lore with Johnny Thunders. But the only junkies Jake ever met were lousy poets and musicians. A suspicious side-note: he had never heard of a heroin addict who enjoyed dancing, a fact that had to deserve a government research grant.

Jake said, 'He's not a junkie. His name's John Quay. You know, like the Fall song: "No Xmas For John Quay".'

Maybe he wasn't a junkie, but it was a racing cert the man who opened the door had problems. He was six foot of unsupported bone, headless behind a sheet of greasy hair. He didn't say a word, just turned around and let them follow him up the stairs of his flat. As Jake reached the first floor, the guy was already heading for the back bedroom.

Johnny, one pace behind on the steps, prodded him forward: 'Keep going.'

The room was filled with TV monitors, mounted on bolt-together Dexion shelving units. There were no windows and the only light came off the screens, a haze of unstable colours, all dissolving into each other. The man Junk sat down in front of a home-made control panel, his mixing desk, with his eyes straight ahead. The general impression, here's a guy who doesn't break his work schedule for anyone, but Jake couldn't tell what he was doing or even if he could see, the way his hair covered his face.

When he spoke, it came out in a flat Manchester

accent: 'Leave the vids with me. You want to come round tomorrow, they'll be ready.' That kind of voice always carried a promise: the user wasn't about to begin caring for anything. With Junk, perhaps, you could take it as it sounded. At least, Jake couldn't see what the guy was living for.

Johnny slung his bag onto the mixing desk, saying: 'Sorry, change of schedule. I got customers set up for tonight. How about it?'

Junk looked through the bag, counting the number of tapes. His mouth moved but he didn't actually speak aloud until he asked: 'How many copies again?'

Johnny pulled a pencil-scratched list out of his back pocket, smoothing it out before handing it over. Junk took it and held it to the light of the nearest monitor. As he brushed away his hair to read it, Jake saw a raw puckered hole where the man's eye should be.

Something like that, coming so early in the morning, Jake couldn't help himself. He turned away, saying, 'Jesus Fuck.'

Even as it was leaving his mouth, he was already backing away, scared what this freak's reaction might be.

All Junk did was mumble 'Sorry' and reach for an eye-patch that lay at the end of his desk. When he pulled the elastic over his head, he did it over his hair so the crown now lay tight to his skull and the rest flared out like a dirt-black mop.

After a few seconds, mouthing a roll of sums, he said, 'Okay, eight-thirty. But I can't do all these Beta-max today. I don't have enough blank tapes.'

Johnny nodded. 'Fucking krauts, all they got is VHS. They don't get that Betamax is the future.'

Junk agreed.

'But you can do the rest?'

'Yeah ... I got to say, though, I can't see you shifting many in the Video 2000 format.'

Johnny said he'd already got a buyer. As they left, he said, 'Eight-thirty.' And to Jake, as they slithered down the stairs, 'Let's hope I got the money to pay for it by then.'

The Arndale Shopping Centre was decorated for Christmas: strips of twisted ribbon slung across the tiers, stars swinging from thirty-foot wires to hover over the main concourse, strings of fairy-lights giving the escalators a little twinkle. There was no single theme or colour; the shiny marble floors amplified the Christmas overload. Jake had split up with Johnny outside, on Market Street, and had to deal with effects alone.

He rode the escalator past W H Smith's, underneath a computerized sign that spelled out Merry Xmas in flashing techno-green. A few years ago that lettering had been used on almost everything, but particularly on seven-inch singles: Kraftwerk and Gary Numan, obviously, but also groups with less programmed identities looking for a timely futurist spin, like the Police or the Tubes. Now, the sign already looked outdated. This was going to be a past-perfect Christmas: post-futurist like it was post-punk, post-new-wave, post-mod and ska. Post-everything. Post early for Xmas.

Another escalator took him to the door of a clothes shop called Venus. The shop was slotted into an architectural overspill on the lower ground floor, which made it practically impossible to pass by accidentally. It was almost as if the mall chiefs had analysed the circulation-flow for the whole site, realized too late they had a piece left over and thought, *sod it*, we can't make it work. Their failure was compounded by the Christmas decorators; the glitz thinned out noticeably in this area: a spot of Xmas alopecia alongside the hairy sights everywhere else. The odd thing, Venus was camp as Christmas, anyway. Though that wasn't the main attraction for Jake. He was always happy shopping for clothes. He was even happier that Johnny had decided to do his Christmas purse-snatching alone.

The shop assistant, a girl called Clare, called out the moment he walked through the doors. 'Are you on your own?'

She sounded as though she was surprised. Jake told her, 'Yes,' but didn't tell her what Johnny was doing. 'He should drop by later, I don't know. Maybe he'll get detained.'

Johnny had wanted Jake to help him: work up-front as a decoy while he rifled through their bags from behind. Jake told him, 'It's really tempting. Let me think.' Then he told Johnny to fuck off. Johnny said, 'Why do you think I got you up, this morning? I should have left you; see how you coped sandwiched between Sean and Domino.'

Clare was perched on a high stool at the counter, behind the glass-fronted case filled with belts, heavy-metal bangles and crucifixes. Jake knew her fairly well. She worked in Venus most weekdays, on her own during the boss's lunch hour. The high stool was her favourite position. Sat there, she could see the whole store and still reach the tape machine. Just now it was ticking into the beginning of a Soft Cell song.

As she turned to adjust the volume one notch higher, she asked, 'You going down Pips, tomorrow?'

Jake nodded. The last week, a DJ had played a few old punk singles and Jake fancied the idea of a punk look: a kilt, a muslin shirt with over-long sleeves, maybe bondage pants and new boots. He was thinking monkey boots rather than DMs, because they looked younger and cuter. What he didn't want was anything that smacked of Oi fans, Exploited punks, all that crusty, metal-studded Barmy Army brigade. He wanted credit for his style; he didn't want anyone mistaking it for an entire lifestyle. He swayed down the length of the store, trailing a hand through the racks, but couldn't see what he was looking for. The shop seemed to be betting on glam, besides the usual witchy Siouxsie stuff most of the girls wore. Clare was modelling a black fake-patent lace-up top and a ragged purple skirt. Her hair was the same shade, pulled into spikes.

She said, 'Are you and Johnny still living together?'

Jake said, 'Yes.' Then wondered why she'd asked. 'You want to know if we're inseparable?'

He put an arch spin onto the question and thought he saw her blush. It was hard to tell; she was wearing inch-thick white foundation.

There was a pair of gold lamé hipsters hanging by

the counter, similar to the ones Iggy Pop wore on the *Raw Power* album sleeve. Jake walked over and picked them out. He tried them against his waist first, smoothing them flat to his legs as he looked in a mirror.

'How about these?'

Clare, said 'Yeah, they'll suit you . . . What size are they?'

Jake checked the tag. 'Twenty-eight. I'll try them on.' Walking to the dressing-room, he said: 'Hey, Clare, you got any Iggy records you could put on?'

Clare turned and skimmed a finger across the tapes on the shelf above the counter: '*The Idiot?*'

Jake shook his head, 'No. Something earlier.'

Her long black fingernails clicking across the ridges of the tape boxes. 'No. What about *TV Eye?*'

'You got that? Yeah, put on "Dirt".' It was a live album with a deeply muddied sound that put some people off, though it was one of Jake's favourites – it sounded so desperate. An uncomfortable fact: David Bowie played keyboards throughout, although there was nothing markedly Bowie-ized about them. A few weeks ago, Jake had got drunk and conceded that Bowie might be talented; perhaps as a musician, although more likely as an arranger. It was only when he had to arrange to drop his own vocals over the top of a record that something usually went wrong.

Clare FF-ed through, looking for the beginning of the track. Jake stripped in the curtained cubicle, worked the tight strides up his legs and zipped the fly. By the time the song started, he was backing out of the changing-room, shirtless and twisting his thin white

body around before the mirror ... ostensibly to see
how the trousers fitted round the back but really to
throw a few Iggy-style contortions.

Clare said, 'Oh, yeah, they look good.'

Iggy said, '*I been dirt and I don't care.*' It was the
voice that Jake was tuned to, the way it managed to
give such an authoritative spin to desperation. Like
something out of *Patton* or *Henry V*. Maybe the word
was stoical, as though Iggy was always gearing himself
up to push deeper into his unholy groove. Jake strutted
round, arching his back to throw out his chest in the
Iggy bantam walk.

He said, 'What do you think? Better without a
shirt?'

'You'd go to Pips like that?'

'Well, I never tried near-nudity before. How'd you
think it would go down?'

'Depends who you're trying to impress.'

The answer was: *everyone.* He said, 'What about
you?'

She pursed her lips, her head thrown back slightly,
the kind of pose where the foot would be tapping up
and down if this was a cartoon. She wasn't too easy to
fool, which was why Jake liked her.

He said, 'I'm not sure. I'll take them off.'

While he was dressing, he shouted his punk idea
through the curtain. Clare reinterpreted him.

'You want to keep it really sharp and clean, like a
mod attitude but a punk style?'

Thinking about it, maybe that was it. Clare sug-

gested he try the Roxy. She'd heard they had some old
BOY designs stored in the back somewhere.

Jake uh-huh'ed. 'I'll maybe try later. I have to wait
for Johnny.'

Clare said, 'He's here.'

He heard Johnny shouting 'Hiya' down the length
of the store, Clare saying 'Hiya' back.

'You alright?'

Pretty soon, Johnny was pulling back the curtain on
Jake's cubicle, asking: 'You indecent enough?' He gave
a wink, holding open a plastic Woolworths bag so only
Jake could see inside it. There were about five purses
lying in the bottom.

Jake was stunned but managed to keep his voice to
a hiss. 'Are you crazy? You want to get caught with all
those?'

Johnny hissed back, 'Give us a chance. That's why
I'm here, to sort them out in the privacy of the changing-
room.'

'Why didn't you use the public lavvies like every
other bag-snatcher?'

'That way I would get caught, doing it the same as
everyone else. Budge over.'

Johnny would have got in the cubicle with him, but
Clare shouted out, 'No carrier bags in the changing-
rooms.'

Jake swished out through the curtain, 'It's okay. I'm
done.' He had the gold trousers slung over his shoulder.

'What's he doing in there, with a plastic bag and no
clothes.'

Johnny tossed the empty plastic bag over the top of the curtain. 'Give us something to try on then.'

Jake said, 'I'm his fashion consultant.'

He selected a tight red dress and a pair of wedge-heeled slingbacks. He threw the dress over the curtain rail and pushed the shoes underneath. 'There you go Johnny. Knock us dead.'

Johnny said, 'Thanks.' A moment later, after he realized what he'd got, he said: 'Jake, I been meaning to ask, you a puff or what?'

But when he danced out of the changing-room, he was wearing everything. The dress pouted emptily where his breasts should have been and his heel hung a half-inch out of the back of the shoes but everything pretty much fitted. Johnny wiggled over to the front of the shop and back.

'This is it, the real me.'

Jake said, 'You're liberated, mate.'

He asked the price.

Clare totted it up: thirty quid.

'You got the shoes in a larger size?'

While she turned to look in the storeroom at the stacks of boxes on shelves, Johnny went back to the cubicle and kicked the pile of empty purses to the side until they were hidden by the folds of the curtain.

Clare came back with a larger size pair of shoes. Johnny slipped them on. 'Maybe the shoes, not the dress.'

While he was changing into his own clothes, Clare asked Jake if he had decided on the trousers.

Jake said, 'Maybe. Where's your boss? Is it his lunch hour?'

She nodded her head slowly. 'He'll be back any moment.'

Jake nodded. She knew what he was going to ask. 'Do you mind if I just take them, then? I'm a bit short at the moment.'

She sucked at her lip. 'Okay, but shove it inside your jacket. I don't want him coming back and bumping into you on the escalator.'

They were on the escalator when they ran into trouble. Johnny's hand was inside a woman's shopping-bag and, when the escalator straightened and she stepped forward, she felt the drag on her shoulder. Johnny pushed past her, running hard. Jake, two steps slower, tried to follow but the woman already had a grip on him. After about three seconds, no longer, Jake pulled a violent twisting shrug and she weakened. He saw, from the beginning to the end, the woman was scared crazy, but she didn't want to let go.

It was another five minutes before he caught up with Johnny. Sprinting through two concourses, weaving round the indoor market stalls and only stopping when he reached the fifth floor of the multi-storey next-door.

Jake, bent double and panting hard, managed to say: 'What the fuck you trying to do?'

'You got away, didn't you?' Johnny was just as short of breath but already feeling through his pockets for a pack of cigarettes. Leant against the barrier rail, there was nothing but sky above his head, nothing but fresh air between his ears.

Jake said, 'I got away? I nearly had to lamp her to do it. Don't fucking do that to me again.' He pulled himself straight, walked over to Johnny and snatched the cigs out of Johnny's hand. 'You cunt.'

'Yeah okay. Sorry. But I'm still short of money.' Johnny threw his Venus store bag to the floor. 'I shouldn't have bought these fucking shoes.'

They were just lucky he hadn't worn them – as he said he would. They couldn't have got far if Johnny had been trotting along in heels. Jake took out a cigarette, lit it and threw the pack back at Johnny.

For a while, up there above High Street, they stayed quiet and waited for the cigarettes to work their relaxation trick. Johnny's only seemed to make him reflective. 'Anyway – how's it my fault? It wasn't you with your hand in her bag. You could have just stood there, making out you don't know me. You didn't need to run.'

Jake undid the buttons at the front of his coat. The Iggy-style trousers were wrapped around his waist. 'And when security searched me, how was I supposed to explain this?' He was lucky they hadn't unravelled while he was running. He had felt them slip a little.

Johnny stared. 'You stole those? Why didn't you take the shoes as well?'

Jake wasn't sure, but Johnny seemed genuinely upset. Maybe he was just tired. He had turned his face away, looking out over the parapet towards the Piccadilly Radio skyscraper and Chorlton Street Bus Station beyond.

After a moment, he said, 'What time is it?'

Jake wasn't wearing a watch. It was mid-afternoon.

Johnny said, 'So what am I supposed to do now? Sell my arse?'

'Yeah, well, don't sell yourself short. About fifty pence should be right.'

Johnny said, 'I'll catch the ones leaving work.'

They didn't talk much on the walk across Piccadilly Gardens towards the Village. Jake was already feeling the hiss of a depression, it worked its way deeper as they closed on the diesel smell of the coaches and the shadows of the car-park above. Hopefully, Johnny wouldn't have to literally sell his arse. If it all went smooth, he'd wring out a few handjobs, suffer the backseat gropes, maybe use his mouth or have someone use their own on him. At least he wouldn't be working alone: Kevin Donnelly was already in his usual place, by the car-park stairs, close to the gents' toilet.

Jake nodded over to the boy, giving him a thin smile before turning to Johnny.

'Yeah, well, I'll see you later.'

It was about as irrational as you could get but he felt he should have offered to help. Johnny didn't ask though, and there was no way Jake could face it, cold or sober, before dark on a Friday evening. They arranged to meet later in Good-Day's. Johnny thought he might be a couple of hours – no longer. He said, 'You're still coming to this party, later? Help me flog the vids?'

Jake said, 'Sure.'

Jake walked round to the back of Good-Day's where the door was on the latch. He knocked first, then pushed it open. At the end of the corridor, he saw Lady Good-Day talking on the phone. Jake rapped again, this time on the side of the staircase. Lady Good-Day looked over and waved him in.

Official opening hours didn't begin for another forty-five minutes or so and, aside from a lone regular and one of Good-Day's barstaff asleep on a bench, the place was empty. Coming in the back way, Jake entered on the wrong side of the bar. He ducked under the counter and waited for Lady Good-Day to get off the phone. As he flexed against the wood-grained melamine rim of the bar top, he tried to remember the last time he saw Good-Day out of drag. This was man's wear: a huge T-shirt that fell to his knees, a string hairnet that covered his Bobby Charlton hair-do.

Putting the phone down, Good-Day said, 'Who's the early bird?'

Jake said, 'You'd have got ready if you knew I was coming?'

'If you were coming, I'd be ready.' The way Good-Day winked, you'd think his face was spring-loaded.

'You want to make amends, I'll have a Bacardi and Coke.'

Good-Day rapped the bar with the back of his hand; his rings made a small-change clank. 'Either you've got cash or you go thirsty.'

Man and woman, Good-Day believed in you paying your way. It was the same code as the Manchester Chamber of Commerce, only Good-Day applied it as thick and slippery as he did his make-up. Not every transaction necessarily had to be in cash; it wasn't like he was claiming to be incorruptible.

'Of course, you can always work for it. I think I've got a vacant spot that needs filling.' The offer came with another wink. A fatman playing the cringing coquette; it wasn't pretty.

Jake said, 'Just a Bacardi and Coke.' He had enough money for now.

Sitting there, watching as the office workers began to drift in, he had a chance to think back to his conversation with DC Green. Aside from the laboured stories and the whipped analogies, the policeman had been straight with him: he was ambitious and while the force was holding up Pascal as a model, then he would play along. Sitting at the bare table in the interview room, he'd said, 'Cards down, son, I need the pinches. There's seven thousand police on the Manchester force and, if I stand still, one of those bastards is going to steal my career. I got to say, with you it's different . . . all I'm offering you is a chance to stand still. Feed me the pinches or I send you down, every fucking chance I get. Think on.'

Soon, Jake would sell someone out; all for the sake of John Pascal's crazy faith in hell & salvation, and the career of DC Davey Green. The way things were going, his first victim might even be Johnny. It wasn't as though the idea of betraying a friend was an alien concept. Sneaking off with Domino last night, that was an act of betrayal. Once Sean got hold of him, it would become a whole fucking drama: Fairy and Rebecca both

playing small, walked-on roles. Jake couldn't claim he
was innocent; he knew what he was doing. The truth
was, if it had been nothing but a two-minute stand-up
shag, he might have resisted temptation and walked
away clean. It was because the stakes were so high, he
had to go through with it. Afterwards, when the whole
thing turned sordid, he wouldn't be able to shrink-wrap
and sanitize the whole affair. It trailed too many betray-
als to be cleaned up easily . . . it would have gone too
far, got too serious.

Good-Day was still out of costume, slobbing
between the beer pumps in his T-shirt and tracksuit
bottoms.

Jake said, 'What am I supposed to call you when
you're dressed like that?'

The man preened and waddled over. 'It doesn't
matter what I *wear*, I'm still a lady. Breeding shows.'

Jake said, 'Why is it being a queen's not enough?
You have to be a raving queen?'

'Call of the fucking wild, dear.'

'It's a call for fucking help.'

It was the grand alibi, camping up the glamour even
though you knew you were on a downward spiral. The
only saving grace, that there was a kind of final,
desperate glamour in the fact that it was all downhill
from here on. Once you started on that trip, nothing
could save you. Jake was ready to sell anyone and
everyone out, and claim that each betrayal had its own
special allure. When he knew, the real allure was that
every betrayal sent him spinning deeper into the hole.
And DC Green stole that last comfort when he made

his promise: *sell someone out, you save yourself.* The deal broke the spiral, putting Jake back on course in a world that was mean-spirited, tight-arsed, un-desperate . . . he couldn't think of enough adjectives. For the past year, he'd been trying to make his life over as one long slow-motion crash. But maybe he wasn't up to it. That moment in the Arndale Centre, when the woman was hanging onto his arm and Johnny was halfway across the mall, Jake was thinking: *This has nothing to do with me. I'm still a fucking bystander.*

One thing DC Green made clear: he had no axe to grind. He thought the whole thing was stupid: 'You kids want to play at nances, I don't give a fuck.' He didn't get Anderton's moral crusade and he didn't believe John Pascal was anything but another brownnose hypocrite. Green didn't believe anyone could take it seriously.

Jake called for another Bacardi. There was no reason to think it wasn't serious. Jake believed it could get serious; at least he was trying.

CHAPTER *NINE*

DI Green was bouncing on the edge of one of the beds, like this was the Slumberland factory and he was the boss spring-tester. He definitely didn't understand the idea of twin doubles. Pointing at the one opposite, he said: 'Shove that out, you got more floor space. I don't get it.'

The man had a point. But Jake didn't know why he seemed so disappointed. Maybe he'd been looking forward to slurping around a water-bed, maybe find a Jacuzzi.

It was the first time Green's patriotic buy-Manchester spiel had faltered since he hitched a ride in Jake's taxi. Now he was almost thoughtful; on the ride to the hotel he had been a one-man promotional extravaganza. Perched on one of the cab's flip-down seats, he over-dubbed every city-centre improvement with his own personal running commentary. If Jake's face showed a glimmer of surprise, he grabbed hold like it was admissible evidence. The pause at the first set of traffic lights, for instance, as one of the new trams stole the junction and slid towards Piccadilly Gardens.

Looking out of his hotel window, Jake got a fresh chance to see a tram. He watched it snake through a choreographed S-bend and rejoin the traffic on St Peter's Square, and he tried to blank out Green and his whole bed analysis.

The man saying, 'Yeah, well, it seems comfy. You should be all right in a mo, you get your head down.'

Jake stayed silent. Just felt the sour aftertaste of vomit in his mouth.

'What was it? Delayed shock . . . what?'

'I'm fine.'

'It wasn't that you're worried about seeing Halliday tomorrow?'

Jake shook his head. 'No. Just something I ate.'

It had happened on the cab ride from Piccadilly Station. Jake got a rush of saliva and shouted to the driver to pull over. He was just in time. Hunched by the kerb, he threw up a bitter mouthful of coffee. There was nothing else in his stomach. Now he was installed in the hotel, he was feeling light-headed, but otherwise better. He carried on staring out of his bedroom window, trying to enjoy that Millennial Manchester vibe without puking.

He turned to DI Green and said, 'What's that?'

Green followed Jake's look, back out of the window, towards Lower Mosley Street. 'That? That was built yonks back.'

What was once the derelict Central Station had now been refitted with a wire-sprung steel canopy and hung with glass. Banners floating outside the building promised a season of *Cinderella On Ice*. 'Book Early for an All-Round Family Entertainment.' The family angle wasn't something they could have advertised sixteen years ago, when Johnny used its broken arches for cover any time he worked as a rentboy. This was his usual procedure, he would flag down a punter on Chorlton Street and steer them across town and into the great hall of the station. For a few parked, packed minutes, they got to buy a ride aboard the dicky-back express.

'Next to it, that's the Hallé's new concert hall.' Green joined Jake at the window, pointing off to the right and another hi-tech dreamboat. 'It's been up six months and it's already supposed to be in profit. I tell you, this Labour council, they really got their shit together.'

Jake looked across, towards something that looked like a dinkier version of the opera house at the Bastille. It looked cute, printed against the skyline. Maybe it was supposed to be a double monument: New Manchester, New Labour. What he'd seen of the city before he got sick, there were a lot of improvements. At least a stack of cosmetic tricks that the coming Labour Government would probably fail to reproduce over the country. Still, the concert hall didn't look right. This was Manchester, not Paris. And the particular view from his bedroom window was something Jake knew well. From St Peter's Square, down Lower Mosley Street, he expected to see a clear stretch of urban desolation. It was his and Johnny's standard route home when they shared a flat together.

'Where are the Crescents? I should be able to see them from here.'

'You won't see them from any-fucking-where, they knocked those shit-holes down.'

Jake stared out, expecting to see a hole at least – a dotted line against the sky to mark the space they left behind.

For some reason he was still holding the man-size tissue the cab driver gave him to wipe his mouth. He screwed it up, aimed it at the bin beneath the dressing-table and scored, first hit. He never expected to get physically sick, and even now he couldn't explain it. The second the cab pulled out of Piccadilly, Green had started planning a full-scale tour of the city. Jake tried to say, *No Thanks* – he could do it alone. But DI Green was a hard man to shrug off. When the sickness caught him, they were halfway through the tour, circling the hoardings that enclosed the bomb-damaged centre of the city. Jake had never expected to see so much damage six months after the IRA bomb. A hole the size of two back-to-back football stadiums had been carved out of the junction of Cross Street and Corporation Street, taking a chunk of the Arndale Centre with it.

Green said, 'Shocker, eh? Fucking IRA cunts, bringing that shit to Manchester when half the city's Irish.'

The blast extended as far as the Corn Exchange. When they reached the buildings' steel-trussed carcass, Jake asked the driver to slow down. He wanted to see what was left of Pips. Fifteen years ago, it was the north's largest nightclub. Built into the underground cellars of the Corn Exchange, the club extended over most of a city block. Now, it was under unsteady rubble. The bomb had lifted the dome off the old building, twisted it round and slammed it back. What

115

was left was so out of kilter, the whole edifice seemed bent with the effort of holding it up.

It was around then, Jake got the cab driver to stop while he threw up. Something in the whole situation, the mix of helplessness and anger, got through to him. At the time, it felt even grander than that: the mix of politics, Manchester and Ireland and all of that place's crazed sense of religion. Jake hated what the IRA had done: not just bombing Manchester but doing it during Euro '96 when the city was full of ordinary shoppers and Czech and German visitors. He'd caught the afternoon TV news specials and seen people staggering round, blood pouring from their heads, seen them stretchered to ambulances. It was horrible, more than horrible.

Six months on, he could see what the IRA had done all over again. And still he wasn't quite able to blame them. It was the way he was raised. The IRA were Catholics and he still, somehow, believed Catholics were too simple to bear any sense of responsibility. At least, not for any longer than it took a hick priest to absolve them. If he wanted a focus, he could project it onto the Ulster Unionists for stoking up a war that made both sides look and act like dumb psychopaths, onto the Tory government that pandered to them, onto the Reverend Ian Paisley and the streaming shites that tailed him, onto the lunatic evil posturings of men that betrayed their faith ... which brought him full circle back to Pascal and his own religious war.

He'd reeled out of the taxi and onto the pavement, his head pounding, squeezing a mouthful of sour puke that seemed to come out of his lungs. He couldn't believe he could still feel so powerfully hopeless or that, when the feeling erupted, it could use religion as its alibi. He was over religion.

He'd told Green, he didn't need a chaperone to the hotel. He wasn't so sick he couldn't manage his one item of luggage. Green told him it was no bother. Anyway, ever since the Midland Hotel had been refitted, he'd been wondering how the rooms had turned out. This was his first chance to see one. He caught Jake's look and said: 'So when am I going to book into a four-star hotel? I fucking live here.'

The room was exactly like any Holiday Inn room . . . that's what it was. Even down to the complimentary tourist book left on his bedside table. Under the words *Welcome to Manchester*, there was a sci-fi sketch of another tram, a sleek electro-glider bulleting through the Piccadilly terminus. Jake picked up the book and flicked to the timetable, checking out the route map and list of interchanges. Across the top of the page, the old legend *What Manchester Does Today . . . The Rest of the World Does Tomorrow*. The book was marginally slicker in its presentation than Green, but it blitzed the same kind of confidence in the city. Maybe the confidence was infectious. Jake just wasn't the best person to feel it. He wasn't really Mancunian, not originally, and certainly not anymore. He might experiment with a tram ride, more probably he'd go hire a Hertz. Though it could be time to economize; so far he was spending money like water.

Green was crouched by the television cabinet, reading the cable guide and trying to program the box to the porn channel. Jake slapped it off.

'I'm not paying for that.'

'Thought you were the last of the big spenders, travelling First Class, staying in swish hotels.'

Jake was ready to spend what it took to be comfortable, but he couldn't throw his money away. He didn't try explaining, though; just opened up his mini-bar and took out a bottle of water to wash the sour aftertaste away. After a two-second exposure to Green's hangdog face, he let the man choose a miniature Black Label and left him playing with the ice shelf. The sound it made, it could have been a slot machine paying out the jackpot.

With his head still inside the cabinet, Green said, 'Seriously, it's all new to you?'

Jake hadn't been back to Manchester at all.

'Because I was going to say you lost your accent.'

He had, he knew. It was just generic non-Southern now, rather than site-specific. He said, 'I only had a Manchester accent for the eighteen months I lived here.'

'You're not from Manchester?' Green stopped, his head clearing the rim of the fridge-style door. Jake took in the look, it was either genuine surprise or a close approximation.

Shrugging, he said, 'I've got some relatives here. But, no, I never was true-blue Manchester.'

'Well, it makes sense, now you said it.' He swirled

his drink around the inside of its plastic beaker. 'So, where are you from?'

'Caldenstall.'

'Yeah? That sheep-shagging burg up in the Pennines. I never knew.' The way Green sucked at the whisky, the ice cubes rattled off his teeth. 'I should have guessed, though. You're such a stroppy git, you had to be a Yorkshireman.'

'It's only just in Yorkshire, less than four miles from the border.'

Green nodded. 'I know. I was up there last month for John Pascal's golden wedding. I tell you, I never even knew he was married, and once I saw his wife, I realized why he kept her under wraps. If someone told me she was a bloke in a twin-set, I wouldn't be surprised. She looked like Arthur Scargill. All in all, though, it wasn't such a bad do. At least Pascal relaxed his teetotal kick for the night and laid on some booze.'

As Green finished his drink, another whisky minia-ture appeared in his fist. 'I could never see why he retired up there, though. I mean, I can see that Man-chester lost its attractions after Anderton left but what I saw of Caldenstall, it was full of hippies, poets, TV producers and same-sex couples playing house together. I wouldn't have said it was Pascal's scene.'

It was true, Caldenstall had a definite arty-liberal demographic. But the original character of the place hadn't disappeared entirely. Built as a pack-mule stop-over on the Pennines, you only had to kick away the rich topsoil and you'd find the unreconstructed North below, sunk deep in bigotry and cast into the millstone

grit of the Pennine moorland. You couldn't erase something like that ... not with a few raffia baskets and a
clutch of tie-dye prints.

Jake said, 'Pascal didn't retire there. He always had
a house in Caldenstall. He was born there.'

'Yeah?' Green had his hand back in the ice-tray, he
came up with a fistful of cubes and dribbled them into
his beaker. 'I knew he was a Yorkshireman. Anderton
recruited him from Bradford after he got the Chief
Constable job here.'

Green used a finger to stir the drink, clinking the
fresh ice, stirring up an old story.

'You heard the one about the old Yorkshire fellah,
his wife's dying on him. She's lying in bed, he's drawn
the curtains, lit a candle and now he's sitting there
waiting for her to go. Well, she's pretty weak but she
starts whispering, "Tha doesn't have to sit with me, tha
knows." He tells her, "Nay, lass, tha's been a good wife
to me. I'll not leave thee now." But she can tell he's
itching to go, so she says again, "I know there's things
wants doing." He says, "Aye, lass, there's a kitchen
shelf needs fixing but tha's been a good wife to me. I'll
not leave thee." Another ten minutes, he's started
fidgeting, so his wife says, "Go down, love. Tha doesn't
have to stay, tha knows." He's pulling at his fingers,
saying, "Well, someone's got to see about those taties
and I been meaning to fettle that old gate, but tha's
been a good wife to me. I'll not leave thee now." It goes
on and on, she keeps whispering that he can go, he's
pacing up and down the room but he still refuses to
leave her. Eventually he's hovering at the door; he can't

stand another second. So he says, "All right, lass, tha's persuaded me. Just promise one thing." She's going, "Yes. Yes?"

' "Promise me, when tha feel thaself slipping away, tha'll just lean over and blow out that candle. I'd not like to see it go to waste." '

Green was grinning. A slow gargle at his scotch and he said: 'How'd you like that?'

Jake gave a polite smile. The couple would be called Jacob and Sarah, too. Take your pick, it was either a Jewish story rewrapped as a piece of Lancashire–Yorkshire chauvinism or it was an original, aimed at Yorkshire nonconformists, brewing up thrifty new biblical virtues to go with their Old Testament names.

Jake said, 'You never believed Pascal was for real, did you?'

'I believed he was a Yorkshire twat.' Green's second glass of whisky was drained to the cube. 'I just didn't go for the religious shit.'

Jake said, 'He was head governor at my school.'

'So what did he do as governor – keep the school on the straight and narrow, make sure no one got a whiff of that new-fangled Darwinian crap, that kind of stuff?'

What he did, his single piece of weirdness, was take the morning assemblies whenever he could. Seizing his chance to be a lay preacher for at least one day a term; not counting sports days, prize-givings and Christmas services. Christmas wasn't Christmas unless you had a high-ranking policeman raising hell about the dereliction of the modern age. Jake could have gone into it.

Instead, he said: 'You're closer than you think.'

'And look at you. All that religion and none of it rubbed off.'

Green had seen everything he wanted. He was ready to go. He scribbled his number on a pad by the hotel bed, and told Jake he'd see him tomorrow . . .

'Get some shut-eye. I want you on form if you're going to get anything new out of Halliday.'

Then, at the door, like it had just come to him: 'You know, the prison's close to Caldenstall. Maybe we should drive through, stop for a drink or something. Some of the pubs there, they look all right: kind of olde-worlde and what have you. Going up for Pascal's golden wedding, I got to thinking. I'd not been that way in years.' Nodding as he spoke, then a shake of the head. 'Still, it's not a surprise. Seeing as the last time I was up there, I was putting labels on bits of your pal Johnny. The state we found him, it still gives me the creeps. Anyway, feel better soon . . .'

Jake wished he was still holding his bag. One sharp crack to Green's side, he could smash all the whisky miniatures the man had stuffed in his pocket.

CHAPTER *TEN*

Johnny got back to the Crescent, stood in the hallway and shouted out: 'Anyone home?' Fairy was in the bath, washing his hair, so he probably didn't hear. But Jake and Sean were in their separate bedrooms and both of them yelled back. The only people they weren't speaking to were each other.

A minute later, Johnny came pushing through Jake's door, asking to know how the geopolitical alliances in the flat were shaping up. Jake told him the Domino incident was still producing fall-out, and he was in internal exile. The last few hours he'd stayed in his room, lying on his bed, reading *The Wild Boys*.

Johnny wrinkled his nose. 'You going to stay in here, you want to think about washing that duvet.'

'You think it smells?' If the duvet was past obnoxious, Jake hadn't noticed yet.

Johnny told him, 'Like a fucking bumhole.'

Jake pulled at a corner and took a sniff. He kept his look quizzical, letting realization dawn slowly: 'Oh, yeah. I know what it is.' Another sniff. 'What's happened, you think its my duvet. But it's you – you smell like arse. How's your ring fitting, tart boy?'

However it was, Johnny wasn't brimming with *joie*

de la viva. But he was carrying his hold-all with him, so he must have made enough money to pay his video-copying service.

Jake said, 'You all set?'

Johnny nodded. 'Just freshen up first. Is everyone coming?'

Nine o' clock, Johnny had got everyone to agree to come on his video-selling trip. One thing he promised, they'd be back by midnight so they could get to the Poly Disco. The only one missing was Kevin Donnelly.

Fairy was crouched on the staircase, a pair of crimping irons plugged into the landing socket while he burned his way through a thick layer of gel and spray, putting a savage crimp on his hair. With half already done, he looked like he was wearing a small corrugated roof on his head. Before he switched attention to his fringe, he took a pause and asked Johnny if they were going to wait for Kevin. Johnny checked the time and said he didn't think so. There was something wrong with that lad; he couldn't stop working.

Aside from the chemical stench off Fairy's scorched hair, the atmosphere in the flat had got a whole lot lighter. Sean was still in a sulk but, since Fairy took on the role of the diplomat, Jake's situation had eased. It was no longer a case of all-way blanket hatred. He could borrow the hair-dryer, eyeliner, whatever . . . it wouldn't end in a fight.

The cab ride to Oldham, though, Fairy had to take the middle of the back seat because Sean refused to sit next to Jake. Maybe Jake should have ridden up front with the driver but Johnny insisted he needed to be there. He was travelling with his bumper bag of porno films between his knees and needed the extra room.

As they crossed the town boundary, Johnny turned round and asked if any of them knew Oldham, because the cab driver definitely didn't.

Fairy said, 'I do.'

Jake said, 'Yeah?' Making out that he was interested. 'So how much is it to Old 'em?'

The house stood at the centre of a stone-built terrace of Victorian villas breasting a hill. As they stood on the pavement, waiting for Johnny to pay the fare, Jake began to get a bad feeling. It wasn't just that Fairy was giving him the big *froideur* all over again. Though that was part of it. Slinking last through the gate, between the defensive line of privet, Jake already knew it was going to be one of those painful nights when he was nothing but an invalid bag of clumsiness. There was a holly wreath hanging over the darkened glass of the vestibule door, and when Jake caught his reflection between the leaves and berries, he saw a turkey made up for Christmas.

A man showed them where to hang their coats. Jake remembered the face and moustache, and recognized the man – the guy was the taller of the two clones he had seen with Johnny last night in Bernard's Bar. Tonight he was wearing a deep-blue shirt and yellow tie, stripy socks and red Kicker shoes. Clearly the T-shirt and jeans had been his Boys' Town look; tonight he was modelling his partying-at-home outfit.

Jake wiped his feet, hung his bunnyman coat where he was told, and followed on down the hall in tense anxiety. He didn't know why Johnny needed them all to come with him, and he didn't care. He was just concentrating on keeping it balanced.

There were another five men cramped in the kitchen at the rear of the house. Sat at the table, grinning down at the remains of their meal, they looked like a cabal of comedy colonels. Paper cracker crowns hid their crew-cuts and the grins they couldn't wipe off their faces were tufted by five identical moustaches. Like wobbly lines of horsehair.

The lover of the man who'd met them at the door swayed to his feet, saying: 'Why don't we go through, Davey? There's no room in here.' Then, turning to them, 'Wine, beer or brandy?'

A clutch of wine bottles stood among the debris on the table but there were fresh, foil-tipped bottles waiting by the sink. Given the choice, only Fairy opted for wine over a tin of Carlsberg. Then they retraced their steps, back towards the front door, and the living-room that lay to its right.

Despite their clothes, the two guys seemed to have tripped on some sense of colour co-ordination when it came to their home. The Christmas tree standing in the bay window was dominant yet restrained, hung with gold baubles and red tinsel and no other colour. The room itself was a shade chintzy but comfortable. The aspidistra on top of the TV set looked too large to be a fixture but Jake guessed its usual place was on a table inside the bay. Come Twelfth Night it would be back in the window, screening out the neighbours.

Jake took a corner seat as the other men traipsed in from the kitchen. The smaller host was bouncing at the rear, yelling that someone should put the music on. When it started, Jake set his mouth into a line and tried to look neither close nor distant. Between him and the hi-fi speaker, above his head, there was a thick layer of Judy Garland and 'Someone To Watch Over Me'.

Later, Fairy caught Jake skulking on the first-floor landing. His fingertips were pressed lightly on a bedroom door, putting on just enough pressure to ease the door open. Inside, it was Laura Ashley decor and stripped-pine furniture. The walls were a swarm of small blue flowers, the matching duvet dropped them in pleats to the floor. Either side of the bed were matching wooden chests: a book, a pair of reading glasses and an alarm clock at one side, a heart-shaped picture frame at the other. The photograph showed the two men standing on a beach with their backs to the camera, side by side and arm in arm, wearing matching butt-cleavers as they grinned over their shoulders.

Jake, feeling uncomfortable, said, 'Someone was in the bathroom. I was just waiting.'

Fairy said, 'That was me.' He didn't see a problem with a little domestic prying. His head was already around the door, mouthing a *whoo!* as he said, 'It's lovely, isn't it? Have you seen the bathroom? They got these bamboo blinds over the windows and a huge rubber plant over the bath.' He held his hand out, three feet above the floor. 'About so big. And what about the kitchen? You see the old cooker thing?'

'The Aga.'

'Yeah. Phil said it heats the water for the whole house. You notice how cosy the kitchen is?'

Jake thought it was on the close side.

Fairy had a licence to nose; he was working on first-name accreditation, saying: 'David and Phil promised to show me around later ... you know how many bedrooms they've got?'

Jake nodded. 'Three.'

'You already had a look around?'

Jake hadn't; he just guessed. All these kinds of houses were the same. If he'd seen a staircase leading up to a loft conversion, he would have guessed four instead. He was kind of taken aback by Fairy's enthusiasm, as though it was all entirely new. Though he was a council-estate boy, so it probably *was* to him.

Jake made for the vacant bathroom. 'I'll see you downstairs.'

Two things Fairy had forgotten to mention about the bathroom: the signed photograph of Pat Phoenix and the stack of books by the toilet. There was a bumper book of quick crossword puzzles, half completed; a Peanuts collection; and a photo-book of fifties muscle boys, none of them particularly muscular or particularly naked but it was all a part of the heritage. When Jake checked himself in the bathroom, he thought he was looking a whole lot less anxious and clumsy.

The way the night was shaping, it was just a suburban Christmas with a bent twist. All he had to do was ride it out. Downstairs, he could hear six baritones agreeing that, yeah, the lady is a tramp.

At the foot of the stairs, he took a sharp left back to the kitchen and the beer supply. He assumed the room was empty. When Sean appeared from behind the door, he tensed, nodded. 'I just came in for . . .'

Sean guessed what he wanted. He passed over a can, his face already blurred and sharpened by drunkeness. 'Here you are, you cunt.' A pause, then a sneered grin. 'What about this place . . . put it on the front of *Ideal Homo*, our little "out-of-the-cottage" look?'

Jake said, 'Have you seen the bedroom?'

Sean gave a shriek, keen edges bleeding into alcohol. He'd not only seen the room, he had memorized every detail. If David and Phil ever had to face a Nuremberg tribunal of style crimes, he had the full rap sheet on them. Jake laughed along but didn't really get the venom. His only problem with the house was that he couldn't tune himself to its cosiness, and he couldn't trust his untuned reactions around it. With Sean there seemed to be something close to real pain. Behind the anaesthetic he was fighting an infection.

'What the fuck do you think they're trying to achieve? Fucking bon-homie-sexuals, doing Judy Garland like it's a rugby-club song and cuddling up under Laura fucking-flora Ashley.'

Jake clicked the top off his can, fitted his lips to the keyhole and tried to remember if he'd ever seen Sean so drunk. And with Sean you could bet he wasn't gorging because the drink was free . . . that was something else that wasn't his style.

'It's like a fucking sitcom. Gay Bloke at home in Sub-bubbly-burbia.'

'What's your problem?'

'I'm a fag. I'm not a fucking joke.'

It was certain, Sean was nothing to laugh at. Fighting drunk now as he slopped wine into a glass and across the kitchen range. Spilled wine steamed off the hobs, cooking up as it vaporized in the air.

Sean sniffed and checked the label: 'Fucking Lambrusco.'

He dumped the bottle end-up in the sink. The washing-up froth turned blood red.

There was a back door to the kitchen, leading out to a narrow garden. Jake tried the handle; the door opened with a breath of winter.

'You want to step outside? Get some air?'

Sean walked over, peered out at the dark. 'If I find any gnomes, those fuckers are crockery.'

Jake banged on a light switch. The garden lit up as a weeded-bare corridor back-dropped by a line of skeletal trees, everything tenderly wrapped to hold together through the winter and wait for a spring release.

Sean staggered out, saying: 'Got it wrong: should be *Homos and Gardeners*.'

The night air raised bumps on Jake's arms. He left Sean to wander alone outside while he stayed within the door-frame. He was still there when Fairy came up behind him, asking what was wrong with Sean.

'He's overcome.'

'He wants to come through to the lounge . . .' Fairy gave the vowels an extra luxurious stress 'Everyone's dancing. He could show us one of his dances.'

Jake moved away from the cold, keeping step up the passageway to the sound of six men chanting: '*We are D-I-S-C-O. We are D-I-S-C-O.*' Through the door, he found David and Phil's party guests all standing in a circle and stabbing their fingers at the ceiling as they rose to an all-male disco crescendo.

Johnny was stood apart by the television, wrapping up his empty hold-all now that business was over. On the muted screen, a video of two men going at each other in dumb lust: one naked but for an astronaut helmet, the other naked but for socks. There was no doubt, porn was made for men by men, and once the sticky business of opening female motivations up to the camera stopped being a problem, the films spun out in wilder directions. With straight pornography Jake could always feel the discomfort: the pornographer pushed into a brutish corner. Filming men on men had to be a relief and a release. With men, you could do what you wanted . . . you never had to worry about it. Jake was gazing at the screen, zoning out the sound of the hi-fi as he stared in straight-faced concentration.

Johnny looked up, 'Jake . . . you okay, mate?'

Jake snapped out of it. 'Yeah . . . I was somewhere else.'

Johnny jerked a thumb over to the screen. 'You should have seen one earlier. A paperboy goes to get his

Christmas tip and the man's standing there in his dressing-gown saying, "How about that?"' He mimed opening up the front of a dressing-gown, his eyes cast down to his crotch and one eyebrow raised for comic effect.

'How many did you sell?'

'All of them. The ones the two guys ordered, and a load more to their friends. I think they're going to be this year's Christmas presents. This is a winner. They can't get them anywhere else.' He had his empty bag rolled under his arm, now, ready to think about his next step. 'Next time I got to get more of these American ones. The German ones, everyone looks like they're following a schedule. The Yank tapes look more fun.'

Good hard fun. The kind of fun you really had to have the stomach for before you could get into it. Fun without any transcendental aim and with no end. The kind Iggy Pop sang about in 'Funhouse', in 'Funtime', in 'No Fun', even. If you had to name the major Iggy preoccupation, this was it: looking hard for hard-looking fun, always sung in sunk block caps – FUN. In a world without end, amen.

Jake said, 'We done here?'

Johnny nodded, he guessed so. 'What about Sean and Fairy?'

'They're out the back, shall I call a minicab?'

Jake was replacing the receiver when Johnny returned from the direction of the kitchen.

Jake said, 'The cab's going to be two minutes. Are Sean and Fairy ready?'

Johnny shook his head. 'Fairy wants to stay on. It's just the two of us.'

'What about Sean?'

'He was out in the garden. Fairy said the two of them could get a cab together.'

Jake paused. 'Did you speak to Sean?'

'No, but Fairy says he'll get him home okay.'

Jake looked down the hallway, Fairy was stood at the kitchen end, waving them off. He was smiling now but just wait until Sean found out he'd been abandoned.

Jake said, 'Shall we wait outside?'

On the cab ride back to Manchester, Jake was already fixed on the speed he was going to buy once they were back in the Village. Johnny sat beside him, talking about the weirdos he'd run into earlier that afternoon. He was shaking his head. 'A guy whose breath smelled of rotten fish. I asked him about it, he said he always made a week's worth of fish-paste sandwiches on Sunday evenings. That way he didn't have to worry about his lunch for the next week.'

Jake was listening enough to say 'Jesus' at the appropriate moment.

'Yeah, well, where he had his head, at least I didn't have to worry about smelling him.'

'You remember to wash up after?'

'Too right. Hey, what about their lav . . .?' He jerked his head towards the back window, and Oldham disappearing behind the cab. 'It had half a fucking jungle in it.'

As they rounded the Express building, Johnny asked what he made of Kevin Donnelly. The kid was still working when Johnny left the Bus Station with enough money to pay for the video-copying services.

Jake shrugged. A sad kid. 'Why didn't he come tonight with us?'

Johnny shrugged. 'He can't think out of his rut. I don't know, maybe he didn't believe I was serious about asking him. Maybe he just likes to earn money.'

'Maybe.' Jake was wondering how much Johnny had earned on the video deal. All he had was a tenner and change, but he didn't want that to hinder his funtime.

'Kevin said he bumped into a guy he knows who needs to get some tapes copied.'

'What guy?'

'I don't know . . . a friend or a regular or something. I told him I could get it done, give him a price.'

'You sure it's nothing dodgy?'

'Well, it's not going to be *Bambi*, is it?'

'*Snow White and the Seven Sex Dwarfs.*'

'*One Hundred and One Fellations.*'

The cab was skimming across the top of Piccadilly Gardens, the terminus for every night-bus in Manchester. It was almost twelve but the buses were sailing out half empty. Catching a ride home, just because the pubs were closing, was unserious behaviour. Friday night was pack night: move in packs, pack a toothbrush. The crowds of straights barrelling through the sunken gardens were all heading in the same direction: towards Rotters Discotheque on Oxford Road. These were the

Rottie-dogs, facing winter in shirtsleeves or stocking-less legs. Only a skinful between them and hypothermia. They had the right urge, they were just applying it in the wrong direction. Jake checked the colours of the Rottie girls' legs as the cab waited for a break to turn left: red, white and blue beneath the glaze of the fake tans. There were so many of them, the cab driver had to crawl through the herd with his hand pressed to the horn. Ahead, Chorlton Street Bus Station rose above the street. Another second and they were back inside the Village at the doors to Good-Day's.

Johnny took the bar; Jake snuffled towards the back of the room, asking around for a dealer. A boy he knew sent him outside; he'd seen Paulo talking to someone outside the fish-and-chip shop. Jake waved a hand at Johnny, mouthing *Two minutes*, and started out the door.

The chippie opposite the Bus Station was full, a queue running along the counter and doubling back towards the door. Along the ledge of the front window, a row of rentboys chatted over their grease-soaked bags. Kevin Donnelly was sat towards the end, his hand dipping from the bag to his lips like a grab-crane in an amusement arcade. He looked up when he heard Jake asking down the line if anyone had seen Paulo. Jake nodded at him.

A red-haired boy said Paulo would be back in a minute. Jake decided to wait. As he took a perch next to Kevin Donnelly, the boy whispered, 'Someone was looking for you.'

'Who?'

'That copper' – a pause – 'you know, from last night.'

'Oh, Christ.' Jake raised his eyes, ran them over the rooftops opposite. 'What did he want?'

'Said "Keep him on his toes".' The words came out flat, a verbatim report. 'Has he got it in for you?'

Jake shook his head. 'I don't know.'

At the end of the street, he caught a glimpse of Paulo coming threading past the Birmingham-bound coach, wobbling on stilettos. Jake stood up.

'Funtime.'

'What?'

'Nothing, I'll see you later . . . back at the flat if you want somewhere to stay again.'

Kevin Donnelly had craned another mouthful to his lips. As he mumbled a 'Yeah, thanks,' the fluffy white innards of his chips showed up like cottonwool teeth dipped in matzo oil. Jake was glad he wouldn't be eating tonight.

He ran across the road, shouting, 'Hey, Paulo. Wait up.'

CHAPTER *ELEVEN*

Jake slept through most of the afternoon. At five, he washed away the last of his sickness under the shower. After a call to the casino to tell them he was on holiday, and another to his flat to hear the empty ring of his answer-phone, he dressed and left. Heading out to the Village. One thing he was missing: he forgot to pack his hair-wax. But he wasn't supposed to be out to impress anyone.

He could have entered the Village head-on, maybe cut through Chinatown. Instead, he looped through a network of alleyways like a regular backdoor trouper. The streets were narrow, foreshortened by the Victorian warehouses that lined the way. The buildings could have been empty or derelict, they showed so few signs of life. What it seemed like, the New Manchester Deal didn't extend as far as the backs of the buildings. Jake couldn't see that the area had changed much in fifteen years.

Then the alley peeled back and Chorlton Street Bus Station sprang up, and it was exactly like he'd never been away. The same dingy piano bar and nightclub set into the corner of the multi-storey, the same National Express coaches pulling round into Sackville Street.

And, opposite the Bus Station, the same row of farm-yard-style cottages, whitewashed in grey: a gay porn shop, a gay pub, a Chinese takeaway where the chip shop once stood. A few whores, male and female, were standing on the pavement, grabbing something to eat in a pause from the after-work rush-hour business.

Back in 1981, it seemed Kevin Donnelly lived on chips. Usually he ate them out of a funnel with salt and vinegar. For variety, maybe off a tray with a curry sauce. That was past history, but there were a few look-alikes out tonight. One boy especially, the way he held his mouth open as he chewed his chips, he could have been Donnelly Mk II. Even his complexion matched, the colour co-ordinated with the curry sauce.

Jake stood there, kerbside, staring out at a street scene that looked so real it could be a TV documentary. The only element out of place was Jake himself. If anyone saw him, they could walk up and pass their hand right through him. Down here he was a ghost. The exact date he stopped belonging: 2 February 1982. Johnny had been dead for almost seven weeks then, and Jake had spent the entire time so alone and useless the only thing he did was buy the *Evening News*, always hoping for an update.

And when the story finally broke – it was something else entirely.

The way it happened, Jake was in town early. He picked up the first edition from the kiosk by the Piccadilly Plaza. The front page led with a story about two men, one a teacher and the other a head nurse. Following their trial, all reporting restrictions had been lifted and among the other background snippets, Jake read that the teacher hadn't worked since Christmas. With the jury returned and the guilty verdict marked down, the man's dismissal was a confirmed fact. The nurse took the resignation route but the way the report stressed the word '*voluntary*', it was clear his letter was expected, even overdue. In the photograph, taken outside the court, both men were trying to mask their faces. They were wasting their time because the newspaper already had a personal photograph, and ran it alongside: the two of them standing on a beach, wearing matching pouches and holding hands. They had similar crewcuts and moustaches, they had their names printed beneath the picture: David Corner and Philip Thomas. David and Phil . . . turn to page three for an account of the pornography found in their possession.

Jake stood under the awning outside Piccadilly Records, creased open the page and read on. According to Inspector John Pascal, the police raid came as the culmination of a successful collaboration between his own task force and the Oldham branch of Manchester Metropolitan CID. Quote: the officers had discovered videos of '*unimagined depravity*'. The report, right down to its syntax-lite style, was routine press-conference stuff, but Jake recognized authentic chunks of John Pascal inside the copy – something Jake had heard in school assemblies and at the Caldenstall Congregational Chapel. Let Pascal loose in front of an audience, he was ready to hijack it and turn it over to the Word, via his own words.

The *Evening News* had a sidebar of Pascal's

thoughts on the *counterfeit* relation between the two men: a pretence that *sullies* the institution of Christian marriage. A separate heading for Pascal's thoughts on the horror of allowing an avowed *homosexualist* to mould the minds of the young. The report stressed that many of the videos were *explicit enactments* along paedophile themes. Jake assumed Pascal was referring to the video of the paperboy looking for his Christmas tip. Jake had watched all of Johnny's Berlin collection and he agreed the paperboy was young-looking – but only for a man in his mid-twenties.

After Jake finished the story and binned the paper, he didn't even bother going back to his flat. He just walked the two blocks to the station and jumped the first train to London.

It was just like Green promised it would be. If Jake sold someone out, he got to save himself. Maybe it wasn't quite the way Green had meant it, but Jake took the chance and saved himself anyway. He hardly even remembered giving Green the names of the two men, at least not until the report of their trial refreshed his memory. The fact was, those past seven weeks, he hadn't thought about anything. Like he told his mother when he finally spoke to her, he was thoughtless. The whole of Christmas, he'd been shivering in his flat, so blind and cold in his fear he never got to hear the greatest irony: his own mother was convinced he was dead.

Johnny's body had been dumped at the edge of Caldenstall village and, though she never knew he was a friend of Jake's, she let his murder play on her imagination. By the time Jake thought to call home, it was summer and he was working at an amusement arcade off Piccadilly Circus. One giant leap, Piccadilly Manchester to Piccadilly London. His mother was crying so hard she barely heard his apology. Maybe he should have listened more carefully because he only spoke to her another dozen times, maximum, before she died in '93.

Jake took a side-step, turning his back on the Bus Station and heading for the canal. There was no plan, only that he wanted to catch a breath and thought he could do that down by the water, so long as he ignored the smell. What he found there was coffee tables resting on a piazza outside a starkly clean modern bar, disco lights blaring out of the two storeys of glass frontage and skidding across the shallow surface of the canal. The canal itself, that was unbelievable. It had been flushed through and turned into a beauty spot. There was even a cutesy Japanese-style bridge leading over to a new waterside cafe. It was still early but Jake felt like he was stepping aboard a carousel; there was so much heat, light, noise. So many people, too, all wearing their fairground best.

Jake checked, left and right, deciding whether to start with the Union, which was old but looked like it had had a revival, or whether to take a punt on one of the new bars. He decided to try the lot.

The third bar along his trail was the Rembrandt, and it was unrecognizable. The close-brick walls had been pulled down and replaced with glass panels in concertina folds. Jake stood with his back to the bar; he had a view down to Canal Street and back towards the Bus Station. He could even see Good-Day's if he leant out thirty degrees. He had a cold beer, he was listening to Handbag House, he couldn't say he was uncomfortable. For the first time in as long as ten minutes, he got cruised.

'You on your own?'

Jake turned, found himself looking at a man maybe four to six years younger than him. Very nice neat hair, a soft Irish accent.

Jake said, 'I'm afraid so.'

'It's deliberate?'

Jake nodded. 'Sorry.'

The man smiled and moved off. Jake repositioned himself. By looking between two pillars, he had a semi-restricted view of Good-Day's. The place wasn't as drastically changed as the Rembrandt but there was a new sign and the windows were no longer blacked out. He couldn't decide what time he should step over there. He didn't know if he should aim for the floor-show or not, always assuming that Lady Good-Day was still running entertainment evenings.

Over another Beck's, he began thinking: was the opposite of seedy seedless? The Rembrandt was so fresh and clean, you could bus in a coachload of Yorkshire pensioners, they'd think they'd found a very nice little brasserie café. Maybe they would complain that the juke-box was tuned a little loud, then a waiter could step over and suggest they adjust their hearing aids. Jake took another pull at his beer and was sure he heard it speak to him: saying it fancied a walk around the room. Anyone asks, just tell them it's the drink talking.

Jake headed for the Canal Street side of the bar, where the sliding windows had been pulled back, and settled among the drinkers that were standing half in, half out of the bar space. Thinking, *Am I in with the out-crowd, or out with the in-crowd?*

Looking at the groups passing up and down Canal Street, he got to check the youngsters, the students, the club types, the shrieking look-at-me's and the disco-bunnies, all of them on the move. The Rembrandt was a kind of calm centre, something between an oasis and a viewing station. Or maybe a heritage site, a place that catered for the veterans. The age range seemed to be around thirty to fifty, which was where Jake was trying to position himself. As long as he could remain reflective, maybe he could keep on top of the buzzing in his head and his stomach. The beer was supposed to douse that feeling, though he knew for a fact it wasn't working. Maybe it wasn't the beer's fault; he just wasn't drinking it hard enough. He sank the bottle and headed on again.

Ten-fifteen, he was leaving the Castro. This was a cellar bar and as he reached the stairs, someone asked, 'You going already?'

'I'm already gone ... howling at the moon and clawing at the gutter. Later days.' He took the steps two at a time and even managed to trip as he reached the top.

These streets, this rigid Village grid like a down-sized New York, he knew every grate, every manhole cover, even the distance in high-heeled feet from block to block. The only thing he didn't know was all the stuff in between. It was like the whole site had been chic-bombed; call it a queer act of God. And on the Sixth Day he created fun fur and saw that it was so goo-ood, he just went right on interiorizing. Jake had the before-and-after pictures playing through his head. Even the old bars like the Union, New York New York, Dickens, Central Park, they all had the same born-again glint. Well, he couldn't actually speak for Central Park, which still looked too desolate to bother with. Nor, yet, Good-Day's, but it was next on his list. He was still on the nostalgia trip, tracing the new cartography onto the old circuitry. When he finished, it would be Hello, Good-Day . . . it was a promise.

There was a whole archaeology of connections, all waiting to be rediscovered. Starting at the Bus Station where Jake used to step on and off the York–Manchester coach until the day he decided that he might be a small-town boy, but it was time he claimed refugee status and got on the council waiting list for a flat in Hulme. Then, from the Bus Station, on to the Dickens where Fairy first got talking to him and persuaded him to try the Poly Disco. The same night, he was sure, he met Sean for the first time. A few weeks later, they got to know Johnny.

From there, take a round trip past Legends Nite Club, where he first bought a gramme off Paulo. And then it was either back to the Bus Station and take ten pounds as you pass Go . . . which was roughly what Kevin Donnelly charged. Or shoot along Canal Street and the exact spot by the canal wall which, until yesterday, was the last place Jake had ever seen DC Green. There was a story to that, too.

He left Donnelly chewing the soul out of a chip and ran to head off Paulo, who was weaving in and out of the coach headlamps, back-lit like a fifty-foot transvestite in high heels and blond wig. At first he thought Paulo hadn't heard him shout, the noise of the coach engines too loud. He caught up with him at the corner of Chorlton and Bloom Street.

'How do you move so fast in those?' Jake was pointing at the shoes.

'I was born to it,' said Paulo. Then, lower, 'It's not a good night, Jake.'

'You not got any speed?'

Paulo was looking up and down Chorlton Street, and Jake should have caught the anxiety. He would have, if he hadn't drunk so much at David and Phil's Christmas dinner party.

Paulo said, 'Walk with me.'

They turned the corner into Canal Street. The whole length of the road, only one streetlamp seemed to be working. Paulo stopped by it, sitting on the edge of the canal wall and looking through his handbag. He came out with a fistful of wraps, saying: 'How many do you want?'

'Fuck, Paulo, I want it all.' Jake wondered if his eyeballs were revolving, the cartoon speed-freak. 'But I can't afford it.'

'How much you got?'

The answer, twenty pound he just got off Johnny, maybe as much as fifteen he had with him anyway. He said, 'Twenty, maybe thirty, but then I'm broke for the whole weekend.'

Paulo said, 'Hold out your hand.' He cupped his hand above Jake's, palmed what looked like ten wraps into it.

Jake didn't get it at all. Paulo just said, 'Sorry.'

That exact moment, the road lit up ahead of them, pinning their shadows to the canal wall. Jake hadn't even heard the car engine. He turned, found himself looking at a fat man, waddling out of the beams of his Vauxhall Cavalier. If he couldn't recognize the walk, he knew DC Green's voice well enough already.

'Nice one, Paul, my son.' Green threw Paulo a salute. Paulo took it with a shrug, said 'Sorry' again and started walking away. It seemed that, out of the three of them, only Jake didn't know his moves.

Green said, 'You reckon I search you, I'm going to get me a haul?'

Jake looked off to his left, a whole empty length of street ending in Piccadilly Gardens.

'Don't even think about running. If I have to go chasing you round in my fucking car, I swear I'll run you over first.' Green was only three yards away, close enough for Jake to get the full benefit of his smile.

Jake stuffed the wraps into his pocket. He said, 'DC Green, I believe I've got information that might be of interest to you.'

'That a fact? It's got to be my lucky night.'

CHAPTER *TWELVE*

Saturday was a cruise. Jake was high on a day's gossip, high on the night's possibilities, high on drugs, on beauty and clothes. It took him a sweet, short seven hours to put together the outfit he was going to wear to Pips that night. It was specialist work but no chore. Jake finished shopping only because the shops closed around him. Now he was alone, zigzagging through the high-rise towers along Spring Gardens, feeling kind of ditzy. He had maybe three hours sleep in the bag since the previous night; three hours or less, ending in an amphetamine wake-up call. No wonder he was feeling a little attenuated; it was a miracle he managed to make any shopping decisions at all. Right now he couldn't decide whether to head back to the flat or just kill time hanging out.

He crossed Mosley Street by the City Art Gallery, sped through Chinatown and descended into the Village. Among the polythene store bags in his hand, the heaviest held a new shirt and a bottle of Coca-Cola with most of the Coke poured away and the space filled with Bacardi. When he hit the bar at Good-Day's, he had a no-lose plan. Either he could scav his drinks or he could serve himself under the table.

Good-Day was serving in male civvies, keeping the first slow hour of the evening ticking over. When the night traffic really started and his staff took over, he would run upstairs and change.

He wasn't fooled by Jake's request for straight Coke.

'I'm supposed to believe you'll make it last all night while you're pouring refills out of your own bottle?'

Jake waved a hand round the bar. 'Then tell one of these old puffs to buy me a drink.'

An early-evening regular was standing close enough to hear. He said, 'Give my young friend whatever he likes.' The man had a mock-Etonian voice, clipped to the fruit and the gin.

Jake got his Bacardi and Coke. He carried on sitting at the bar out of politeness, listening to the guy speak.

'I'm a refugee in these parts . . . the pace of life, alas, too much in my preferred climes . . .'

It wasn't like Jake was concentrating. All day, he'd made regular speed drops as he skipped from changing-room to changing-room across the city. In the mirror behind Good-Day's bar, his reflection was pared down to two wide eyeballs set in a sulphate stare.

The old man clicked for another two drinks, letting Good-Day take the money from a pile of change he'd left dumped on the bar-top.

'. . . this was in the Colony Room of which you've no doubt heard? Darling Francis was rolling, positively steaming, when he met us that night. The other guests I now forget, but for the unwanted presence of Fatty Farson, refusing good vodka because he claimed –

accurately as I was unfortunate enough to discover – that he could not be held responsible for his behaviour when vodka became an added factor to his usual diet.'

The man was a recognizable type, clinically boring to an exact standard. Maybe he shared his Soho stories with all the others like him, working on a time-share basis: tonight you can have the *Francis & Me* story; tomorrow it's all mine.

Jake's glass was empty and he was ready to move on. As he stood, Good-Day waved him to a quiet corner at the far end of the bar.

'Someone was looking for you.'

Jake thought: DC Green. He stammered, 'Who?'

Good-Day said, 'Gary Halliday.'

Jake didn't know the name. 'What did he want?'

'I don't know. That beat-up kid who hangs around the Coach Station sent him here.'

'Kevin Donnelly sent him?' It was one of Good-Day's peculiarities not to notice what the boys at the Coach Station were doing there. Maybe it was delicacy. Perhaps the idea of buying what he wanted, so close to his own door, took all the fun out of coercing his own staff into providing the same services.

Good-Day said, 'I think it was something to do with videos.'

'Oh, right.' Jake got it now. 'That's nothing to do with me. He wants to speak to Johnny.'

'He asked for you both.'

Jake shrugged. That was Donnelly's fault if it was true. He said, 'Nothing to do with me.'

'Yeah, well, watch out.' The warning came from nowhere. Backed up with a free drink, it was a stone shock.

Good-Day must have read the surprise. As he put the glass down in front of Jake, he said, 'Just take care.'

The TV adverts for Pips Discotheque always ended with the words '*Behind the Cathedral*', rolled out in the drawl of a late-nite American DJ. There was something about the words and the tone, the spin of passé cool following on a clunking description, that should have sounded preposterous. The result, though, whenever anyone mentioned Pips was that the words 'Behind the Cathedral' seeped through too, as a subliminal coda. The Victorian gothic cathedral and, behind it, in the catacombs beneath the Corn Exchange, a nightclub filled with neo-gothic Siouxsie girls and Berlin-age Bowie boys.

Jake arrived around ten-thirty, ready for anything but still not dressed. He headed for the toilets on the lowest of five floors at different levels. These were the largest ones in the club, but it was still a squeeze to get by all the boys at the mirror. When Jake found an empty cubicle, he left the door swinging open so he could keep up with the chat.

Someone shouted over, 'Hey, Jake, you had any problems getting in?'

Jake recognized the voice: Stevie, a nineteen-year-old hairdresser from Rochdale. He shouted back, 'No.' The bouncers were always sweet with him . . . not *sweet*

sweet; they just nodded and stood aside when he rolled to the front of the queue, and said, 'Alright.'

'They were bitches with me. I came in a kilt and they said they were stopping men from wearing dresses. I said, It's not a fucking dress' – he gave the word an emphatic hiss – 'but they wouldn't budge.'

'What happened.'

'Oh, I came with Louise, you know her, and she suggested we swap; I wear her trousers, she wears my kilt and we change back once we get inside. Only, she's got these big butch hips so the kilt doesn't fit. We're struggling inside her car. I'm trying to be all discreet and she's slapping around saying, "It's too tight, it's too tight." I'm going, "Hold your breath in, dear." It's no good. I don't know what to do. Anyway . . . *luckily* . . . she has this tartan dog blanket in the car, so she wraps that around her and I wear her trousers.'

'You got in, then.'

'We got in, yeah. After standing in line for about half an hour with her smelling like a dog and whining that she's itching . . .' He did a whole number on her list of complaints; you had to imagine the pain Louise put him through. '. . . then once we get inside and I tell her I left the kilt back in the car, she gets even worse. She's going like we have to change NOW. And she expects me to wear the dog blanket. I tell her, "No fucking way. It's your dog. You wear the fucking blanket. What do you think I am?"'

Jake was laughing. 'Where is she now?'

'Oh, don't ask. On the warpath, so if you see her, don't tell her where I am.'

Jake was wearing his new clothes. He took a sly drink from his Coke and Bacardi bottle and teetered out of the cubicle – let everyone see him and weep: a soft velvet blouse in black, flowing sleeves and strap-like lacing at the front, tied loose to show his bony white chest, tight mock-croc hipsters skinned from a black-and-grey faux crocodile, and high, high Cuban heels.

Hairdresser Stevie said, 'Oh, very rock-and-roll.'

'I don't know. I think it's more louche and dissolute.'

Someone else suggested: 'A rock-and-roll vampire.'

Jake compromised on that, and asked Stevie if he could borrow his hairspray.

'Take it. I get it free.'

Jake borrowed a comb too. As Stevie was leaving, he asked if Sean was around yet. Jake didn't know . . . the last time he'd seen Sean, the boy was even madder at being left stranded in Oldham in suburban homo hell than he had been over the Domino episode.

'I won't tell Louise about you, you don't tell Sean about me.'

'Oooh, it's like that. Don't worry, if I find Sean, I won't be talking about you.'

Jake hustled himself a little room at the mirror and started back-combing his hair, holding it up with toxic sheets of extra-firm-hold spray. He darkened his eye-brows with a kohl pencil and whitened his face with a pale foundation. After a last swift side-step into a cubicle for a drink and a snort, Jake came swaggering out of the toilets, just another gothic wreck.

There were five dance-floors in Pips, each with a different theme and not all of them dedicated to gothics, romantics, queer boys, glamour pusses, starlets, cross-dressers, or whatever Jake's group looked like that week. In descending order, there was the Roxy Room, the Bowie Room, the Electro Room, the Perry Room and, finally, Floor Five – the only one without a name and without its own regulars. As Jake came out of the toilet, the DJ there was experimenting with a glam rock sound, playing 'Ballroom Blitz' by the Sweet but no one was dancing to it. Jake passed by.

He met Domino on the stairs to the Perry Room. The first thing Domino asked was whether he'd seen Sean.

Jake twitched annoyance. 'Everyone's asking. I haven't seen him.'

Domino said, 'No, I meant have you seen him. He's up there.' A hand pointing upwards. 'He's turned into a Perry; got the Lacoste sweater, the jumbo cords, everything.'

'Really?'

Jake scooted up the steps, Domino turning to follow. 'You see him?'

Jake shook his head.

'Over there by the pillar.'

Jake squinted against the lights. The room was already full and nearly everyone wearing cord jeans, Pepe or Lee, in either burgundy or tan. The look was finished off with matching golf sweaters and Italian loafers. Everyone looked so utterly similar, it took a while before he picked out Sean. Then he saw him, stepping around to the Gap Band in the weird Perry dance . . . a kind of forward/backward strut.

'Jesus Christ! Where'd he get those clothes?'

Domino shrugged, 'You seen his chain?'

Jake had seen it. A gold chain that flickered around the crew neck of his sweater.

Domino said, 'Any second, he's going to turn around. I'm off.'

As he disappeared back down the steps, Sean did turn, sweeping his long Perry fringe out of his eyes as he glanced over. Jake waved him over, too curious about the transformation to worry about how much Sean hated him today.

As Sean stepped off the dance-floor, Jake said, 'What's happened to you?'

'Nothing. I just got fed up with the music down there.' He jerked his head off to the side, over towards the Bowie and Roxy Rooms.

'What's with the clothes?'

'And I got fed up with looking like a queer boy.'

'You *are* a queer boy.'

Sean swept his huge fringe back again. His hair was fresh cut and the soft curtain of his Perry flick covered half his face; the back was trimmed to a neat comma at the nape of neck. He said, 'You're queer. I'm gay.'

Jake looked out on the Perry boys and girls, all in boyish cords, a few still wearing the Fred Perry shirts that were fashionable earlier in the year but most in Lacoste or Tacchini sweaters. 'You think they're going to be impressed by the difference.'

Sean grinned, 'I'm doing okay. And at least they've got better taste in music.'

An Earth, Wind and Fire track was starting. Before Sean danced away he said, 'I'm moving out, too. I've got a place in Flixton.'

It figured, him and his brand-new flick in Flixton. Sean lifted his hand, palm up, and snapped the fingers smartly down in the Perry-boy wave, 'See yah.'

Jake waved back, 'Yeah, see you mate.'

He dropped down the shallow steps into the Electro Room where they were playing 'The Model' by Kraft-werk. The Bowie Room was through the next archway and, as Jake entered, he saw Fairy by the bar, wearing silk pyjamas with an embroidery of a Chinese dragon on the back. Fairy had worn the outfit once before. Jake had said then that it was ludicrous, but Fairy claimed there was some special Bowie significance to it. Jake couldn't imagine what, he'd never seen Bowie wear anything remotely like it.

Johnny was sat close by with a couple of girls Jake knew because they worked in clothes shops. As Jake walked over, they looked him up and down, saying, 'Great, yeah, you look really good.'

Johnny said, 'You got a refill?'

Jake nodded. He sat down and slipped Johnny's glass under the table. When he put it back, it was full of Bacardi and Coke. The girls were drinking what looked like Pernod and black. They got their refills from under the table, too. They all clinked glasses.

Jake said, 'Have you seen what Sean's done to himself?'

Johnny nodded. 'He was always a soul boy. Have you seen Kevin?'

Jake hadn't. Had he missed anything?

'He's in the lavs. You'll have to wait.'

Out on the floor the DJ was playing 'Golden Years', and Fairy was running through his scrapbook of mime. Bowie had studied mime in Europe at some time in the early seventies. Soon, Jake knew, the DJ would play 'Port of Amsterdam', which had a mime for every line ... even the one that went, '*He gets up and laughs and he zips up his fly.*' Jake didn't know how many times he had seen Fairy, po-faced and oblivious, stroking his fly. Too often to find it funny any more.

He said, 'I'm going to look back there.' He nodded to the Roxy Room.

Each of the separate dance-floors was set into a grotto, their walls painted in coarse white stucco. The Bowie Room was decorated with different portraits of Bowie wobbling unevenly across the Polytex surface. The Roxy Room had similar pictures of Bryan Ferry, as well as one enormous painting of Lou Reed taken from the back cover of the *Transformer* album. Unlike the Bowie Room, there was less of a hard connection between the Roxy Room and its given name. Jake passed through a low arch and, for a moment, two different songs blended together ... Bowie singing 'Golden Years' and, beneath it, the bass-heavy hum of a darker track. Jake hovered before moving forward, trying to guess what he was going to hear.

As he stepped through, he heard the last bars of 'Warm Leatherette' by Grace Jones slowly segueing into

'Homo Sapiens' by Pete Shelley. Out in the rough circle of the dance-floor, Kevin Donnelly was dancing on his own, floating gracefully across the music but always, always in time with the beat. The boy was wearing a tight plastic T-shirt and Clash pants, both of them cast-offs from Johnny's clothes pile.

Jake crossed from the carpet to the wood-parquet floor and started feeling for a time signature, knowing it would be much, much slower than he expected . . . the speed was blowing through his body, gale-force five. Kevin Donnelly turned to smile at him, the boy was wearing blue eyeshadow, a slash of disco glitter across his cheeks and an artificial beauty spot high on his cheek. The style was white disco-trash, Debbie Harry reborn as a boy. Jake winked and then tried to refocus, concentrating on finding the beat.

It was closing in on one o'clock before they played 'The Passenger'. Jake was steaming drunk, speeding like a maniac. Johnny wasn't any clearer in the head but he was ready to argue any point Jake wanted.

'What's the matter with the song, I thought you liked Iggy Pop?'

The chorus thundered through the speakers, the bierkeller chant of *La La La La-La La La* that Jake blamed on Bowie. The dance floor was full, arms and legs swinging like a skeltering cancan.

'Listen to the words – they're just ripped out of some novel. It's all Bowie, hardly any Iggy at all.'

Everything in the lyrics was about watching things

and doing nothing. Main themes of alienation and all the other allergies you got in the scrawling pretence of Bowiedom. Nothing like Iggy who sang stark simple lines about *being* and *doing*, even if it was just being bored, being desperate, out for FUN.

Johnny said, 'What the fuck are you talking about?'

Jake's mouth was moving, but so full of words, and the words so chock-full of venom, nothing was making sense.

'Bowie. Crawling after Iggy, like because he can't do it himself – can't get in there like Iggy.'

'Crap. It's Bowie who's bi. Iggy's straight.'

'Bowie isn't anything. He's the dumb-jerk friend who has to chase after someone else's charisma, catching onto their reputation because he's too timid to push out there himself.'

Johnny was reeling around, saying to anyone who was close enough to hear, you want to listen to this: 'He reckons Bowie has to run around after Iggy Pop because . . . what is it?'

Jake was convinced. Rotating on the spot, his eyes blazing on the people around him, on their hair and their clothes and the kind of music they tried to dance to; everything, the whole fragile night-style. Looking at it all with speed-sharpened vision, he knew that without Iggy it was nothing but a faggoty pantomime. It needed something like the *Ig* to make it desperate, serious stuff. If it all came down to David Bowie, it was just tissue-thin, ludicrous . . .

Johnny, still talking: 'So, what you saying? That

Bowie's the jerk, friend, trying to look cool by tagging after Iggy?'

And someone else was there, saying, 'What, like Jake does with you?'

Jake saw his own fist fly out, cracking against the boy's nose. He put the next one into his gut and, as the boy started falling, he followed it with a kick. Around him, a girl screaming, someone shouting, *'Psycho! He's gone psycho!'* Yeah, well, psycho was serious. Better than limp-wrist mime boys in pyjama pants. Two pairs of hands were dragging on Jake's shoulders, trying to pull him away from the boy on the ground. Jake tried to make his last kick count, but only grazed the boy's head.

He tore himself away, heading out across the dance-floor and up the steps, two by two. One more flight of stairs and the exit door was in front of him.

He ran through Manchester, end to end. The freezing winter rain couldn't touch him. In the trough of Piccadilly Gardens he saw a straggling group of girl late-goers, en route for Rotters. He shouted 'Slags!' and they turned their faces briefly out of the rain to shout 'Puff!' back at him. Their wind-chapped legs hardly slowed.

Jake hurtled on, through the stalls of the night buses, sneering at the Saturday-night drunks heading home. Across the road, at the foot of the Piccadilly Radio tower, he saw others eating bags of chips, sheltering from the rain in the night light of the Plaza. His amphetamine eyes saw them like bit-part scenery, a sheet of rain in front of them like a curtain. He flicked a V at them, calling them 'Greasy shites!' They threw chip bags at him, all of them falling short of the line that separated the rain-slick dark from their little square of light.

Jake ran on diagonally through the traffic as he aimed for the Coach Station. The cars that swerved around him, they were shites too. He danced out of their headlights as he made for the opposite kerb.

The gang that followed him from the bus shelter were only a few yards behind him when he finally caught the wet slap of their feet. He turned to meet them, three puke-faced kids about his age but smaller. They didn't expect a fight. He swept away the feet of the leading one, and as the boy skittled across the road he met the second with a side-handed cut to the throat. As the boy trembled and began to sink, Jake put a boot to his groin, kicking on automatic as his eyes sidewinded to look for an easy attack on the third. He was too slow bringing his arm into a block as the third boy lashed out. Jake took the blow across his face and slipped on the wet road. Still, he got hold of a foot as the boy tried to follow his punch with a kick. All it took was a twist, Jake brought him down.

Now it was a scrabble across the road, a flailing, lizard-like movement as the two of them wrestled for a footing, Jake still looking for a disabling blow before the lad's friends got it together and rejoined the attack. When the shadow of a stick flashed across his eyes, he reared back, expecting to feel crunching pain on the forearm he'd raised to protect his face. It never came; the stick landed square on the skull of the other boy and broke it open.

Jake was still only half aware of the man with the stick. There was no time to look at him as Jake turned to face the first boy – on his feet now from his long slide across the road. Jake wanted the boy to come on to him, to get close enough for short work to the kidneys. Across the road, the man with the stick was whaling on the remaining kid, who was still on his knees from the boot Jake had put in his groin. As Jake met his opponent and grabbed hold of his lapels, the stick man ran over.

Jake let go his grip, the stick swiped across his eyes one more time, then the boy went down. A squirt of blood hovered against the rain and disintegrated.

The stick man had hold of Jake's arm. 'I've got a car.'

Jake was laughing now. Adrenalin and amphetamine, amphethalin and adrenaphine, a heart-choking mix.

'Inside.'

A car door opened. Jake collapsed into the front passenger seat. When the driver's side opened, the stick came first, tossed onto the dash so it skidded and rested in front of Jake's eyes. It was an old-fashioned policeman's truncheon. A lathe-carved handgrip at one end, black blood glistening at the other.

Jake turned. The man was panting but grinning. 'Jake Powell? I been looking for you.'

'Yeah?' Jake shook his head, he didn't know why. The man was regular-looking: clean, regular features and straightforward smile. He was maybe in his mid-twenties.

'Didn't Kevin Donnelly say I was looking for you?'

Jake was still trying to catch his breath. What had Donnelly said?

'He told me you could copy some videos for me. I was about to talk to you last night, but the police hauled you over.'

The car was moving now. The man reached round blindly and pulled a plastic bag off the back seat, and through the gap between their seats. 'The videos.'

Jake took the bag – three unboxed Betamax tapes. 'Oh, yeah, I can get these copied.'

The car turned at the end of the street. Out of his window, Jake saw the bodies of three boys on the road. 'Thanks for that.'

'No problem.' The man flashed an open grin. 'You were lucky I was just leaving Benny's bar.'

Jake must have looked confused.

'Benny Silver. Lady Good-Day.'

Jake clutched the bag of videos. 'Oh, yeah, the tapes. He told me all about them.'

CHAPTER *THIRTEEN*

The sign above the door used to give the licence-holder's name as Benny Silver – not Benjamin. Jake had always wondered about that: why Good-Day chose the diminutive of a name he never even used . . . there had to be a story there. But that was fifteen years ago and someone else had their name above the door now. Jake didn't have a back-up plan so he pushed on, at least to see how much the place had changed. He found himself in a large square room more than semi-full. The place was a little dingy and the music was still too loud. Basically just like it ever was. A squad of ageing queens were trying to get a party mood going in one corner. They were whooping, breaking into snatches of song and dance. Jake glanced their way as he tramped for the bar, and caught a few over-the-shoulder looks in return. Maybe he was double-focusing, but one of the men looked familiar. Then the face was gone again.

Jake swayed for the toilet. The one guy standing at the urinal nodded a greeting. Jake stepped up and, after a moment, said, 'This place hasn't changed much.'

'Since when, darling?'

'1981.'

'No, the old place hasn't changed much since then.'

Jake took another look at the man. In the dim light, he hadn't realized just how old he was. He had to be a good person to ask about Good-Day.

The man was still talking: '. . . 1978, during that huge discotheque craze, we had a complete redecoration . . . 1985, I think, we laid a new carpet, which was a big thrill. Then, it must have been '93, the boards came off the windows . . . orders of the new management. I believe they wanted to let a little light on the matter, but it was a horrible mistake. Most of us, we look our best at thirty watts and below. Not you, of course, dear . . .'

The last line came with a smile. Jake managed to return it. Not so drunk that he couldn't smile and zip up at the same time. Before moving over to the wash-basin, keeping it casual, he said, 'Good-Day sold up, then?'

'Oh, yes, sold out for a million. Lucky bitch.'

A third man had just entered, so short and squat he had to elbow extra room to stand at the urinal. He had a nasal voice, apologizing for the crush. 'Excuse me, darling.' Then, as he got himself settled: 'Good-Day? Who's asking about that cunt?'

Jake said, 'He got a million for this place?'

The second man: 'Oh, at the ab-so-lute least, believe me.'

'So what happened to him? He moved to the Bahamas or something?'

'Good-Day move? You have to be joking. Who'd have him?'

The first man again: 'Who'd love him like we do?'

'The cunt.'

'Ha-ha.'

Jake said, 'He still comes here?'

'He's buying the bloody drinks, darling. Champagne all round.'

Jake headed out of the lavs, aiming for the queen mothers' corner. Ahead of him, a dapper, baldheaded man rose out of his seat, a shade unsteady on his old bandy legs. As he wobbled for the back door, he showed the slimmest ring of trimmed grey hair around the base of his skull and ears. That was the reason Jake hadn't recognized him. If Good-Day was ever seen wigless, his hair was always combed in the Bobby Charlton flick-over. Then, again, the guy was now a lot older. In fifteen/sixteen years, a middle-aged man can become a geriatric. It had happened to Good-Day.

Jake easily caught up with him. They were in the back corridor, Good-Day halfway up a staircase, but Jake grabbed him by the wrist.

Good-Day sat on his chair, his head turned to the net curtains and the street below. The table between them had a rich walnut surface, a lace doily spread at its centre. Jake curled his fingers round his glass of whisky, looking down at its full-length reflection in the deep glaze of the wood.

He said, 'This is where you live?'

'One room. I rent, but the furniture's all mine.'

'You ask me, the furniture's a mistake.' The problem was there was so much of it. Besides the bed, the table and its four dining chairs, Good-Day had a cabinet-sideboard affair, a settee and a big old radiogram.

Good-Day shrugged. 'I know. When my mother died, I was only going to keep a few of her things. I guess I was too distraught to think rationally . . .'

'You could always get somewhere bigger. I hear you sold out for a million.'

'Did I fuck! Still, it was quite a bit.'

'There's not been many improvements.'

'It's a joke. All the bright new bars opened around here, getting the bright young men, and this one's full of sad cases.'

'Why do you stay?'

'It's home. In fact, it's better than home; it's a hotel. I get my bed made, breakfast too. I eat in one of the new restaurants, or walk into Chinatown. As far as the bar goes, I leave it to the new manager. Maybe he'll show some imagination if he's allowed to get on with it.'

The man – Jake found it easier to think of him as Benny Silver because he looked so unfamiliar – shrugged sadly.

'I'm retired. Leave the international corporate homosexuals to run the Village. How's that for change?'

Jake still wasn't sure this old man recognized him. He'd said his name, earlier, as he twisted his arm. Benny Silver just nodded and asked him to come through to his room. The room was a complete surprise: all this clunky Deco, specially tailored to the dark Manchester suburbs by being as dark and as heavy as possible.

Jake said, 'When did your mother die?'

'Four, five months.'

'This what her house looked like?'

Benny Silver looked around. 'Pretty much – the parlour anyway. Sick, isn't it?'

Jake nodded. It was an old woman's place through and through, even to the smell of damp face-powder. The smell reacted badly with the whisky.

Benny said, 'She was ninety-two, would have been ninety-three last week.'

'That's old.'

'Uh-huh. So maybe I'll be here for another thirty years. I should find the energy to do something. Start afresh.'

The Jewish candelabrum placed on the doily, that was Art Deco too, solid, cubic and silver. Jake was left staring at it while Benny bustled over a Teasmade in the corner. When he returned, he was short of breath but that was only his fatness, not any disease.

Jake said, 'You do remember me?'

'Of course. Jake – Johnny's friend.'

'Johnny was killed fifteen years ago.' He didn't have to say it. The way Benny trembled with the teapot, it was clear he knew.

'What about Kevin Donnelly?'

Benny didn't look up. Just said: 'He's dead too.'

'I meant, did you know him?'

'Yes, I knew him.'

So, there was only one question: 'Who killed them?'

'Gary Halliday.'

And the police had *him* safely locked up in prison. Jake poured his whisky into the cup of tea, took a sip and said, 'You always knew about Gary Halliday, didn't you?'

The man nodded. Jake took another sip from his cup. Even with the whisky, it tasted like old woman's tea stewed in globby cream. He flung the teacup out into the dead space of the room. It seemed to hang for a moment, reaching the tip of its arc beneath the lightshade, then accelerated into the radiogram. The cup shattered, the tea steamed off the Bakelite panel.

Jake said, 'You want to do something about this room, I got ideas.'

Benny was saying, *Oh no no no*. 'I'm not up to this.'

'You're only, what, in your sixties. I bet you could cope with a lot more than you think. You knew about Gary Halliday and you didn't do anything.'

Benny was chewing the inside of his mouth. When at last he spoke, he said, 'I didn't do anything. How many times have I heard people say that: they didn't do anything – they knew, yet they did nothing? I've heard it all my life. I'm Jewish, so you imagine what they were talking about. So how do you think I feel? I knew about a monster and I kept quiet about it. You want to know why?'

Jake nodded.

'It's a story, so please be patient. I don't want you smashing things because you think I'm going too slow.'

'I'll wait until you've finished.'

He began, 'Okay. When I was a kid . . . is that too early for you? Well it started when I was a very little kid. People used to say, "They think we eat babies." I remember I had an aunty, she would bounce me up and down on her knee, hugging me and saying: "They think we eat little babies." And I'd get maybe a kiss or maybe sent to the kitchen where I'd be given a biscuit, and my mother or another aunty would be there to give me another kiss. "They think we eat little babies" – you imagine? And so I knew right from the beginning that They were out there and They were spreading these ridiculous lies and probably They even believed them. Then, when I was older, maybe nineteen, I read this history book about the old days. I found out, back then, the traditional way to perform circumcision was the rabbi would make the cut, take a swig of red wine, then lift the baby up and gargle with the baby's dickie in his mouth. It was the best way to sterilize the cut, probably anaesthetize it too. But can you imagine some dumb Slav peasant creeping up to a Jew's hut in the middle of the countryside and looking through the window? He sees everyone standing around an altar, the candles lit, and, at the centre, some weird priest, half in robes and half in undertaker's clothes, his hair sticking out in all directions from under a great big hat, gnawing at a baby's groin and the blood and wine running over his huge grey beard? What the fuck do you think they would have thought? They run out, they start scream-ing: "Those Jews eat babies." Reading that, I couldn't believe it was all so simple. It could be explained . . .'

Benny Silver was shaking his head, like he'd come into the world gullible. It wasn't how he was leaving it. 'I know now, because so many stupid things are getting revived by the Hasidim; gargling wine with the baby's dickie is the traditional way. I've even seen it done. But

I know why no one's ever bothered to explain how it was the gentiles came to think we ate babies. Because it wouldn't do any good. I'm not saying it's because they already decided to hate us, so they wouldn't ever listen. That may be true; it maybe isn't. I don't know. But I do know the whole thing sounds too awful. Gargling a baby's dick after you cut it up, how are you supposed to explain that? What can you say?'

'It's disgusting.'

'Yeah, and *you've* been around. Imagine how it sounds to other people. It wouldn't do any good because they'd think, well, it's not eating babies but it's disgusting enough. So – to cut back to the point – I knew about Gary Halliday and the reason I knew was because he thought I was like him, another kiddie-fucker. When I found out why he was cultivating my acquaintance, I kept well out of his way, but it scared me. If *he* thought I was like him, what would everyone else think?'

Now he was going for the confessional. 'I'm a dirty old man. What I like are what I always called boys. But I didn't really mean *boys* boys. I meant people like you. I was a dirty old man, and what I liked were nubiles. I did my best to persuade them to get naked and get in my sack. There must be millions out there like me, maybe a majority of men. The difference, though, most of them like girls. Meaning inappropriately young women. And because I like inappropriately young men, I was scared to say anything. To most people it sounded disgusting enough, what does it matter that I'm innocent of that specific charge when I'm guilty as hell of something else? How old were you back then: seventeen, eighteen?'

'Seventeen and eighteen.'

'Suppose I ever managed to worm some favour out of you, I could have been locked up for that.'

'You could have. Though the law's changed now, eighteen's okay.'

They sat in silence for a moment until Jake said, 'Basically you're saying you were scared.'

'After Johnny was murdered, I was terrified.'

'Gary Halliday told you he killed Johnny?'

'As good as.'

'He say why?'

'Johnny had videos of him and his friends doing what they did. He was going to take them to the police.'

'What about Kevin? Why was he killed?'

'Same reason. Somehow he managed to get his hands on the same videos – or copies of them.'

'Halliday told you this?'

'He screamed it at me. He was running around looking up everyone who might know where Kevin Donnelly was, trying to get to him before Kevin got to the police.'

Jake couldn't think. He didn't know whether to smash up the whole room, or whether he could justify doing it. Maybe he would be doing the man a favour, making him reassess everything one more time.

CHAPTER *FOURTEEN*

Jake set the bag of videos down on the smoky-blue cover of the hi-fi. The room was almost dark and wherever he stepped there was party debris underfoot: cups and cans, up-ended saucers full of cigarette stubs. There was a boy and girl asleep on the settee, someone else spread on the floor and covered in a coat. As Jake walked by, an eye opened.

'Alright, Jake, how's it going?'

Could be a great deal better, but Jake just nodded, *fine*, and stepped over the lad's body.

Fairy's lean-to was still standing intact at the back of the room; the party couldn't have been that wild. Jake pulled back the pink, furry-swirled bedcover that made the opening flap and looked inside. It was Kevin Donnelly lying there, and he was on his own. Jake let the cover fall and walked out to the stairs. He remembered now, Sean had moved to Perry-loving Flixton. Probably Fairy had taken over his old bed. He had first bagsies on it.

At the top of the stairs, Jake saw a slash of daylight around the edge of Johnny's door and pushed it open. Johnny was in bed with two girls. It was a moment before Jake recognized them as Rebecca and her friend

Debs. In that flush of embarrassment, he was just glad no one seemed to have heard him.

But, as he began to close the door, Johnny lifted his head and said, 'Jake, that you? What time is it?'

'Nine-thirty.'

'Jesus.' Johnny's face was screwed against the daylight, although it was still weak. 'What happened to you?'

Jake didn't know what to say. He thought, I got stoned and ran around.

'You got a black eye?'

Jake knew all about it, though he wouldn't have said it was a black eye . . . it didn't go deep enough. He guessed he got it in the fight last night, outside the Bus Station.

He said, 'I ran into the guy Kevin Donnelly told you about, the one who wanted some videos copying. I put them downstairs on the record player.'

'Right. I'll take them round to Junk' – Johnny waved a hand over the girls – 'later. What price did you give him?'

Halliday hadn't seemed worried about price, just discretion. Jake shrugged, 'I don't know.'

'Well how many does he want?'

'Four of each, all VHS.' He remembered that. 'I'm fucked, Johnny. I got to crash. I'll catch you later.'

Rebecca stirred against Johnny's body and opened sleep-mired eyes, as buggy and vulnerable as a baby ET doll. Strange since her night-time eyes were her best feature. Even so, her Cleopatra make-up was still in place. Jake pulled the bedroom door behind him before she wakened completely.

The door to his own room was closed. Jake pushed it open, feeling the soft weight of clothes piled carelessly on the other side of the door. They were Domino's clothes. It was Domino lying in his bed. Jake stared at him for a moment without knowing what to do, then turned and tried Sean's room. He was right about Fairy: it was his room now. The boy was asleep there, lying naked on a near-naked bed, just a tartan dog blanket and the hairdresser Stevie to keep him warm. Jake could smell the breath of the animal but not the smell of sex. It didn't mean that it wasn't there, only that he carried it too and was already numb to it. He turned back to his own room, swept along on a bellying wave of nausea.

Jake kept a sleeping-bag at the bottom of his wardrobe, below the shelf with his folded shirts. He shook the bag out, laid it on the floor in the shadow of his bed, and crept inside. For half an hour the tinny jangling of the amphetamine in his blood and brain kept him from sleeping. Then, suddenly, it didn't any more.

Once, and briefly, he was pulled out of sleep by Domino but he buried his head and the boy gave up. It was much much later when Johnny came and woke him, sitting above him on the edge of the bed, an arm stretching into his dreams to shake him awake.

'Jake, Jake.'

He slurped into the light. Someone had drawn back the curtains on his window. 'What?'

Johnny had a plastic bag at his feet. The video tapes.

'Jake. Do you know what's on these?'

Jake shook his head. 'Porn?'

'No. Not porn.'

Jake tried to pull himself up. There was a headache deep behind his eyes. 'Not porn?'

'It's real stuff, real abuse. The man fucking the kids in his home.'

Jake was awake now. 'You've seen it?'

'About a minute's worth. Junk refused to copy them. He couldn't look at them. What I want to know, why did Kevin Donnelly send the man to me? What the fuck's up with that lad?'

Johnny was out of the room now, stamping down the steps and into the living-room. Jake slithered out of his sleeping bag and followed behind.

He found Johnny hunched over the settee talking to Fairy. No one knew where Kevin Donnelly had gone. Fairy suggested he was working. Johnny couldn't believe that.

'It's fucking Sunday. What's he going to be doing on a Sunday?'

Jake said, 'Anyone want tea?'

'Tea? I couldn't hold it down.' Johnny was waving a video out of the bag. 'A little fucking kid, bawling his eyes out. I don't get Kevin. The same man who fucked him up and now he's helping him out. Helping him while he does the same thing to someone new.'

In the end, Johnny did have a cup of tea. Over the next hour he had several, thick and syrupy mugs, and he held them all down. Kevin Donnelly returned while he was sucking at the third.

Stood in front of their settee, the three of them staring up at him, he looked smaller and more feeble than ever. He was back in his everyday clothes now: Harrington jacket and tight jeans. A little Borstal-boy shoplifter and they had him in the dock.

Johnny said, 'Who the fuck does this man think he is?'

'Gary Halliday.'

Johnny said he didn't give a fuck what his name was, why had Kevin sent him to them? The kid had nothing to say, his thin lips twisted under his biting teeth. Johnny told him, 'I don't fucking get you . . .' and to Fairy, 'Do you fucking believe this?'

Johnny felt unclean. He said it more than once and, sitting on the settee, he looked uncomfortable in his clothes, in his skin. Jake had never seen him like that before.

Donnelly said, 'He tells me what to do.'

'And you do it?'

'If I don't, it's always worse.'

Jake remembered the story again, that after he'd spent a year in the home, Kevin's social worker had suggested it might be time for him to leave. Gary Halliday had said, no, the kid wasn't ready, another few months and maybe . . . but not yet. And that was that. What would something like that do a fourteen-year-old kid? Another story: every time Kevin ran away he got another few months added on to his total. Forget everything else, just that one thing alone would convince

Donnelly he had no choice but to go on and on doing whatever Halliday told him.

Johnny's voice was clear and firm, even pompous. Again, Jake had never heard him sound like that. 'You don't live there now. You live here. You're seventeen, you make your own money, you do what you want.'

Kevin was twisting on the carpet in front of them. 'He tells me what to do, I try and do it if I can.'

'No. No. No.' Johnny's voice was getting even slower, even louder; like he was explaining the obvious to an idiot. 'This fat, bald cunt comes crawling up to you and you do what he says? No. Listen to me, the next time you kick him in the fucking bollocks. You put a glass through his face. Do you understand?'

Kevin was shaking his head. 'He's not fat and bald. That's Mr Ford, not Gary.'

'Who?'

'Mr Ford, the man in charge of Drake Block. Gary's the housemaster for Raleigh.'

Johnny still didn't get it, he'd seen the guy on the video.

Donnelly was still saying, 'Gary's not fat and bald. Is he?'

Jake realized the boy was staring straight at him. He shook his head. 'No. The guy's youngish. He's got hair.'

Johnny was saying again, 'So who's Ford?'

Kevin explained in a breaking mumble, there were four housemasters: for Drake, Raleigh, Nelson and Scott.

'All four of them are kiddie-fuckers?'

Donnelly nodded, 'Four of them at Colchester Hall. Sometimes they took us to parties at other homes.'

Johnny's voice had lost its pompous edge; he was beginning to understand this thing was too complex. He couldn't go out and bottle one man – castrate the problem in one easy step. But he couldn't believe the truth either.

'Why's no one done anything? You can't keep this thing secret when there's so many of them.'

Johnny was forgetting he knew it about it, too. Long before today. Or at least he'd heard the rumours. The difference now was that he'd seen a video of a fat bald man whaling on a crying kid. It had got too graphic. He wanted to know why had no one gone to the police?

Donnelly said, 'I think the police know.'

'Why?'

'They have to. They send us there, they take us back there. I know some kids have told them. They either know about it and don't give a fuck, or they don't believe it.'

Johnny was waving a video. 'You got the fucking proof here. You *make* them believe.'

Donnelly was fast shrinking into his clothes, disappearing from the head and feet, as though he was being sucked down into the most abused part of himself. He didn't care about proof; he didn't want to know what Johnny had seen on the video tape.

Johnny flung the tape down. 'The Manchester police hate gays. How can they let this stuff go on, and still go out raiding the Village every other night?'

Johnny couldn't let it go. Two hours later, he was

still ripping at the blind stupidity. No one had an answer.

'The hypocritical fucking bastards.'

It was just Jake and Johnny now, walking across the stretch of dirt, grass and diesel tarmac, back towards Junk's flat at the other side of Hulme.

Jake had one suggestion, the only thing he could think of. 'The police can't see it. What's happening at Colchester Hall, it's like a blind spot.'

'Fuck that. It's happening right under their noses.'

'No. It's happening behind their backs. What they've got under their noses are places like Moss Side, Whalley Range or the Village. They think they're fighting a war against evil, so they aren't going to start looking into the remand homes and stuff, start questioning the places that help them do their job.'

Where they were walking, beside the five-a-side pitches, the fence was half ripped down and the concrete uprights stolen. They were probably taken in the riots earlier that year and used as battering rams. Across Moss Side and Hulme, walls had been reduced to rubble as they were pulled apart, brick by brick, and used as ammunition. There were scorch marks on the road where cars had been set alight and barricades built. One night it was like a replay of *Fort Apache – The Bronx*: TV cameras out in force as a mob swarmed on Moss Side police station and threatened to burn it to the ground. *That* was a war. The police believed it and so did everyone else, whichever side they were on.

179

'Anderton knows everyone hates him. The City Council's full of Trots, the student union's campaigning against police brutality, half the city's had riots. He's locked in a siege, so why's he going to go after people like Halliday?'

'It's not a fucking siege. It's a game,' said Johnny. 'It's got to be in the police's favour to play up the risks of Black Trotsky Race Rioters just so they can scare ordinary decent twats into supporting them.'

'Raiding the Village every night? That's war. After Moss Side they treat the Village as a second front.'

Johnny didn't believe it. 'Bollocks. People like Pascal don't hate the Village. It's just an easy target.' The way Johnny saw it, the police force was a home for pragmatists and hypocrites. An institute for the dumb with just enough political savvy not to show how stupid they were.

But Johnny had it wrong, Jake was sure. If they were talking about the essence of the police, about its core and about its values . . . he had to understand there were real principles at stake. Maybe the police in general, the foot-sloggers, were hazy, shady chancers. But Anderton and Pascal were zealots. The way their world worked, it was good versus evil. He wasn't saying they were geniuses but they had an unswerving plan: bad out there, good in here. He tried to get it through to Johnny, but Johnny hadn't had his say.

'Fuck that, Jake. If they got any deep reason to focus on the Village, it's because they enjoy prowling us so much they assume everyone else is on the sniff. They think we're infectious and want to make sure the contagion doesn't spread. Because they think it's what the world wants, to give in to people like us.'

Maybe Johnny had something after all. Jake could see Anderton or Pascal falling for that: the idea that temptation is the one earthly power that's all but unanswerable and always irresistible without spiritual grace. It was the one point where their faith could cross with his and Johnny's one unshakable belief: the conviction that everyone in the world wanted to shag them.

'People like us,' Jake said. 'So what about people like Gary Halliday?'

'Evil fucking bastard.'

'What do you think he looks like? He's got horns? He's swinging a fucking tail? The man's young, he's smart and he's fit . . .'

Before Jake finished Johnny was ready to spit. 'He's *fit*!'

His mouth turned into a snarl. It wasn't what Jake meant – not fit as in fit between the sheets. Jake could feel it all going wrong, whatever he was trying to say.

'I meant he doesn't look like us. He's not some raving faggot. He's not a punk, rentboy, speed freak. He's plausible. If it was him against Kevin Donnelly, you wouldn't take Donnelly's word. No one would. And if you were Donnelly, you'd know you don't stand a chance against Halliday.'

'I'm not Donnelly.'

'You'd rip out his balls?'

'I'd watch him fucking eat them.'

'Yeah, well, you're not Donnelly. You've not been through what he has. He isn't normal any more. He probably doesn't believe he was ever normal. The way he thinks, if he was, Halliday would never have singled him out in the first place.'

'It doesn't mean he has to go out of his way to help the bastard. Ask me to copy the man's horrible fucking tapes.'

Jake thought, *He didn't ask you. He asked me.*

What he said was, 'You can't blame Kevin. He thinks it's what he deserves. Look at him, the hardest-working rentboy in Manchester. You think he's ever stopped to wonder if that's where he really wants to be? He doesn't know anything else.'

'So he wants to get back with the guy who kept him locked in a room for a year as his personal fucking pet sex toy? That's his fucking destiny?'

Jake didn't know exactly what Kevin Donnelly thought. What Jake was doing was just pushing on in the same old direction. It's what everyone was doing, pushing on, and the only thing that matters is how you do it. Whether you drag the crap of the past behind you like a cripple, or you shrug the pain away and outrun it. Go out first, in a desperate blaze.

CHAPTER *FIFTEEN*

Jake woke. He had a shrieking headache. The shrieking turned out to be his bedside telephone, but when he picked it up there was no one on the other end, just a disconnected buzz. He lay there, the piece to his ear, for a full minute before he realized it was the wake-up call he never asked for. He reached under the bed for his glasses and his watch; it was eight-fifteen.

Another twenty seconds later, a full English breakfast arrived at his door. Jake knew for sure this was none of his doing. The state he rolled in, last night, he couldn't have planned anything like this. While he was sipping his coffee, the phone-call came from DI Green. The man was ready to confess, he thought maybe Jake needed help waking.

'You alone?'

Jake looked over to the left-hand side of his bed, then across to the twin double. 'Yeah.'

'Only, the way you were spreading yourself round the Village last night, I thought you might have picked up company.'

'No.'

'You're not exactly talkative this morning. I tell you

what, you take another half hour. I'll be waiting in the lobby.'

Jake reached the lobby at nine o'clock. The policeman was drinking a cup of tea, with three bourbon biscuits, but when he spotted Jake he dropped some coins onto the coffee table and started off at a jog, tracking Jake between the pillars of the foyer until he ran him down at the concierge's box.

'Don't forget your car.' Green nodded at the concierge, who was standing there with a grin.

Jake said, 'What?'

'Show the man your room number. He'll give you the keys for your hire car.'

The keys came in a bulky envelope. A Xerox sheet inside carried a description of the car: make, model and registration number. Jake opened it and found he had a Lexus, credited it to his hotel room. Jake nodded a brisk *thank-you*, with no show of surprise. He didn't ask why he needed a car or how Green knew his driving-licence details. He just tried to maintain the same tundra-esque profile as he had the whole of the last two days . . . at least when he knew he was being surveilled. He was surprised Green didn't persevere – maybe suggest that he'd looked a little less zipped the previous night. Jake'd been careering drunk round the Village; there was always a chance he couldn't now remember what he'd got himself into. But the man obviously wasn't in the mood for gossip –

didn't even ask what Jake learnt from Benny 'Good-Day' Silver.

The car was charcoal grey, understated, and parked outside G-Mex. It was a Lexus, as per the photostat instructions. DI Green took the passenger side and settled into the seat. The impression he seemed to be going for was that some people drove, some had got used to having drivers. Jake didn't ask Green if that really was his game-plan. He didn't even ask for directions.

They travelled maybe six miles before Jake turned to him and said, 'You're a hypocrite.'

The way it came out, as a flat, uninflected statement, it sounded hostile. Green didn't exactly spin in his seat but he shot Jake a look, trying to gauge the mood before he decided on a response.

Jake rephrased: 'I mean, what did you really think of the Village, back then?'

'As a hypocrite?'

'Yeah.'

Put like that, what could the man say? He gave the slightest pause and said: 'I thought, this shit is going to get me promoted.'

'What about those gay men in Oldham – the nurse and the teacher? We ruined their lives.'

Green shrugged. 'I know. But I ruin lots of people's lives. That's what I do for a living. Mostly I try and ruin the lives of bad people, but if I started weighing every single case, I wouldn't be able to do the job at all.'

Jake knew the man didn't mean that the paradoxes and contradictions would eventually get to him, undermine his sense of self. So why Jake even bothered asking . . .

'Fuck, no.' Green laughed out loud. 'Just, if I started into that shit, I wouldn't be letting the wankers in the Crown Prosecution Service do their job. I'm just a simple copper, me.'

The man leaned back in the seat. Like he was waiting for Jake to look over, just so he could throw him an inscrutable expression. It worked: Jake couldn't decide if the look was smug or if it was supposed to be ironic, so he turned his eyes back to the road. They were pushing up into the hills, now. Behind them, Manchester was nothing but a matt blanket, cross-hatched with designer scars. Another few miles, even the motorway would end. They'd turn off, and there'd be nothing but hills and sheep. Already the windscreen was divided along its length: one half coloured with the purple and browns of the Pennines; the rest with cold blue sky.

It all made Green fidgety, at least enough for him to quit with the laconic act. He didn't have the temperament for it anyway.

He said, 'What you were asking, what do I think of the Village now? I got to say, I think it's great. Nice and clean, good for tourists. It brings money into the city and it's a piece of piss to police. I couldn't be happier.

And if you want to know if I regret the way we used to tear it up, then *no*. It was a mad time, and it gives the place a bit of cultural heritage. Gives everyone the opportunity to say: this used to be a ghetto and now look at it; it's an urban-planning-zone theme park.'

Jake said, 'What did you think about Anderton and Pascal?'

'Yeah, well, they had a different view. I tell you one thing I remember. I was beered up once with the lads, back when I was still a DC, and some drunk bugger turned to Pascal and said, "It's a load of wank, isn't it?" Maybe those weren't his exact words, but it's the gist. Pascal cut him dead; said it's down to the police to give a moral lead to society. I don't know what the arsehole was even doing in the pub, seeing he didn't drink.'

Green shook his head, but only because he was laughing. 'There were some fucking funny ideas about policing in those days. Still, all that talk about what we were for, it got us some whacking pay increases. You know, there was a time in the eighties when a junior copper – not even twenty years old – got paid more than a teacher with ten years' experience and previously another four at university. Not that I gave a fuck. It's just weird seeing some kid in an expensive sportscar and thinking, fuck me, that arsehole's a copper.'

The motorway junction was coming up. One side of the road, they were approaching the scratchy ends of Saddleworth Moor, where Kevin Donnelly was dumped. Soon they'd be at the edge of Caldenstall

Moor where Johnny's body was found all those years ago. Green made sure he pointed out the landmarks as they passed them.

Jake just gripped the wheel, let the words fall unheard – Green's story of how they had to break open the peat with pickaxes before they could recover all of Johnny's body, the ground was frozen so hard.

Green said, 'When we get there, look at his hands.'

Jake jerked round. 'What?'

'At the prison. Take a look at Halliday's hands, see if he's guilty. It's an old police trick.'

'You think they'll be red or something?'

'Fuck, I don't know. It's never worked for me. I only just remembered it. I was standing with John Pascal at a conference once, thinking, *How the fuck do I excuse myself when he knows I'll only be going as far as the bar?* Then this old chief inspector from Devon or somewhere came up and started asking about Anderton. You could tell the old guy couldn't believe a man like that had been given the job of running the country's second biggest force. But he tried to play it subtly . . . just muttering something about the intellectual rigors of the job. Pascal gave out this smug smile, saying the Chief's not an intellectual, he doesn't have to be – just look at his hands. Pascal had some idea they were plain-dealing hands, they showed a sense of destiny. You believe that?'

Jake did. It sounded like Pascal.

'So, what about it? You going to tell me if Halliday butchered your pal Kevin Donnelly?'

'Benny Silver thinks so. He told me Halliday was

running round the Village a few days before, asking everyone he could think of if they'd seen Kevin Donnelly. He was scared Kevin had evidence against him.'

'That's what I heard, too. Though I never thought of asking old Good-Day about it. He say anything else?'

'He said he wanted to be thought of as a dirty old man.'

'That's some ambition. You'd think he'd be happy just being a millionaire.' Showing Jake he knew the rumours – Benny Silver's vast wealth.

They were off the motorway now and the road was even steeper. Around the place it flattened out, they'd be able to see the prison.

Jake said, 'Do you have any more police tips? Anything to tell me if he's guilty?'

'Ask him what proof Donnelly had.'

Jake said, 'Video tapes.' Then wished he hadn't. The look on DI Green's face, coming up as though it was news to him.

'Is that what Silver told you?'

'There were always video tapes. Johnny got a man called John Quay to copy them for Halliday.'

'Really? He got old piss-eyed Junk to do it?'

'Maybe you should be having this talk with *him*?'

Green shook his head. 'It'd be difficult. He got caught in another police action. In the confusion, some-one blew half his head away.'

'He's dead?'

'No. He's in the hospital in Prestwich. Apparently, he's running courses in video-making, though only the really hopeless cases understand what he's going on about. I doubt whether Junk could say anything that would hold up in court.'

'If you don't have the videos, what case have you got against Halliday?'

'Statements, confessions, the usual shit. I was wondering why you never told me anything, seeing you knew all about it. What sort of piss-weak excuse for a stoolie you turned out to be.'

It wasn't even funny.

CHAPTER *SIXTEEN*

Johnny nodded forwards and back in time to the music, his hands jabbering across the rim of the steering-wheel like he was a spoolful of nervous energy about to pull loose. Jake waited. It was thirty minutes now they'd been sitting in the dark of the stolen Volkswagen Golf, guessing the weight of the iron security gates. And, despite all his crackling energy, Johnny didn't seem to be in a hurry to press the buzzer and make the delivery.

Up ahead, Colchester Hall stood spot-lit at the top of the driveway, its two wings spread out like a back-drop behind it. Warm and inviting as a psychie-ward shower.

It didn't matter that Jake didn't want to be there. When Johnny asked, he agreed to go with him. If Gary Halliday tried anything, then there would need to be two of them. From the start, they were trying to fence this whole thing with caution. They stole a car rather than pay for a taxi. They didn't want to become a name on some radio-man's pick-up list, or get I-D'd as the dimly recalled drop-off of an insomniac driver. And if they needed to get away in a hurry, they didn't want the nightmare of a lonely suburban call-box while they waited for another cab.

Johnny needed driving-music so it was lucky the car got stolen before its stereo. Since Princess Parkway, they'd listened to the 999 album *Separates* on continuous play. Now they were parked, the song 'Homicide' was on another run-through, the chorus of '*homi homi homi homi*' how many times, over and over. Jake never understood why the band was so popular with skins or the sub-moronic Oi punks. Half the songs carried suspicious undertones; just read the titles: 'Feeling Alright with the Crew' or 'The Boy Can't Make It with Girls'. Above all, 'Homicide' and that chant of *homi homi homi* that wasn't about homicide but other desires, barely suppressed under the too-high voice, shot through with neuroses and desperation. The singer was no killer, except in the William Burroughs sense of a boy that looked like a sheep-killing dog. A too-punk kid.

Another two in the dark of a stolen car, nothing but their profiles showing, haloed by the loose glare of the security lights. When Johnny nodded that he was ready, the decision came like a spasm. He got out of the car and Jake watched him pass through the range of the rear-view mirror. The videos were boxed in the trunk. Jake got out of the car to give Johnny a hand.

The intercom was set into the right-hand post, one side of the gate. After Jake pressed the button, they stood waiting until a voice threaded through the grille. Jake didn't recognize it.

'Gary Halliday?'

'Who's this?'

'Kevin Donnelly's friend, from the other night.'

The gate didn't open. They stood in the freezing night air, holding a cardboard box each, and stamping their feet to keep warm. Jake only realized then, hearing the high-speed stiletto chatter, that Johnny was wearing his new slingbacks. His bare toes were curled under with cold.

Johnny said, 'Press again.'

Jake was about to – scared Johnny would die of pneumonia. Then they heard a steel wheeze, and the gates began to clockwork apart. They walked through the gap and up the hill, tracked by a halogen spotlight and the shadows of the rhododendron bushes along the driveway.

Colchester Hall was a pre-war detached house, not so very old but built to resemble something Scottish and baronial. The roof was surrounded by blunt castellations. The front door was wide enough to drive the Golf through, if no one cared about the wing-mirrors. There was another intercom on the doorframe. They buzzed and stood. There wasn't even the sound of footsteps yet to reassure them.

Johnny juggled the box of videos until he'd turned his wrist far enough to read his watch. 'You think they're all in bed?' After another few seconds, he said, 'Together . . . ?'

Jake took a step back from the stone-arched porch and looked up at the house. There were lights on the upper storey. He said, 'Donnelly said there were eight boys in every house. So that's thirty–six altogether counting the housemasters.'

'There any other staff?'

Jake shook his head. 'No. There's a cook during the day, but the cleaning and stuff are done by the boys.'

'What were those we passed: tennis courts?' Johnny pointed back to the bushes, and the wire fence that stood behind them.

Jake nodded. Two tennis courts.

Johnny said, 'Yeah, well, I fucking hate tennis.'

'Yeah?' It struck Jake as weird, to actually have an opinion on tennis. But if you ignored the high heels, tried to imagine Johnny in training shoes, he could pass as a county athelete. They both could, though Jake was built like a long-jumper, not an all-rounder like Johnny. Colchester Hall prided itself on athletics; it was one of the little nuggets they had got out of Kevin Donnelly.

'You hate tennis? What *do* you like?'

Johnny looked round, surprised at the question, then almost coy. 'Everything else. Or I did, when I was at school.'

He was talking about team sports. Jake tried to imagine him as a schoolboy striker, a prop forward, maybe a spin bowler. Jake himself was fourteen years old when he realized he could never play any team sports. Around that age, self-analysis was his main obsession, so he was amazed it had taken him so long to figure it out. He didn't have a single character attribute to be a team-player. He got a school badge for swimming and won a medal for cross-country running. There was no school karate champion but for almost five years, right to the moment he left home, he trained three nights a week at Caldenstall civic hall. That was something he hadn't mentioned to Johnny, so Jake guessed he had his own secrets too.

The door opened. Gary Halliday smiled at them through a wave of soft brown hair. 'Sorry I kept you waiting, Jake.' Then a mild frown as he turned to Johnny. 'Who's he?'

'Johnny.'

Halliday turned, looking Johnny up and down slowly and pausing at his feet and the ten dirty toes, black with dirt, bluish in the cold.

'Oh, yes,' said Halliday. 'It's Johnny's business, isn't it? I'd forgotten. Come in.'

Johnny hadn't lightened as the man became more polite but he hadn't yet spoken either. Perhaps he was worried how his voice would sound against the clear un-dialected voice of Halliday. Jake could tell Johnny was thrown, despite what he'd told him, in the car and earlier, that the man was no identikit creep. He was more than plausible: wearing a V-neck jumper and check trousers, Halliday looked like a second-league model; the guy to sell aftershave on the back of a Sunday newspaper. There was even a hint of cologne as he nodded his head and turned. They followed three steps behind, to the right of an ornate staircase and down a corridor towards a warm and brightly lit kitchen. Halliday waved a hand at the chairs pushed under the heavy kitchen table.

'Have a seat.'

Looking at him there, with his casual gesture and only slightly informal clothes, Jake realized they'd been kept waiting so long because Halliday needed the time to dress. The man carried a sense of being comfortable. He underlined it constantly to keep them unbalanced. They were seeing him at home, in his own kitchen: how did they expect him to look?

Johnny let his box of tapes drop to the table with a sullen clunk. Gary Halliday grinned and pulled the box over. Inside, the tapes were sleeveless and black, stacked together.

Halliday glanced across the upturned spines, the arrow of a frown brushing the top of his nose. He waved for Jake to slide his box over, and looked at them, too. 'Where are the labels?'

Johnny was still standing. He said, 'You've given them titles?'

'They were numbered.' There was a pause before he said, 'I'll just have to watch them all before I give them to my colleagues.' The way he broke open a smile, he let them know he wasn't complaining about this extra work.

Johnny had to look away. He still hadn't taken a seat and, when he started talking, his eyes were always somewhere else: on the floor tiles, the kitchen range, the dog basket tucked behind the kitchen door.

'How long you been here?'

'Must be . . .' Halliday's eye flickered over a calculation '. . . just coming up to three years. After university I did a year's voluntary work overseas, and then came here.'

He had international experience in what he did.

Maybe that's what gave him his confidence. Jake dropped to a chair and kept his head down, too ... apart from a swift look at Johnny as the boy finally decided that he needed a seat.

Halliday was moving around the kitchen. He lifted a hob cover on the kitchen range and reached for a kettle to stand on top of it. In the silence, Jake heard the whirring rattle of a washing-machine on spin-cycle and, after a second or so, another one. There was a whole Laundromat of soiled clothes, working away in a room somewhere behind him. Everything about the house was clean and efficient, free of evidence. Apart from the tapes.

The kettle boiled inside a minute, it had been waiting primed on a cooler ring. Halliday poured out three mugs and slopped the bags into the sink. Before he handed them over, he took a bunch of keys from his pocket, selected one, and opened a padlocked cupboard above the work surface. Inside were two bottles of whisky and one of gin.

'Anyone care for a drop in their tea?'

Jake waited for Johnny to say something. When he said, 'Alright,' Jake just nodded.

Johnny was chewing at the inside of his mouth. Finally, he said: 'So who's the boss here – you?'

'Not officially, but I always seem to get my way. It's the fuhrer principle.'

'The Nazis?'

Halliday shook his head; the arrow frown made a short reappearance. 'Just a figure of speech, Johnny.

197

The theory that leaders emerge naturally, when the times call for it. The other masters here, they're that little bit older, a little more timid.'

'You turned them on to this?' Johnny nudged a hand towards the box of videos.

Halliday laughed. 'Christ, no. The bastards had been at it for years. During my first month here, I used to hear them shuffling about the corridors at night, trying to avoid each other. It would start soon after midnight. They'd hiss at the boy they'd had their eye on, and lead him back to their room. Then, around six in the morning, you would hear the alarm clocks begin ringing and it would happen all over again in reverse.'

'You brought them out into the open?'

The laugh again. 'Something like that. I mean, I took this job because it appealed to my sensibilities, but I was never exactly open about it, not even to myself. It was only when I realized the others shared my tastes, I was able to validate myself and take responsibility.' He flashed the whisky bottle again. 'A little more?'

They shook their heads. Halliday just shrugged.

'I think the situation here is remarkably free now. We each have our favourites, what you might call stable relationships, but that needn't imply exclusivity. We're pretty open in that sense. All of us, the boys and the men, are prepared to share. But I suppose you know that?' He tapped the top of a video. 'You've probably seen one of our parties.'

Halliday stood his mug down, empty on the table. As he rubbed his hands, he said, 'So, what do I owe you?'

'One-sixty.'

'Okay, then. You'll have to come along. I don't have the money on me, and you'll understand that I can't leave you here on your own.'

'Because of what we'll see?'

Another laugh. 'Christ, no. Because this is a secure care home. The government has rules, you know.'

They followed him back out of the kitchen to the front staircase. His room was on the first floor, left along a corridor. As they walked, Halliday continued to talk. His voice wasn't exactly soft but it was unforced.

'Since I arrived, I've encouraged the feeling that we share something unique. And as long as everyone understands that sharing means we're mutually implicated, we can foster a deeper sense of security. The parties and videos help ensure security.'

He had the key-chain in his hand again, a bright new silver deadlock for his own door. The room wasn't large but there was enough space for a bookshelf, a desk and two beds. Halliday's bed was the larger, wide enough for the steel cot to run across its foot.

The cot was made up with a few grey blankets. The boy lying under them didn't move and didn't open his eyes. Maybe he was asleep. Johnny gave the boy only a quick glance, as though he was cross-checking, seeing if anyone was filling Kevin Donnelly's old place. The scene was just as Donnelly described it; they didn't need to look twice. Johnny walked to the window at the far side of the room and fixed his eyes on the grounds outside. Jake followed.

They were up above the tennis courts now, looking

across to the one-storey changing-room block at the far side of the grounds. The building there was a pre-fab painted a dumb white that held out against the dark.

Halliday slid behind them. 'Do you want to take a look over at the clubhouse?' He pointed to the pre-fab building. 'I'm sure I could get a party together tonight.'

They jolted round. Halliday continued giving them that same, even smile. Now he was fingering a roll of twenty-pound notes, twisting them into a tight tube before passing them to Johnny. 'How about it?'

Johnny didn't say anything. Halliday turned to Jake. 'How about it, Jake? Anything you want to do? I could wake up William for you.'

Jake shook his head, but Halliday wasn't through. 'Come on, I know you could wear out two or three of them. William for starters, perhaps. I know I've been neglecting him recently.'

Johnny started towards the door. Halliday turned aside to let him brush past.

'Just an offer – no strings attached.'

As Jake followed Johnny into the corridor, Halliday added, 'And it stays open.'

Johnny didn't look back. Jake did.

He saw a hand go out to William, and heard Halliday saying, in that same voice, 'Come on, Billy boy. Let's show these two men out.'

As they walked down the stairs and to the front door, the two sets of footsteps followed them. Halliday's confident footfall, the scampering of a barefoot boy alongside him. Johnny opened the inner door but, once in the vestibule, they had to stop and wait for

Halliday to unlock the main door. The jangling of the keychain made them turn. Halliday was there with his smile, standing tall, his hand in the hand of a thin, young-faced boy of fourteen. The boy was wearing a pair of Speedo swimming trunks and nothing else, his ribbed chest shivering in the tiled coldness of the vestibule.

'Do you want William to walk you to the car?'

Now the outer door was open, the fierce winter cold raged through full-blast. Johnny was muttering, 'Fucking hell,' striding, head hunched into his shoulders, as fast down the driveway as he could without slipping in his high heels. Jake skipped out to catch him. At the bottom of the drive, the gates began to haul open.

CHAPTER *SEVENTEEN*

Standing outside the prison gates in the handy car-parking area, Jake was struck by the mean use of space. The prison was so isolated up here, the grounds could have rolled out as far as the horizon. Yet the distance from the prison wall to the perimeter fence was barely thirty feet. There didn't seem to be any reason for this. At least, Jake couldn't see one but, like DI Green said, he was no penological expert. Ha ha ha!

The teenage guard inside the Portakabin gatehouse looked down his clipboard list. 'See Gary Halliday?'

Jake nodded.

'Okay . . . Mr Powell.' The guard dipped slightly, maybe to pull a lever or twist a dial. The gate swung open. 'They'll ask for your name again at the main door.'

Jake nodded. He wasn't likely to forget his name between here and there. He gave a salute to DI Green, sat waiting in the hire car. The man's last piece of advice: 'Don't get detained.'

The prison was a new-built block for remand prisoners, owned and operated by a private security firm. They couldn't have chosen a better place. On the only road up to the prison, Jake had asked what the building used to be. Green thought, a farm. If that was true, there was nothing left of the older building. Jake tried to think if he ever knew what had originally stood there, but gave the job up. He was born over the crest of the hills to the east, and had rarely walked this way. Even if he had, he wouldn't have recognized it from this side. All moorland looked the same until you found a definite viewpoint.

The same brown-suited guard that took his name at the main door led Jake to the visitors' room. Climbing the staircase that only non-prisoners could use, Jake slowed to take another look over the moors: the unflattened stretch of a Pennine dip, green and purple as a bruise except where the peat broke through the overripe grass. Those wounds gaped like black mouths. He lifted his eyes to the mid-horizon where the sky caved down to touch the earth. The sky as white as a bleached-out filmscape, the ground as heavy as lead.

'Mr Powell.'

The guard was looking down at him, lagging on the staircase. Jake nodded and took the last flight, three steps at a go.

'Through there, Mr Powell.'

Another guard was waiting at the door to the visitors' room. Jake found himself a seat while the two guards nodded soundly at each other, doing the dance of transferred responsibility.

The new guard said, 'The beast is being fed. He'll be five minutes.'

Jake okayed. He beat his fingers softly on the melamine table-top and waited. His chair was a plastic bucket-seat like a school chair. Before it got too uncomfortable, the guard brought out a prisoner. Jake wondered: is this him? The man was narrow-shouldered and wide-hipped, carrying a pot belly that swelled out of the hollow of his chest. The hair was mostly gone, too. Jake looked him over. In the twenty seconds it took for the man to shuffle round the room and take his seat, Jake decided he recognized him. It *was* Halliday, only the man had lost his build somewhere along the line.

Jake drew a packet of Rothmans out of his inside pocket and said, 'I guess you've taken up smoking?'

The cigarettes were Green's idea, though Jake didn't mention that. He held the pack open, one cigarette standing proud. It was there, ready for plucking if Halliday wanted it . . . a chance to develop a fresh bad habit to replace the ones he now had to do without.

Halliday looked at the pack but didn't touch. He said, 'Jake Powell?'

'You remember me?'

Halliday nodded. 'You look good.'

'You look like shit. What is it: someone found the portrait in your attic?'

Halliday snorted, making a sound that was close to being a laugh. 'Well, no one's found yours yet, have they?'

Maybe he thought the ice was broken. Whatever, he took the cigarette, gripping it between slick, ticcy fingers.

Green had tried to ensure that when Jake went in, he was fully primed. At least he had a disposable lighter to go with the Rothmans. Jake used it to light Halliday's cigarette. Halliday nodded a thanks.

With his long first suck, he dragged the smoke to where it could do the most damage, and held it there. With his lips sealed tight and thin, he held the cigarette out vertically in front of his eyes and fixed his concentration on its burning tip. With a slow-burning will-power, he finally kept his hands from shaking. A practical lesson, if Jake wanted it, in smoking for pleasure when smoking's the only pleasure left.

As he exhaled, Halliday thanked Jake again, adding, 'You know, I'm only on remand. The currency's still cash money – I'm not bargaining with cigarettes yet.'

'Yeah? Though I imagine you have problems getting to a bank.'

'Well, that's true.' Halliday spread his hands. 'One of the problems of being a bachelor. So, Jake, why are you here?'

Jake didn't answer, his eyes drifting to the bluey wisp snaking off the cigarette. A little nicotine Caspar ghost out playing between them.

Until he said, 'How long will you get?'

Halliday shrugged. 'Who knows? Maybe they won't even find me guilty.'

'What's that – clutching at straws?'

He shrugged again. 'Maybe. But my lawyer's experiencing some police obstruction. If it goes on, it might work towards a retrial – who knows? My fingers are crossed.' Then, again: 'Why are you here?'

'You approved me.'

'I'm desperate for visitors. But why you? I haven't seen you for fifteen years.'

'I'm surprised you remember me. We only met twice.'

'Yes, but that first time, it was such a memorable night. I replayed the moment over and over again.' Halliday's smile came with a flash of teeth and a glimpse of coyly bitten tongue.

Jake blinked slowly but kept his breathing even. He was determined to show nothing that could be inter- preted as a flinch. He said, 'It was memorable, yeah. But what came later, I remember that better.'

Halliday nodded. 'The night you came back with your friend Johnny?'

'The night he was murdered.'

'Is that right? It was the very same night? You know, all I can see from my window here are the fucking moors. It almost makes me glad I'm inside, rather than out there – among the elements.'

'Johnny didn't notice them. He was dead before he reached the moors.'

'Was he?'

Jake held Halliday's eyes until he forced the man down, made him flicker and look away. Jake almost welcomed it, this confirmation that he wasn't a boy any more. What he didn't know was whether it meant he was an adult now or just that he'd lost the ability to react like a normal human being.

He said, 'The police want to pin Johnny's murder on you.'

Halliday flinched back up, like he'd had a battery

shock to his spine. His mouth open, 'No. How?' Then pulling himself together, 'They aren't serious?'

Jake sat back, giving Halliday just long enough to run through the idea one more time. He could almost see it doubling back across the man's skull; there wasn't enough hair to hide the flickers and pulses beneath his scalp.

Finally, Halliday said, 'Is that what they're working on? What they're not letting my lawyer know?'

'What is this?' Jake held out his hands, an open question. 'If you're practising a courtroom number, go ahead. But I don't get why you should be surprised.'

'That I killed your friend?'

'What? You think, because it was a few years back, they don't go through their records? They're computerized now; it doesn't take them for ever to put cases together.'

'Why would they drag up him?'

'Because it was you who killed Kevin Donnelly?'

The surprise sent the man's arm scurrying in a spasm across the table. Even when it came to rest, it still trembled slightly. The other hand was fingering at the lapel of his prison jacket.

'I didn't kill Kevin Donnelly.'

'The fuck you didn't. You know how many people can testify against you? The only thing they're missing is an eyewitness account of you stabbing him . . . though maybe that's something else you kept on video.'

'Christ almighty. This is the biggest . . . the most . . .'

Two things Jake hadn't seen in a long while: someone trembling in fear, someone lost for words.

Jake said, 'Talk to me.'

'What can I say? Have the police been to talk to you?'

Jake nodded. 'About Johnny? Yeah, they have. I admitted I'd met you, but I told them it was fifteen years ago. They'd better speak to someone else. It turned out they already had: like Lady Good-Day.'

'Benny? What could he say?'

'Fuck this roundabout, Gary. You know what he said. Talk to me.'

'He told them I was looking for Kevin?' Halliday stopped shaking; he had a thread now, he could see the way things were spinning, he could hope to pull it apart. 'I was running around looking for Kevin. I never caught him.'

Jake felt the frown tighten his scalp, his ears tingle coldly. 'You didn't catch him? What's that supposed to mean? If this is your defence, you'd better forget it. It's not going to play.'

'It's true. I never caught him. Even if I had, you think I could have killed him? I just wanted the videos he'd stolen off me. I'm not a murderer.'

'If he had your videos, then you had to kill him.'

'Maybe. Maybe. I don't know.' Shaking his head. 'This was Kevin Donnelly. I know I wouldn't have had to kill him.'

'Donnelly wasn't a kid any more. We're talking about a thirty-two-year old man. He'd had half his life to think it over; he wasn't going to be persuaded by you. I mean, take a fucking look at yourself. Touch earth.'

Halliday was sitting there saying, 'No, no. I wouldn't have had to kill him.'

'Of course you fucking would. The videos are the only evidence. You had to kill Donnelly. Just like I had to kill Johnny.'

Jake's voice flattened until it was nothing but uninflected desperation. And it broke open the scene they were playing. Halliday's arms slipped off the shiny table top: there was nothing to hold them there.

'*You* did it.' Halliday, in a whisper. It wasn't even a question.

'You know I did.' As Jake said it, he saw Johnny's body again, screwed around on the floor, the head twisted backwards around a broken neck.

'The night we left you, he was all for going straight to the cops. He gave you copies of your video, he made another set for them. When they raided you, they'd have matching documentary evidence. Party night at Colchester Hall, starring the masters and boys . . . and me.'

'Johnny made copies for himself?'

'He had them with him, you arsehole. That same night, they were in the boot of the car.'

'Where did you . . . where did it happen?'

'Where did he meet his end?' Jake pointed to the grilled window. It happened out there. Halliday followed with his eyes, looking across Caldenstall Moor to the far hills.

'You couldn't . . . persuade him? Make him reconsider, for *your* sake?'

'He never saw more than a few seconds of the tapes,

209

so he never knew about my role.' Jake shook his head, trying to lose the tinny buzz that was racing between his ears. 'But there was nothing I could say. Not that night – not the state he was in. And I know for a fact you wouldn't have had a hope with Kevin Donnelly.'

Jake reached forward, his voice at a hiss. 'So tell me, you cunt, what happened?'

Halliday's story started out slow. Five cigarettes burnt to his lips, and he only got to the beginning point. One month ago, Colchester Hall was burgled. Nothing was stolen except the videos.

'I kept them in boxes under the floor of the boiler-room. They were the only copies. I didn't let the other masters have their own copies any more. The thief tried to make it look like a real robbery: everything was broken up and smashed. But I was sure one of my boys had something to do with it, and I finally got it out of the little bastard. Kevin Donnelly had got hold of him and persuaded him to make a stand.'

Jake thought: fifteen years of abuse, all on tape. Kevin Donnelly must have watched it through, pushing on rewind until he was primed and insane.

'So you went looking for Kevin?'

'I tried. I went to everyone I could think of who might know him. One of his sisters told me he was living between Crumpsall and Cheetham Hill, subletting a room in a council flat. The place was disgusting: nothing in his room but a blanket on the floor, a TV and a video-player. But when I got there, he was already gone, the TV was kicked through and the video had been stamped to pieces. I found some of the tapes there, or what I assumed were the tapes. He'd pulled them open and strung the insides across the room like Christmas decorations. I knew there were more. He'd stolen so many, he could have decorated the whole shitty block. That's when I started going to Good-Day's again, every night for more than a week. I heard rumours that Donnelly was bumming round London, but I waited. I don't know why but I was sure he was coming back. Then I got lucky. He phoned ahead for somewhere to stay and I got the news off one of his friends. I was there to see him get off the train at Piccadilly. I only had to wait for eight hours before I got the right train. He was carrying a bag, nothing else. I knew it wasn't large enough, so I followed him. He walked to the lockers, I circled round. I guess I was too confident. When he opened the locker, I saw the stacks of tapes inside and called out his name.'

Jake could just imagine the way he said it: the master's voice.

'He went for me. I was so stunned, I didn't have a chance. I thought he'd broken my nose, there was so much blood. Even when I was on the floor, he was still hammering me. He cut my face open ...' Halliday touched a pinkish scar that ran across his eyebrow; it didn't look so bad. 'He did that with the edge of one of the bloody videos.'

'He got away?'

Halliday nodded. 'I think it was a passer-by ... someone pulled him off me. But before I could get to my feet, he'd run. I was surrounded by a crowd, all of them asking if I was all right. I couldn't see Donnelly anywhere.'

'He still had the tapes?'

'Most of them. I managed to get outside the station. The traffic was backed up as usual and as I ran down the hill, I kept looking in the taxis. I finally saw him as I reached the traffic lights; he was still on foot. I wouldn't even have seen him then but he was nearly hit by a truck coming round the corner from Great Ancoats Street. I guessed he was heading for one of the car-parks. I was lucky there, as well, I suppose. I got a taxi, then all I had to do was wait. The one-way system brought him swinging in front of me, driving this old yellow Capri.'

'Where'd he go?'

'Here.' Halliday tapped the prison table. 'Well, almost. I actually lost him in Littleborough.'

Halliday pointed over his shoulder, back in the direction of Manchester where Littleborough village lay, pressed hard to the Yorkshire border. 'I told the cabbie to keep circling. Eventually, I saw his car again, parked in the central car-park close to the bus terminal. I paid off the taxi and I waited for him to come back.'

'You got him?'

'No. That was it. I just waited, across the road, watching from a pub. He never came back. After it got dark, I went out and broke into his car, hoping he'd left the videos there. I didn't find them.'

'That's it?'

Halliday nodded. He was telling the truth.

'So you lost him?'

'I don't know what happened. Maybe he got a taxi or a bus somewhere.'

'Or stole a new car?'

'I suppose so. He knew how to do that, didn't he?'

'You were the one with access to his records. But, yeah, I'm sure he knew how to steal a car.'

'You know I didn't kill him?'

Jake nodded. 'You blew it, though. You're just lucky the tapes never turned up.'

He signalled to the guard. Halliday remained sitting there, staring out of the window. Pinning everything on the appeal, a second trial, and no evidence.

CHAPTER*EIGHTEEN*

Even driving after midnight, it took Jake and Johnny more than an hour to reach Littleborough – one side of Greater Manchester to the other. The rain fouling up the route didn't help. Then Johnny took a wrong turn and took them into a jigsaw detour around the outskirts of the city, finally clicking on the right road past Hollins. Johnny was slamming on the clutch and the wheel, driving the car like it was a tug in an Atlantic spray.

But it wasn't just the weather. Johnny couldn't get over the boy in the Speedo trunks, shivering in the doorway of Colchester Hall. As long as he carried the image, he couldn't concentrate on Jake's directions. Jake suggested they switch seats at the next petrol station; let him take the wheel for the last eight miles. There were spectre swirls of sleet mixed into the rain, and Jake knew the weather would only get worse as they climbed Caldenstall Moor.

Johnny said, 'What's with this fucking weather?'

The heater was running full-blast and Johnny was still shivering. The sleet had begun to stick to the windscreen, making sugary patterns to snare the wipers. Instead of a smooth arc, they were wiping at a slow bump and grind. As Johnny pulled onto the garage forecourt, Jake asked if he'd seen any de-icer, maybe in the boot? Johnny couldn't remember.

Jake said, 'I'll get some. You stay there.'

The garage sold more than just car accoutrements. Jake took a look around, found a gift rack of sock-slippers and bought a pair for Johnny. The boy was still barefoot in slingbacks. The next leg of the journey took them up into the hills, but Johnny missed out on the scenery because it took him twenty minutes to strap his shoes over the top of the socks. Not that there was anything to see; visibility was lower than zero. Jake cleared a porthole in the windscreen, about the size of a football. When that frosted over, he just drove even slower. It was too late and too cold, they weren't likely to meet much head-on traffic. The whole journey was nothing but a mad, blind steer.

Jake said, 'This is fucked.'

'Not doing anything – that would be fucked.' Johnny had his plan; they were going to see it through. He was sure the Manchester police didn't care what went on, just so long as they were seen to be policing. If it was a straight choice between the hypocrites who enforced the anti-queer line and the man who directed operations, they were better off with Pascal: the inflexible zealot.

Jake said, 'We really going to hand the tapes over to John Pascal?'

Johnny nodded. 'You convinced me the guy's for real. And if he hates puffs so much, he's not going to be able to ignore the evidence.'

They approached Caldenstall on a ridge road, slipping around the skirts of the moor. One side, there was a cliff of millstone grit. Below them, a valley so full of fog it had lost its depths. The headlights were doing nothing but throwing a white haze into their path; anything that appeared out of it, loomed in a soluble grey block that never recovered its definition. They weren't going any faster than zimmer-pace, Jake only wanted to catch sight of the fork, and the road that led up into the hills. When he reached it, it was easy to spot. Staggered either side of the road, snow-signs flashed out of the night.

Jake turned to Johnny and said, 'The road's closed.'

'What's that mean? There's a gate closing it?'

It didn't mean that. It meant the road might become impassable, the higher they climbed. It certainly would be by morning. He left the decision to Johnny.

'You're saying, we drive on and we might never get the car back down, or we walk through this?'

Johnny pawed at the windscreen, trying to gauge the weather conditions. It didn't require guesswork. The car was rocking in the wind. Johnny was wearing a sleeveless T-shirt under his frockcoat but at least he had a coat. Jake was wearing nothing but a suit and shirt.

Jake said, 'If we manage to drive up there, we're definitely going to have to walk back. And then we don't have a car.'

There wasn't any choice, in fact. Jake did the best he could, turning the car at the fork and reversing as far as he could up the hill of Caldenstall Road. Looking backwards, the hill seemed twice as steep. As they inched upwards, they seemed to be hanging nose-down into the white pit in front of them. The car finally stalled.

'Okay.'

They climbed out of the car into a wall of blistering cold. Jake turned up the lapels of his suit and held his hands to his throat. Johnny fetched the box of videos from the boot and joined him.

'How far?'

'Only quarter of a mile.'

It would seem further, walking on near-ice up a one-in-twelve hill. Jake in gripless Cuban heels, unable to rip his hands from his throat and use them for balance. Johnny in his slingbacks. Three steps, Johnny slipped on the road and began skidding on his back, the box of tapes smashed open and his feet in the air. At least he had the socks now.

Johnny didn't want to be told, again, he'd made a bad shoe choice. 'I didn't know about no fucking mountains.'

Jake bent to help him collect the videos. The box was torn, soggy and useless, but there were only four tapes. They took two each, forcing them into their pockets, and started climbing again.

Jake knew they were at the edge of the village when he caught sight of the Jericho Chapel, a squat sentry pillbox buried into the hillside to guard the only road in and out of town.

As the hill flattened and widened into the village, the snow got deeper. Now they were wrapped to their shins, paying for every step. But they were close. Jake knew all the Chapel Elders' houses. John Pascal lived past the row of shops in a terrace of black stone cottages. A bare mile past his house, the road would turn back into a packhorse track, over the moors to Haworth and beyond into Halifax.

Jake stopped. 'What now?'

'This is it?'

Jake pointed to the second house in the short terrace, a Cavalier choking in snow outside. 'That one. And he's inside. This is his car.'

The door was child-size but studded with heavy metal nails. It looked as strong as the stone lintel stuck across it. The windows on either side and on the two upper floors were tall and narrow, all diamond-crossed with lead.

Johnny said, 'What kind of fucked-up doll's house is this?'

It was a weaver's cottage: an odd, squashed building of three floors fitted into the height of two. Johnny was peering over the low wall, getting a scan inside while he worked on his plan.

'You any idea which floor he sleeps on?'

Jake thought probably the top floor. That contained one large room and had the best light. It was the room where the old weavers worked on their frames. He pointed Johnny towards the row of windows under the eaves, and asked, 'What are you going to do?'

The door had a narrow letterbox hacked out of its centre, maybe wide enough to post a tape, but it didn't play any part in Johnny's plan. The boy stepped over the wall and pushed his face to the leaded window and said, 'Guy's got a video-player, I can see it winking.'

What Johnny wanted to do was set the tape running in the machine so it would be the first thing Pascal saw when he came down to breakfast. See if the man's appetite ever recovered after that.

'We can't just leave the tapes with a note?'

Johnny shook his head. 'We got to rub the bastard's face in it.' He was a step away from the window, looking to the door and then up at the side of the house. 'What about the back – you reckon that's safest?'

Jake nodded grimly. He knew, anyone who could afford it always built a kitchen extension on these kind of houses. Pascal had built one years ago. It would be a lot easier to break in at the back rather than through the two-hundred-year-old fortress door at the front. Jake hitched his jacket tighter to his neck and led the way round the last house of the terrace, to where the backyards of the cottages formed a last line of defence against the moorland. The wall to Pascal's yard was high, the height of the outdoor lavvy. Johnny leapt up to grab a handhold on the lavvy roof, his slingbacks scrabbling at the wall. Jake reached up, pulled him at the shoulder and brought him down.

Johnny started. 'The fuck's the matter with you?'

'If we wake him, Pascal's going to recognize me.'

Johnny stamped his feet on the ground, looking round while he rubbed at his forearms. Getting some friction heat for his thoughts. 'That's right.' But if Pascal put up a fight, there'd need to be two of them. 'It's up to you. What about you keep right to the back? If the guy wakes, he'll only see me. If he starts anything, you hit him with something?'

It wasn't a plan, but Johnny was over the roof now. The snow at the other side muffled his drop into the yard. Jake followed. He was set to jump down, when Johnny stopped him.

'He's not got a dog?' Johnny was pointing to the plastic hood of a dog-sized trap fitted into the door.

Jake shrugged. 'He didn't have – but I don't know. I've not been round this way for nearly a year.'

They stood there: Johnny in the yard, squinting at the house; Jake looking down the back path where their footprints slurred through the snow, ended at the lavvy wall, and began again across its roof. Two pairs: Cuban heels and slingbacks. The snow carried its own light. Up on top of the outhouse, it was like Jake was caught on a stage, lit up for anyone to see.

He turned back to Johnny. The footprints didn't matter, what was behind them was over with.

He dropped into the yard, close to Johnny, and said: 'If they had a dog, it'd be barking by now. But give me your knife. If there is one, I'll kill it.'

'You'll kill it?'

Jake pointed to the trap. 'The size of that, we're not talking about a Doberman. It'll be a terrier, and not even a Yorkie. That would definitely be barking.'

Johnny reached inside his coat, pulling out a screwdriver and a scout knife. 'Alright, country boy!'

Jake took the knife and balanced it on his palm. It wasn't what he'd wanted at the beginning, to be actually *equipped*. But if he was supposed to watch Johnny's back, then it was better like this.

Johnny was looking over the kitchen windows for

somewhere to use his screwdriver, but this was a policeman's house with locks on every handle. It was Jake who suggested climbing to the extension roof and going straight through the old windows on the first storey.

'What difference will it make?'

'Leaded windows – you can pull them apart without making much sound. Also, we get up and have a look, we'll know for sure what room he isn't sleeping in.'

Standing on the flat roof of the extension, the window was at chest height. Johnny forced the blade of his screwdriver under the lead surround to one of the diamond lights and started working it back and forth. His fingers were raw cold, but pretty soon the lead began to slip free and the window started to buckle.

As Johnny pulled a piece of glass free he said, 'How do you kill a dog?'

'Same way as a sheep?'

'How do you kill a sheep?'

'You run it over with a car, but I'm hoping I'll think of another way.'

Johnny ripped away at the window, peeling it back until he had a space like an imploded hole, big enough for him to slip through. Jake put the knife in the inside pocket of his jacket and followed on behind, head-first through the hole, just like Johnny. When he was half inside, half out, his hand touched a scalding radiator, and the burning jolt carried him the rest of the way. He ended head-first in the drying softness of a bedroom carpet, suddenly aware of how wet his hair and suit were, plastered in quick-melting snow.

Johnny was at the door, looking up and down the landing. He waved for Jake to follow him.

The staircase had a signature creak, the low wheeze of a house that was solid and settled but was ready to flex and accommodate new pressures. Jake watched Johnny test each step as he edged his way down. Johnny gave a thumbs-up sign before disappearing into the living-room below. When Jake followed, he spent a minute casing the front door, locating the key on the hall-stand and then slipping open every lock and bolt so they had some chance to escape. When he finally pushed through into the living-room, he found Johnny knelt by the jagged tower of a Christmas tree, lit blue in the rays of the buzzing TV set, his fingers ready and waiting to receive an old tape from the mouth of the VCR.

'It's VHS.' Speaking in a grinning whisper, Johnny was all systems engaged, everything going super-slick. Jake only felt sick. He tried to pull the two videos from out of his jacket pocket but they'd split the lining and the damp cloth had stretched and clenched again, sealing them tight. Jake couldn't free them with his frozen-banana fingers, so used Johnny's knife to cut his pocket open. When he handed the tapes over, Johnny placed them under the tree with one of his own two tapes, making a stark black pyramid against the glitter of the other presents. Johnny's last tape was ready slotted in the machine.

Something jarred with Jake. He said: 'Four tapes?'

'Yeah, I took copies of all of them.'

'I thought there were only three.'

'No. Four.'

Jake said, 'Oh, right.' He must have been mistaken. He slipped into the space behind the living-room door, tucked between the settee and the wall, with the knife in his hand. If John Pascal came down, Jake was hidden.

Jake hissed, 'What time is it?'

Johnny checked his watch, held up three fingers. The clock at the front of the VCR was flashing the right time. Johnny was setting the timer for 7:00 a.m. He had Pascal figured as an early riser. If he wasn't, the tape would still be running at ten o'clock. He had his finger on the FF button, checking to make sure the whole of the three-hour tape had been used. On the floor beside him was a photocopy of the note he'd spent an hour assembling, ransom-style, from letters cropped out of the *Evening News*. A *Pistolero* demand: *RaId tHis pErvERT!* Gary Halliday's name and the address of Colchester Hall underneath.

Jake said, 'Stop. Forget it. We get out now.'

'It's okay, mate. I'm almost done.'

'I mean it. We get out now.'

Jake tried to keep the desperation out of his voice but he knew for sure: that night as he sat in the car with Halliday, still breathless from the street fight, Halliday handed him three video tapes. The next morning, when Halliday walked him to the gates of Colchester Hall and said, winking, '*You won't forget these now,*' there were four tapes in the bag.

Johnny was staring up at him. 'Keep it down, mate. I told you, I'm about done.' The tape had reeled to its stop and his finger was now pressed to the rewind so he could play the last few seconds and make sure they were full.

'Don't play the tape.'

Jake's hand tightened around the knife in his hand.

Johnny's finger hovered over the PLAY button.

Jake finally said it: 'I'm on one of the tapes.'

'You what?'

'One of those tapes . . . I'm there, me and Halliday and . . . some others.'

'You.'

Johnny's eyes rounding out of his wet blond hair.

Jake didn't want to have to say it again. 'Please. Just forget it now. We just go.'

'No.'

It was definite, Johnny's last word, and it wasn't in a whisper.

Jake lunged across the settee, his hands outstretched for the pile of tapes beneath the tree. Johnny shouldered from the side, taking him down in midair. Jake swiped back, not even realizing he was using his knife hand, but he was blind-sided and hit nothing. His face hit the carpet. Two hands gripped tight to both his wrists.

He felt Johnny's breath in his ear: 'Quiet, you twat. Listen. We'll find your tape, okay. We'll find it and leave the rest. That's it.'

Jake nodded. As Johnny swung off him and returned to the VCR, Jake slid backwards until his back touched the edge of the settee. He huddled there, watching glumly as a boy appeared on-screen, flitting from an open doorway to a kitchen table, naked on the table-top.

'This one?'

Jake shook his head.

Johnny waited for the tape to eject, already reaching for another. His fingers poised on FF and PLAY. The long wait before a raft of figures cartwheeled across the screen, made indistinct by the line of static that wiped, north to south, across them, blurring the differences between fat grown men and fleshless boys.

'This.'

Jake in head-down shame, muttering 'No' into the fold of his jacket.

Johnny pressed EJECT. The carriage mechanism wheezed through at its too-slow pace.

In the silence ... a soft creak from somewhere above them. Jake said, 'What's that?'

Johnny's nails scratched at the tape nosing out of the VCR slot. He had another tape ready in his free hand.

'What?'

Jake was ready to scream but held it to a whisper. 'The man's awake. Forget the last two, just get them and go.'

Jake was already on his feet, urging Johnny on from the living-room's doorway.

Johnny shook his head: not refusing, just confused. He couldn't get out of the rhythm he'd set himself: FF-PLAY, STOP, EJECT, out, in. He had a tape in either hand; one pre-viewed, one fresh. Mouthing *okay, okay* as he looked from one to the other.

'Come on, Johnny.'

The footsteps were falling on the upper landing but Johnny had it figured. The first tape slotted back in the machine, the PLAY button down. The unseen tapes clenched in his hand.

'Okay, let's go.'

Jake knew it was too late. He had his hand on the front door, he pulled it open and stepped out into the snow. Behind him, Pascal's feet were clattering on the stairs, but Jake was out and clear.

The black of a figure passed across the slim gap between the door and the jamb. Jake followed it across and watched, through the window, as John Pascal stormed the room: dressed in a long brown dressing-gown, Terylene like monk's sacking, holding an axe.

There was nowhere left for Johnny. He was caught, scootering across the carpet on his backside as he tried to get out of the way. Pascal stood there, axe heaven-wards, his eyes on the screen where two men held a slim, struggling boy down to a massage table: hands on back and bottom, head and shoulders, penises in hand. The tape was moving in regular time; it was Pascal who was caught on pause. When he started yelling, it was a slow whirr, gathering momentum only as the words began to spew out: 'Outrage of Satan. Child of Sodom . . .

'You bring this to my house – this evil to my house.'

The axe lashed down, cutting through the tinderbox of the TV and shattering the tube into a cascade of sparks.

'My house. *My house.*'

Pascal's face was underlit with pinprick explosions, coloured red and blue in fairy lights. His mouth twisted and his head seemed carved into slabs of heavy colour, heavy shadow.

'Spring this serpent here, out of Gehenna, out of Sodom . . . Into my home!'

Johnny was clattering, hand over foot, trying to dodge the swinging axe. Shouting, '*Not me!*'

Pascal was flailing in a prophet's rage, speaking in a voice that filled the entire room with booming judgements, past inarticulate, talking straight to God. 'He knows thee, as the beast knows thee. As thou hast no mouth to hear nor lips to speak nor sign of righteousness.'

Johnny's arm was up, protecting his face from the swinging axe. The arm broke under the shaft, and the axe-head met his head in a sheet of blood.

'Yea, as the Lamb commands, flesh as flesh, as my eye offends. Strike it out.'

The scream of a woman was coming out of nowhere. And the axe kept on falling, blunt side like a golfclub onto the side of Johnny's neck.

'The Lord everlasting, screed of his dawning, the Lord ever-reaching.'

The axe shuddered from tip to shaft. On the floor, Johnny's head was bent around in a right crook . . . as a woman wailed at the doorway.

John Pascal raised his axe again. One more time it thrashed down. 'To the last word.'

Jake pushed out into the blizzard. Into a trackless gulf of fog until the road widened to a square. He slipped to his knees, dog-crawled, panting, to where the houses on the lower side broke open. In a passageway, hidden from the wind and the banking snow, he sludged to the doors of the Jericho Chapel. The doors were unlocked.

This was sanctuary. He skirted beneath the shelter of the circular gallery until he reached the vestry. There, in the corner where the poles for the marching banners leant upright, he found the old chapel wardrobe. He moved the poles to the side, careful not to let them fall, and found a hiding place among the embroidered banners that were folded at the bottom of the wardrobe. After he pulled the door shut against him and drew the banners over his head, he waited for morning.

CHAPTER *NINETEEN*

Less than an hour after dropping DI Green off in central Manchester, Jake was back in Caldenstall. He left the hire car in the car-park, on what used to be church land. Jericho Chapel stood in the corner, its door shut and the plain, leaded windows as blank as tired eyes. Jake stood and stared until he had the same look pat. He used it himself, turning it onto the moorland that was spread below him like a sun-drenched blanket, and stood above him like a dark cowl. This was where Pascal had dumped Johnny's broken body, leaving the night's snow to bury it. The corpse stayed there, Jake wasn't sure how long. It was finally sniffed out by a sheepdog digging for strays in the snowfields.

There were always a lot of sheep, but they were spindly and ragged-arse things. Whatever image you had of a flock, these didn't fit. They were dumb stragglers, ugly loners. Like DI Green had said on the drive back to Manchester, 'What is it with these sheep? I see them every time I drive this way, but they've got crap fur and I know no one eats them . . . what the fuck does a hill farmer do?'

There was a sheep scrabbling across a breach in a farm wall, its hind legs like skinned black bones, blurring as they tried to find some purchase on the stone. Like all the sheep round Caldenstall, it was too wretched to be believed. But Green hadn't thought it through: it wasn't the sheep, it was their lambs that were farmed. When Jake told him, the man slapped his forehead for effect: 'Fuck, yeah. And I call myself a detective.'

One piece of detective work Green did admit to: he'd found Jake because his name appeared in Kevin Donnelly's address book. Green asked if he and Donnelly stayed in close contact.

Jake shook his head: no, they never did. But he knew Donnelly had his address – and had seen Donnelly the week before he was killed.

Donnelly came to London to find him. He had seen Halliday's tapes and needed to know more. He at least wanted to hear Jake's side of the story. What he never expected to hear was Jake confessing to the death of Johnny. The exact same story Halliday would swallow whole, Donnelly wouldn't even listen to. Jake didn't know why; it was more than plausible. It fitted every aspect of his life, because everything Jake had done was shaped by a killer's despair. This was his hell and he walked through it, his eyes fixed at a spot he would never reach, his crime unpunished and unpunishable. It was an endless spiral in a world without end. A vacuum where his own death had become meaningless and what life he had ticked along in killer's time, beyond judgement.

Here in this miserable hill town, fifteen years ago.

Jake watched at the window as the axe fell. Play it in slow-motion, the axe falling one-time, two-time, and

the soundtrack drone of Pascal's insane preaching.
PAUSE – REWIND and PLAY. Johnny struggling backwards across the floor, skating on his arse as Pascal
comes for him, a pantomime and then the horror:
kicking through the pyramid of tapes and then lunging,
the axe blade connecting. And on-screen: Halliday's
party . . . the figures moving deliberately in and out of
the TV frame as the axe kept falling. Jake made it
happen, he couldn't replay the scene without proving it
to himself over and over again. *He killed Johnny.* It
wasn't a point for debate.

Jake turned, making his way up the chapel car-park
to where a passageway cut through to the village centre.
There used to be a red telephone box by the white-
painted pub. It was gone now, but there was a brushed-
aluminium replacement. As Jake walked over, he
rehearsed his lines. The answer-machine clicked on so
fast, he was caught off balance, but the sound of her
voice often threw him, especially when he hadn't heard
it in a while.

'Jacob and Sarah Powell are out right now. We'd
like you to leave a message, so do it after the beep.' It
was so up-beat, accentless and welcoming, but still a
stranger's voice. He told himself it was a long-distance
call and she was using her telephone voice . . . two good
reasons for it to sound so distant.

He waited through the rush of beeps for the longest
tone. When it came, he began awkwardly: 'I'll erase this
message if I . . .'

But she didn't need to know that. He coughed and
began again.

'If this message is still here when you get back, it means I'm not coming back. I don't know where I'll be. Christ knows, I've no idea where I'll be. But I want you to know how much I loved you. I know you always thought I was kind and considerate because you always told me. I never lost my temper with you because I was scared what would happen if I did . . . and because if I ever did, it wouldn't have been at you. *I never wanted to use you as an excuse for something else.* And I know you sometimes got frightened because I always seemed so distant. You didn't have much proof I loved you. I'm sorry. It was never anything to do with how I felt about you. I was just cold to myself.'

It was more than he wanted to say, without saying anything that he wanted her to remember him by. But he didn't want to be seen crying, here in the only public phone-box. So he hung up.

At a strictly automatic level, he was a good husband. While she was out of work, he held down a good job that he hated. When she got herself a good job, he kept on working, because her money was her own and he didn't want her ever to worry about money as much as she had during the months she was unemployed. Anyway, she never knew he hated the casino. She assumed – if he was so good at the job that he couldn't keep from getting promoted – he must like it. In lots of other ways he never told her how he felt.

When they got married, he hadn't loved her. He wanted to. He desperately appreciated her patience and her conviction: she loved him so much. But now that he loved everything about her, he always stumbled whenever he tried to put it into words. It was partly because of that bad beginning when he didn't quite love her. But it was chiefly because of everything that had happened years before they met.

A month ago, Jake was leaving the casino at maybe three in the morning. Someone appeared on the steps outside a bank and called his name.

As Jake turned to look upwards, a short and stocky man stepped out from the recessed doorway. He was dressed in a scrappy T-shirt and jeans, but Jake only saw his face as he reached the footprint of the streetlight.

It was Kevin Donnelly, Jake was almost certain, though he still hovered. The man wasn't skinny; he was short and bullish. His shoulders strained at the caps of his T-shirt. The other difference, he was wearing spectacles: large, plastic, red-framed circles, out of style and barely supported by his pug nose.

But it was the same voice – trying to be cheerful, normal. 'Hiya, Jake. You alright?'

Jake's first thought, standing out in the street, was: *Donnelly's flipped.* There was something vacant and misdirected about him. He at least should have been wearing a coat; it was a cold night.

He said, 'I got the tapes of you and Halliday.'

He wasn't threatening; there was no blackmailing wheedle . . . nothing like that. But he didn't have the tapes on him either. He wasn't carrying a bag: it was just him in his T-shirt and jeans. Maybe Donnelly *was* deranged, but Jake couldn't leave him out there and he couldn't think of anywhere to go.

He left it to him to choose, saying: 'I live round the corner. Either we go back to my place, which is fine, but my wife's asleep. Or we go back to the casino, I've got an office.'

Donnelly said, 'You're married? You're not gay?'

Jake didn't know what to say. But, because Donnelly seemed somehow upset, he forced a grin and said, 'No. Billy-both-ways, mate.'

Donnelly nodded, like he was turning it over and over, but it was an alien concept as far as he was concerned. Finally he said, 'Would you mind, Jake, can we go to your place? I think I need somewhere to kip.'

That settled it. Kevin Donnelly wasn't an operator; he couldn't put on a face to cover his feelings. He didn't want to cause any trouble. Jake had no idea why he didn't want to cause trouble.

They sat in the front room of Jake's apartment, drinking tea. Jake lit the fake fire without asking Donnelly if he was cold. Donnelly still seemed too dazed to feel anything, but staring at the fire was a painless way to get intimate, watching the flames seep around the edges of the black-painted bricks. It put Donnelly's getting-to-know-you questions into a context. The way he asked them, he could have been running through the all-terrain script of a game-show host. He asked Jake how long he'd been married, did he have any children. Jake's answers: three years and not yet. Sarah had suggested they should maybe get to breeding but the whole idea of children terrified Jake – though he didn't

say so to Donnelly. He wasn't looking for a real
exchange. He hardly even tried to keep the ball rolling,
keeping to *yes* or *no* or whatever was the next shortest
reply.

Donnelly didn't seem to notice he was being curt.
He listened to all Jake's answers, nodding and saying:
'Really, yeah really?' Maybe this was as close as he ever
got to an in-depth soul-baring session.

Kevin's turn: 'I was living with a guy but he was a
bit of a twat.'

'Yeah?'

'I don't know what was up with him. He left,
though.'

'I'm sorry.'

'Well, he was a twat.'

Jake thought, so Kevin was one of those: the kind
that hoped for something more than zero. When he was
younger, Jake always thought the difference between
men and women was you didn't have to give a man the
time of day. When the sex was over, you just got out of
there. No reason to feel guilty that the ending was so
abrupt. You never shared anything warmer than the
heat of two pounding bodies. The idea that anyone
could be looking for more than a brute connection, it
made Jake's skin crawl.

Even now, he still believed there was only one
difference between an unreformed homo and someone
who'd made the transition. Women took a lot of time
and effort; anyone who stayed with a woman had
committed themselves to a long haul, and sacrificed the
idea of being alone. It was his opinion, which probably

meant it wasn't worth squat. Jake had always found women alluring and attractive. Once he learnt to go slow and commit, he began to find them immediately and powerfully erotic also. Especially his wife.

As they sat there trying to talk, Jake began to think two things. He was right about Kevin Donnelly: the man was so steeped in sadness he'd become deranged. But also – and this wasn't exactly a revelation – Jake knew he himself was much closer to genuine psychosis than Donnelly would ever be. He couldn't see any serious flaws in his analysis of love, homosexuality and commitment. But he believed Donnelly deserved something better than a life of pure shit, and that he shouldn't have to change himself to get it.

Anyway, Jake was a psycho. So what did *he* know?

Kevin Donnelly said, 'That night you and Johnny went to see the copper, what happened?'

Jake said, 'We got caught.'

He explained how they stayed too long. Johnny had the cassettes all neatly stacked and labelled, the VCR timer was set, and the explanatory note was taped to the television. And it was only then, in those last few moments, that Jake realized what Gary Halliday had done. He had bought Jake's silence by implicating him.

Donnelly listened, nodding. 'It's what he does. How do you think he got away with it all this time?'

He didn't believe Jake had got Johnny killed. The way he saw it, it was a no-fault tragedy; there was nothing to forgive. It was just a result of the principles Halliday used. That was Donnelly all over . . . still so fucked he was convinced his old housemaster operated on a different level.

The truth was, Halliday almost got it wrong. He never thought Jake might be so stoned that he wouldn't even notice he was being videoed.

After the street fight, when Halliday tossed his bloody billy-club across the dashboard, he should have taken a moment to lean over and look in Jake's eyes. Jake had taken so much speed, he was nearer to pure psychosis than he'd ever been. He was so close he could taste it . . .

. . . and what's more, it was better than he'd dreamed.

When Halliday said, You want to go somewhere, Jake told him: 'Fucking *drive*.'

They hit the roundabout on Kingsway, the street-lights ink-blotting into the night, Jake soaking it up in his wide-eyed frenzy. There was a half bottle of vodka in a bag at his feet. He didn't bother to ask Halliday, he just drank it down. It wasn't alcohol any more, nothing but perfumed water. As they passed under the tangle of the motorway junction, he drank it dry and tossed it in the back. Halliday told him not to worry: he had more back at the home, as much as Jake wanted. The motorway slipped away behind them, the new road was panned with flecks of moonlight, sieved out of the over-clinging trees. Halliday skidded the car to the left and his outstretched arm beeped at a pair of iron gates.

The car circled round the house and parked out by a pair of tennis courts. Jake opened his door and slammed his feet to the tarmac, saying: 'Where now, boss?'

Halliday was using a fat key-chain on the door of a low white building. 'You wait here, I'll get some drinks and fix up a party.'

He slap-patted a bank of light switches, Jake walked through into a room strobing fluorescent white. The walls and floors were brilliantly tiled; in the centre of the room was a massage table, and to the side were showers. Jake threw his shirt onto a hook and started swaggering about the room, his back curved and his chest sticking out in a rock-n-roll bantam strut. He still had wraps and wraps of speed in the back pocket of his jeans. He pulled them out and returned to his discarded shirt to tuck a few in the top pocket. The rest he emptied onto the massage table and just lapped them up, tongue to the cool tile surface.

He was walking through the jetting steam of the showers, every head turned to full blast, when Halliday returned. Jake heard him yell and came swinging out of the steam in hipster jeans and Cuban heels, hair swept back and white, bare chest still out proud.

Halliday stepped to the side, saying: 'This is Don Ford.' A fat man in a bathrobe and unlaced shoes followed through the door and nodded hello.

'And these are William, John and Stanley.'

Three boys with slept-in eyes, rubbed red dry, standing in anoraks, with bare legs.

Halliday tossed over a bottle of vodka. Jake grabbed

it, snapped the cap, and took a hard drink. As his eyes refocused from alcohol-induced watering, he saw the three boys hang their anoraks on hooks. Underneath, nothing but swimming trunks.

Halliday said, 'In the shower, boys.'

They trudged passed Jake into the steam. In front of him, Don Ford was hanging up his bathrobe and slipping his shoes under the wall benches. His gut round and pendulous, a bubble of penis and balls hanging in its shadow. He slapped his hands together, 'Me for a shower, too, I think.'

Halliday took off his jacket and hung it on a hook. Next, his shirt, trousers and vest. He was also wearing swimming trunks. He sat down to unlace his shoes, smiling up at Jake. Jake held out the vodka bottle, but Halliday shook his head.

'Come sit down.' He slapped the bench.

Jake sat, about head-height with the man. When Halliday leant in for a kiss, Jake moved in too. Halliday pushed straight forward with his tongue, prising Jake open-mouthed, the invisible bristles of his beard now scouring like sandpaper. Halliday's tongue never seemed to slacken. Jake wasn't kissing back, just holding there, trying to breathe.

When Halliday eventually pulled away, he said, 'You get first dibs.'

Jake followed his eyes. Don Ford was swinging out of the showers. Two of the boys were naked now and Ford's erection was bouncing against the underside of his gut. Ford was leading one by the hand; he twirled him out and around so Jake could get an all-round view.

Jake looked at them: three pairs of eyes. The first time, in how long, he'd seen anyone who didn't want to shag him. Who didn't want to be anywhere near him at all.

Halliday was on his feet, hand inside a sports bag in the corner. He came up with a bottle of oil.

'Have you chosen one, Jake? How about William?'

He pointed to the only boy still wearing trunks. The oil bottle was open and he was pouring a liberal portion onto his palm. As he recapped the bottle and tossed it to Don Ford, he pushed his hand inside his swimming trunks and began massaging his penis. Jake watched it swell beneath the trunks. Halliday never lost his smile.

Jake turned away.

Don Ford slapped the bottom of the smallest boy, 'Onto the table, laddie.'

The boy shrugged away towards a corner, but Ford came after him – a firm hand on his arm to drag him over to the massage table.

'Get up there, now. Or you'll know about it.'

The boy walked over and flopped forwards. His thin chest lay flat to the tiles, as bony and as fragile as porcelain. Don Ford walked forward, rubbing his hands in oil.

Jake stood up, the bottle of vodka swaggering in his hand. 'Get off the table, kid.'

The boy turned his head around, looking towards Jake but not moving.

Jake kept it slow and firm. 'Get off the table. I go first.' As he moved, he unbuttoned the top of his trousers and pulled the zip.

The boy stood up. Jake turned and dropped to the table backwards, slithering out of his pants by arching his back then kicking them to the floor. He looked over to Don Ford. The man was surprised, but Jake gave him a grin: 'You want it?' And over his shoulder, 'How about you, Halliday?'

Halliday was still smiling. 'Okay. Get widthways across the table – boy.'

Jake got in position, legs slightly bent, his chest to the table top. His bottom raised at one end, his head lolling over the other side. Halliday came up behind him, one hand on his back. What felt like a smooth, peach-sized nugget pressing at his arsehole. He was dead to pain; he was drunk and speeding and loose. Halliday pushed inside him to the bowels and started pumping. Jake groaned and pushed back, getting a thump across the top of his arse cheeks.

In front of him, Don Ford – looking from Jake to a boy. As Jake caught his eye, he swelled over, took him by the side of his head and eased Jake's mouth over his erection. Jake spluttered; the fat man had bathed his penis in aftershave. As Jake gagged for air, he managed to get out the word 'Vodka'. Ford nodded, unscrewed the cap, and poured into Jake twisted-up mouth. Then he pushed his penis back into Jake's throat.

Backside and head, Jake just pushed back to the motion until he wasn't anything but responsive meat. Inside his head, Iggy's 'Funhouse' playing over and over, one loop: *all night long.*

As Halliday yelled and slipped out from inside, with a last thrash across his buttocks, Don Ford moved to the rear. Jake lifted his head and saw Halliday walk over to the showers; he wasn't smiling now. His face was bluster red; the man was trying to catch his breath. As he passed, Jake caught the eye of one of the boys. Just looking at him, more *against* him than *for* him. Jake thought: it was right. Don't think I'm doing this to save you. He was doing it to himself. Even when it was fat Ford pounding up his hole, Jake wanted the senseless repetition, the waving sensation of looseness, the insensitive violence of it all.

When Halliday stepped out of the shower, Jake caught his eye and swivelled his open mouth. Halliday nodded and walked over, lifting Jake's head and pushing his half-formed penis to the back of Jake's throat.

By the time Ford had finished, sitting gasping for breath on the bench, almost dead from the exertion and the steaming heat of the showers, Halliday was erect again and working up into Jake's behind.

And maybe, somewhere along that night, as Jake proved he was inexhaustible, he remembered seeing the boy William holding a video camera and filming him. Was that real? Or something he imagined?

After he showered quickly, dressed and started to leave, Halliday called him back, saying: 'Don't forget your bag.' Jake said, 'Yeah.'

And, when he picked it up, there were four tapes instead of three. Jake never noticed. He just walked off, the ten miles into Manchester.

CHAPTER *TWENTY*

Jake was in the call-box in Caldenstall, talking to directory enquiries. As the automatic voice read the numbers, he repeated them over and redialled immediately.

'Mr John Pascal? I'm sorry to bother you. I wanted to look round the old chapel but the doors are locked. The minister gave me your number.'

The voice on the other side, gruff and Yorkshire, a twinge of uncertainty. 'Why'd she do that?'

Jake hadn't thought it would be a woman. He was careful to check the notice-board outside the chapel before he made the call, but nothing had suggested the minister's sex.

He said, 'She was going somewhere, so she gave me the names of a couple of committee members.'

Still suspicious. 'She gave you my number?'

Jake couldn't imagine John Pascal getting on with a woman minister. He leapt for a possible formula. 'She gave me a few but I don't have a pen. Yours was the last so it was the only one I could remember. I hope it's okay. If it's inconvenient, maybe you can give me another name.'

Pascal said, 'Where are you, son?'

'In a call-box outside . . .' He paused to go through the motions of looking up at the sign outside the pub '. . . the Tup.' It was a good job he'd looked; that only used to be its nickname, not its given name.

'Okay, son, give me ten minutes. I'll meet you at the chapel.'

Jake hung the receiver, picked his mac off the shelf and stepped out of the box. There weren't many people on the streets, though there were a lot more cars parked up and down the road than there used to be. Most of them were newish, the latest or next-to-latest letters on their registration plates. The whole village looked cleaned through, but in a too calculated way.

He took the passageway back down to the chapel. The last time he was up here, it was after his mother died. He'd waited until he was very late, and then made an excuse about the trains. He deliberately missed the service, the burial, everything except one curled sandwich on a plate in his mother's house.

His relatives had believed him; they clucked around being sympathetic, saying, 'Today of all days.'

'You should be able to sue those bastards in British Rail.'

He nodded. He should, yeah.

He couldn't have gone into the chapel. Not after the night of Johnny's murder, when he crawled under the banners in the cupboard at the back of the wardrobe. The next day he stepped out to see the sun cracking open the heavy roof of clouds, throwing spot-beams onto the snow that covered everything. That special kind of light that he'd never seen anywhere but in the Pennines. The celestial light, a light sabre of promise. That day it was a sick joke.

Today there was no snow, but the sun was always there, ready to pull its trick in the clouds. Looking south from the chapel, transporter beams hit the earth and recoiled in pillars to the sky. Jake grimaced and shivered. He took another look at the board in front of the church. The board looked old, with its weathered wood, but it was nowhere near as old as the chapel itself. Across the top it said: Jericho Chapel, Caldenstall. In its centre, an old poster flapping at its corner read 'Jesus Is Lord' and 'If You Assume, It Makes An Ass Out Of U And Me'. The words were printed in black across the harsh, fluorescent violet paper. Right at the bottom of the board, in hand-painted letter, the minister's name was given with her initials. Her telephone number was written underneath, and Jake realized it had a Halifax code. She wasn't even local.

He turned and walked to the edge of the chapel, where it overhung the hillside. The hill fell away, right under his nose, two hundred feet or more to the valley bottom. The grass there was richer and greener, and the hill was crossed with dry-stone walls. The hills on the opposite side of the valley mirrored the same arrangement. And, clustered at the bottom, a rival town stretching either side of the shallow river ford. Actually, it wasn't much of a town. It was just larger, with better shops. And more life.

Jake looked back up the car-park. John Pascal was

coming through the alleyway. Jake let his eyes just slide past the man and on towards the hilltops, doing nothing that suggested he recognized the older man.

Pascal crossed in his direction, stopping a few yards from the old wooden doors. 'Are you the lad who wants to look around the chapel?'

Jake nodded and walked towards him. The man was around sixty, robust and unstooped, but maybe florid. His size and colour couldn't have anything to do with drink; it had to be home cooking and the fresh hill winds.

Jake held out his hand. 'James Osterburg.'

Pascal didn't meet it. He just tossed a key over and Jake converted his handshake to an open mitt. The key was heavy and looked too new to work on the door, but it was the right size and turned easily. Jake pushed the doors open and stood back. Pascal nodded that he should go through.

Jericho Chapel was unusual. A tourist might want to look at it. It was built as a hexagon, with the preacher's pulpit and the altar set against two of the chapel's six inner walls. The pews fanned out around two main aisles like slices of cake, their sharp ends pointing towards the pulpit and the brassy tubes of the organ, which rose like a crown from the gallery above the altar. Choir stalls and extra seats spread out from the organ pipes to complete the circle above Jake's head. To the left of the door, underneath the gallery, a closed-off space formed the vestry and, beyond, the committee's meeting room.

Jake walked down the main aisle towards the pulpit,

but stopped halfway to look up at the roof and the windows around the gallery.

Pascal said, 'What's your interest in the chapel?'

Jake said, 'Architectural.'

'So when was this place built?'

Jake smiled. 'I thought you'd tell me. It's eighteenth-century, George the Something.'

'The Second. Built during the Evangelical revival, though there was a Congregationalist community here long before . . . at least from the 1690s.' Pascal said the words semi-automatically, if not from practice at least from familiarity. 'Are you a church member?'

Jake shook his head. 'My grandmother, I think. Or Methodist.'

'Wesley preached here, 1780. We've always been a friend to other dissenters: independent but liberal.'

Jake circled round the altar. 'Yes? What size is the congregation now?'

'About six.' Pascal said it flatly. He'd followed Jake as far as the centre of chapel. Now he watched as Jake moved into the shadows of the gallery.

'Six?'

'The minister holds a service once a month. The rest of the time we have to travel to her – over in Halifax. You spoke to her, didn't you?'

Jake said, 'Uh-huh.' He didn't want to get caught up in anything.

'She's from your part of the world, isn't she?'

Jake ducked out of it. 'Manchester? I wouldn't have said so.'

'I thought you were southern.'

Jake wove behind the pillars supporting the gallery, keeping his face turned towards the walls, reading the plaques: one of them dedicated to Wesley. 'I live in London. Maybe I've lost the accent.'

'A Manchester lad, huh? You know, I was thinking you look familiar.'

Jake said, 'I was thinking the same about you.'

'Maybe. But I was a policeman. If you met me, you'd have been up to no good.'

'Maybe in the papers?'

'I didn't look for publicity.'

Bollocks, he didn't. Jake kept quiet and continued walking. Pascal turned with him. Jake was approaching the door now, his feet almost touching the wedge of light that flooded through it. One step and he would turn into a black silhouette against the doorway and a shadow across the floor, measuring a length to the place Pascal stood.

Jake said, 'God's Cop.'

Pascal's arm came up from inside his coat. In his hand some kind of pistol.

Jake kept still between the shelter of the open door and a pillar. Pascal was squinting into the light but his arm was steady. If Jake moved, he would try to shoot.

Pascal said, 'I knew you were one of them.'

'One of what?'

'Another queer boy, come looking for me.'

'I'm a tourist from London. You're not going to shoot me in church.'

'Wherever the Lord's enemies take the battle.'

Jake said, 'Who are you, the village lunatic?' He looked across the sweep of light from the door – how many paces was that? Pascal was still holding his right arm firm, so rigid that it should have begun to shake. Maybe his craziness gave him a superhuman rigor.

'I know you, queer boy. The suit doesn't fool me. You got the same look as the other two.'

Jake leapt across the path of the door, trailing his mac out behind him so he looked like something swooping through the light. The mac pulled free of his hand as Pascal fired: the only thing he hit.

Sheltered in the doorway of the vestry, Jake waited for the echo of the blast to die in the shallow dome of the roof, then said, 'I think you got a bystander out in the car-park.'

Pascal's footsteps sounded across the stone-paved floor. In truth, there didn't seem to be anyone out in the car-park. At three in the afternoon, the village was dead. No one actually worked in it, anyway. Anyone who heard the shot – and its echo – would assume it was a shotgun out in the fields or on the moor.

Jake ducked away, back through the vestry. The only weapons he could see were the banner-poles resting against the wardrobe doors – just as they had been the last time he saw them. He grabbed the shortest one as he ran through the next door and into the committee room. Pascal stayed a steady pace behind him, following on.

The committee table was draped in dustsheets, protection from the same dust that covered his pole and stuck to his hands, mixing with the sweat there. The

only cover was beneath the table, or behind the dust-
sheeted chairs stacked around the back wall. Jake didn't
trust either place. He pushed through the next door,
back into the main body of the chapel. Behind him,
Pascal's hand struck the inner door between the vestry
and the committee room.

The stairs to the upper gallery curved away to his
left, squeezed between the chapel wall and the pulpit.
Jake ran for them, his feet clattering on the wood until
he reached the top. Standing framed against the organ,
he realized he had made a mistake. There was no other
way down. Pascal could back him round and round the
gallery until he got tired of the game and shot him dead.
Already the man was pounding across the chapel floor
to the foot of the stairs. Jake turned and climbed up on
the rail of the wooden balustrade, steadying himself as
he held his pole like a javelin, hoping he had the height
to spear it into Pascal as the man reached the top of the
steps. Only now, he noticed the brass fleur-de-lis insig-
nia topping off the pole. Only the middle of the three
leaves resembled a spear point, and only bluntly. Pascal
was nearing the top of the steps.

Jake looked down; the top of the pulpit lay below
him. It was a good leap away, both down and across,
but the open face of the lectern gave him something to
aim for, a landing place. Jake resettled his spear in his
hand, trying for a firmer grip. Pascal came head and
shoulders above the step, and Jake let it fly.

The pole wobbled in midair, there was a damp warp
in its length . . . perhaps it had never been true. The

brass tip struck Pascal with no more than a glancing blow as it veered from him and skittled down the steps. Pascal, unharmed but unbalanced, fired wide.

Jake leapt out into the chapel below. His leading foot – his left – landed square to the top of the pulpit lectern. The heel of his brogues jammed on its lip as the lectern teetered, then sheared from its mooring against the pulpit rail. Carried forward with the momentum of his leap, Jake swung his arms forwards and pushed off from the splintering lectern. He grabbed at the edge of the gallery walkway, holding for a second as his whole body swung forward. His knee smashed into the under-side of the steps, and he crashed down in pain.

Pascal was above him. But hidden beneath the gallery, Jake couldn't see him or be seen. He heard a curse, a clatter of feet. The man shouting, 'As the others, so shall thee be. You fucking puff.'

Jake hobbled to the foot of the steps where his pole lay. He picked it up again; maybe it was better as a crutch.

'Vengeance is mine, saith the Lord, I will repay. Yea, to the eye as it offends and even unto the last word. Not for thee where righteous walks, but the valley where the lamb will devour thee.'

Jake held the pole like a kendo stick. Pascal – blundering on the steps – ran into the downstroke. It was a good stroke, anyway. Pascal's head snapped back as the shaft cracked. Jake brought the shattered pole back to his nose in a salute, swung it round in his hands, and drove the point through the man's chest. This time it pierced, Jake's full weight forcing it down. When he couldn't force it another millimetre, he snapped it off.

He locked the church behind him and threw the key out of the rental-car window on the stretch of motorway between Salford and Prestwich. Pascal's body was in the wardrobe, folded amongst the old church banners. It would either be discovered within hours, or within the month; it all depended on whether Pascal had told his wife that he was going to the chapel.

As he passed Salford Quays and followed the canal around Deansgate and behind the G-Mex centre, he wondered again whether he should have visited Mrs Pascal. There was a chance the video tapes were still in her house: if not the ones Johnny left under her Christmas tree, then at least those Kevin Donnelly had brought with him, just under a month ago. By the time he packed and made the 7:30 from Piccadilly, he knew he'd made the right decision. Let someone else find the tapes – he was through trying to protect himself. Travelling first class, in the rhythmic daze of the InterCity train, he remembered that the funny thing about regret is that it's better to regret something you have done than to regret something you haven't done.

It was true, he was feeling better already. He could even smile, although that was due to the circumstances in which he had last heard this same advice: at the start of an album by the Butthole Surfers, the first track of *Locust Abortion Technician*. On the record, a a boy asks what regret means. His father feeds him the 'better regret something' line but ends by chanting: _SATAN! SATAN! SATAN!_'

Maybe he should have run up to Mrs Pascal's house and shouted '_Satan! Satan! Satan!_' through her letter-box. If he was ever asked, he could always claim that was his only real regret. What else? He was alive, his wife loved him. It was time he stopped living a half-life fogged by old regrets. Time to invent some new ones.

CHAPTER *TWENTY-ONE*

Davey Green chose the Range Rover; there was more room in the back and he wanted to read the autopsy report on John Pascal. As he drove out to Stockport, he kept it open on his knee. A note clipped to the first page asked for a reply by return post, but that was two days ago. The only reason he had the report with him now was that he wanted some light reading. God knows, he didn't want to have to talk to either of the two bobbins sat up front, bickering over whether the Playstation or the PC was the better games engine.

When he looked up, DC Draper stopped mid-sentence. He must have been watching Davey in the rear-view mirror.

Green said, 'One of you cunts, when we pass that drive-thru McD's, go fetch me a coffee. And a chocolate donut.'

Draper jerked his head up and down. 'Three sugars, boss?'

What did he think, that the order might have changed since the last coffee half an hour ago in Bootle Street nick? Green told him, 'Yeah, three sugars, and get a couple of fruit pies for you and Collyhurst.'

'Aah, boss.'

He always made his team eat a pie every time they went to McDonald's. It was a good laugh: they always scalded the rooves of their mouths. The whole team was sick of the joke, except Davey.

DC Draper hauled the Range Rover into the McDonald's car-park and ran to get the coffees. Davey never used the drive-thru option; it seemed undignified somehow. While he was gone, Davey told the other lad – DC Peter Collyhurst – to get out his notebook and take some dictation.

'To DI whoever, name and address on this sticker . . .'

Davey waved the front cover of the autopsy report. Collyhurst looked up, took a sken at the sticker on the report's cover, and nodded. Davey swept on.

'. . . West Yorks Police blah-de-dah-de-dah, writing to say we have no interest in the death of John Pascal, retired twat-in-chief. Can't think of any leftovers of his glorious career still infecting Manchester. We believe his death is a local matter: the old guy freelancing as a security guard down his local church. We're just glad the loony had something to tide him over in his declining years. Blah Blah Blah. Delete most of it, type it up, and pop it in the e-mail. You got it?'

He wasn't worried. He knew Collyhurst would end with something suitable. The main reason Green kept him on the team: say what you like about the lad, he could pass as literate.

Davey reread the note attached to page one. He couldn't imagine West Yorks were serious when they asked for help anyway. It was just form. Davey ripped the note out and passed it over to Collyhurst.

'If you get stuck for what to say, you can always recycle some of that.'

'Okay, boss.' Collyhurst gave it a glance through, memorizing the niceties. A second later, he said, 'You read the back of this, boss? The West Yorks DI asking if he'll see you at Pascal's funeral? You going?'

'No. I went up and paid my respects to Doris Pascal the second I heard her husband was dead.'

Collyhurst didn't know that. Come to think of it, no one did.

'How's she taking it, boss?'

'Oh, you know. What can you say? I went up, shared her grieving. I think she felt I'd taken some of the responsibility out of her hands.'

The responsibility – and the video tapes Mrs Pascal had found in her dead husband's desk drawer. The old witch knew what was on the tapes. She definitely knew about the killing of John Conway, even if she didn't know about Kevin Donnelly. Maybe she even believed Pascal's fantasy justification, that a feral queer boy had broken into his house, determined to corrupt and infect him, his sanctuary and his virtue. Though maybe not – she looked mad, but not as mad as Pascal.

Draper returned with three coffees, a donut and two apple pies. Davey told him: careful, he didn't want any coffee spilled on the upholstery. 'You feel you spilling it, make sure it goes in your lap, not on the seat. I don't want it anywhere it's likely to do damage.'

He waited until they were eating their pies before he asked if they'd had any luck with the fingerprints.

Collyhurst spoke first, spluttering round a lava-flow of fruity stuff. 'Hing-her-prints?'

'On Kevin Donnelly's car, you bobbin.'

Green was off-hand when he presented his team with what he called his *hunch*, asking them to ring round local forces until they found Donnelly's car. It turned up, as he knew it would, in Littleborough.

Collyhurst swallowed hard. Davey gave him one more moment.

'Speak up, son.'

The fruit pie bulged in his neck and disappeared. Collyhurst said, 'I don't think forensics have finished with the car yet, boss.'

Well, when they did get round to finishing, they should find the fingerprints of Gary Halliday. If they didn't, Davey would just send them back. The man told Jake Powell he had broken into the car, so there was going to be some kind of evidence. Davey wasn't even worried about it. He could tie Gary Halliday to Kevin Donnelly in other ways. He already had a couple of witnesses who remembered Donnelly and Halliday fighting at Piccadilly Station.

Back on the road again, Draper said, 'This is almost over, isn't it?'

Davey nodded. Just about.

'You think you'll find the videos, boss?'

Davey looked up from his coffee. Playing it dumb. 'Which videos are these?'

'The ones Halliday and Donnelly were fighting over, at the station.'

Davey shrugged. 'How should I know? A couple of witnesses think they saw something – what's that worth? I'll believe there's some videos when I see them.' Or when he decided to unveil them. At the moment they were in a carry-all, on the floor of the Range Rover. Davey had his feet rested on top of them.

Collyhurst said, 'So why we going back to Colchester Hall?'

Davey stared him out, slowly chewing his choco-donut. Collyhurst finally dropped his eyes, but Davey had to give him credit: he was a fucking clever cunt.

Colchester Hall had already been searched, numerous times. Green spent the past two days building a head of steam before he finally pulled out a rare piece of theatrics, ranting and railing that the place could never have been searched properly. The only thing that was going to satisfy him: he was going over and doing it himself . . . *Properly this time, mind.*

They parked at the front of the Hall and had to walk around the building to reach the tennis courts at the back. Davey looked over to the courts; it looked like the whole of the Manchester CID was there, lounging against the chicken-wire fence.

Davey hissed over his shoulder to Collyhurst, 'Who invited all these buggers?'

'You wanted a fresh search. They're all volunteers.'

'They volunteered? My big fat arse.'

Draper, walking on his other side, said, 'They just

wanted to see a legend in action, following one of his famous hunches.'

Davey grunted, tried not to look their way. He just strode over to the shower block, swinging the carry-all in his hand. Draper and Collyhurst were with him every step. The policemen lined against the tennis courts, they all stiffened and straightened, waiting for the big event.

Davey threw up his hands. 'Fuck this circus.'

He slammed the carry-all into Collyhurst's hands.

'You go and search it. Me and Draper will wait outside.' He glared over his shoulder at the the rest of CID. 'Leave us to guard the door, make sure the integrity of the scene isn't violated by their great fucking feet.'

Collyhurst said, 'Where shall I look?'

'Tear the fucking place apart. But don't take too long over it.'

Collyhurst took less than ten minutes. When Davey saw him coming, he started shaking his head. Telling him to get the fuck back in there, he hadn't left it long enough.

Collyhurst just sailed past him with a big fuck-off smile on his face, holding the video tapes above his head. The rest of CID started peeling away from the tennis-court fence and crowding in on him, stamping and cheering.

'Thank you, thank you.' Collyhurst making out it was Oscar time and he was *just so, so overwhelmed.*

Davey knew this had already gone too far.

'SHUT IT, THE FUCKING LOT OF YOU!'

Davey could at least be grateful his voice was so loud. Once they were quiet, he could tone it down.

'Collyhurst, you done well. It's like I always say, you need to think like one of these cunts if you want to catch them.' And, turning to the crowd: 'Of course, with Collyhurst it obviously took less of an imaginative stretch, but let's give him some credit anyway.'

Back into Manchester, Davey started to relax. He told Draper and Collyhurst that he reckoned the investigation was over. He asked which one of them wanted the job of putting it all together and sending it over to the CPS.

Collyhurst said he'd do it. Not entirely sure that ordering and classifying evidence for a report to the Crown Prosecution Service constituted real detective work, but it was the closest he'd come so far. Anyway, if he wrote the report, he got to put his own gloss on the final search of the Colchester Hall shower block. Another of Davey Green's mottoes: half the job of detection was in the presentation.

The tapes would be logged as evidence in both of Davey's current investigations. The pictures on the tapes added weight to the child-abuse case. The bloodstains on the new videos would link Halliday to someone's murder . . . whoever's blood it turned out to be. It might even belong to Halliday himself. Apparently, Kevin Donnelly had bust the guy's nose with a video while they were fighting in Piccadilly Station . . . at least, according to the account Jake Powell finessed out of Halliday on his prison visit. There shouldn't be any trouble finding witnesses to corroborate the scene in court.

Davey said, 'It'll all stand up.'

'No loose ends?'

He shook his head. 'If there are, I don't want to know about them.' Davey put all the emphasis he could into his words – even though he knew Collyhurst would never take the hint.

Around lunchtime tomorrow, the lad would come in and say: 'About this abuse case, I'm not sure we traced everyone involved.'

Davey would nod. Yeah?

'There's an older kid, taking it sideways from Ford and Halliday.'

And what Davey planned to say: 'So? Who really gives a fuck? Whichever way you look at it, he's got to be under twenty-one. The law's changed now, but at the time it makes him underage. On the other hand, he's not a juvenile, so what was he doing at the home at all? It's too fucking untidy. Which is why we drop it.'

It would work.